Don't Summon Necromancers

Jeni Conrad

This book is dedicated to Alene, a mother who welcomed four scruffy kids into her home without a second thought and loved us more than we knew what to do with

Author's Note

As a teacher who has dealt with teens for many years, not to mention was once one herself, I wanted to bring up an issue in this series that many people struggle with. But for some, reading about it may be uncomfortable or even triggering. This story contains themes of an eating disorder. I am not trying to promote it or glamorize it in any way but rather trying to highlight the struggle a person might have with it and how damaging it can be. The issue does get resolved, but it takes several books to do so. If you or anyone you know struggles with an eating disorder, there is help. https://www.edreferral.com/

Contents

1.	Chapter 1	1
2.	Chapter 2	16
3.	Chapter 3	27
4.	Chapter 4	42
5.	Chapter 5	51
6.	Chapter 6	62
7.	Chapter 7	73
8.	Chapter 8	82
9.	Chapter 9	99
10.	Chapter 10	108
11.	Chapter 11	127
12.	Chapter 12	145
13.	Chapter 13	153
14.	Chapter 14	167
15.	Chapter 15	184
16.	Chapter 16	196

17. Chapter 17   207

18. Chapter 18   229

19. Chapter 19   250

20. Chapter 20   269

21. Chapter 21   284

22. Chapter 22   292

Don't Hex Witches   302

About the Author   303

Also By Jeni Conrad   304

Chapter 1

T he house looked a lot better than it had the first time I'd seen it. It helped that it was daytime, and while it wasn't quite sunny outside, it was brighter. I didn't want to remember the night at this very same house where I'd condemned those spirits without knowing it, but it haunted me more than any ghost ever had.

It also helped that whoever had bought it and paid Rose to banish all those ghosts, had spent a fair bit of money renovating it. All the shutters were brightly painted a happy blue and were screwed in tight and straight. The windows had been cleaned, the siding replaced, the grass mowed, the garden dug out and cultivated, and even the old roof had been repaired.

In short, the place looked good. I wondered if Frank was enjoying his new digs.

"I'm still not sure what we're doing. Who lives here?" Emma, one of only two girls in the entire school who would talk to me, excluding my sister who didn't count, asked as we stared up at the house from the sidewalk.

"I don't know who they are."

"Oh? Okay." Emma fidgeted with the strap of her purse, too kind to ask me if I'd taken some crazy pills that morning.

"We've only got to get on the grounds, I think. Shouldn't be too hard as long as there aren't any nosy neighbors staring out at us right now." I took a slow spin, taking in the houses on the block, trying to see if there were any old ladies peeking out from behind lacey curtains.

Being kind enough to indulge my crazy—bless her heart— Emma followed my example and took a spin as well. "It looks pretty chill for a Monday morning. People are probably out working and stuff."

"It's Thanksgiving break though. There could be kids off from school." I zipped up my warm jacket to help prevent more of the early winter wind from sneaking in.

"Yes, that's true." Emma nodded.

"Oh well. Let's get to it. We won't be here long enough for the police to catch us anyway." I turned back to the freshly painted gate and opened it with purpose as if I belonged there and wasn't trespassing.

"The police?" Emma's voice squeaked as she followed me into the yard.

I waved off her concern and headed toward the back of the house, hoping there wasn't going to be a lumbering guard dog bounding around the corner at any second.

"Frank?" I said, loud enough that he might be able to hear me, but quiet enough that the neighbors wouldn't come to investigate why I was hollering.

"Who's Frank?" Emma whispered, her voice strained as she followed behind me.

It probably hadn't been fair to bring her on this trip, but there was no way I was going to be alone. At all. Ever. Even going to the bathroom was dangerous. I'd taken to bringing my phone and immersing myself in social media while I peed and washed my hands.

I was rarely at home unless Mom or Trina were there. If both of them left at the same time for some reason, I could text Gryphin to come hang out with me or yell for Caleb who I knew was always within hearing distance.

They probably all thought I was becoming a super-dependent mess of a human being, but I couldn't even begin to explain how empty every second was without Brandon's stupid charming grin, infuriating snarky comments, or dumb calming presence during a panic attack in the unyielding darkness of night.

"He's a ghost I met some time ago. This is his haunt, so I was hoping to check in with him."

We arrived in the backyard where there were still signs of construction going on. A pile of wooden beams laid to one side while some bare dirt sat growing a few weeds in the corner. They'd probably made the front of the house a priority since that was the most visible.

"Oh, well, you know how I support your ghost hunting, and also how I like hanging out with you, but I'm having trouble figuring out why you would bring *me* to this kind of thing," Emma said as we both surveyed the backyard.

Thankfully a large hedge of overgrown bushes surrounded the area and gave little visibility to the neighbors.

Trying to dig around in my heart for kindness and consideration I knew I'd had at one point, I gave Emma a small smile. "I just thought maybe you'd like something different to do."

She responded to my smile with a warm one of her own, way warmer than the one I was struggling to present. "Oh! For sure! Just let me know if I can do something to help. I feel kind of useless compared to what you can do."

I patted her awkwardly on the shoulder a few times. "Nonsense. Your presence is helpful."

I left her still smiling happily as I walked around in a circle. "Frank? Buddy? Are you here?"

Even if a ghost had worn itself out for some reason or another, my presence in their haunt was usually enough to help give a charge to their ghost batteries. Most of them would perk right up, appearing out of nowhere, feeling a renewal of energy in their quest for revenge or to find their true love or whatever unfinished business they happened to be obsessing about was, but the backyard remained quiet.

I frowned and turned back to Emma. "I'm not sure what is going on. He's not answering."

Of course I could have summoned him, but as he was probably upset with me from our first meeting, despite the fact that I'd later set him free, I was afraid pulling him to me against his will would have the opposite effect. I was trying to get on his good side, after all.

"Oh. Maybe he can't hear you from outside the house? Maybe we need to go inside?" Emma asked, shrugging helplessly.

"Maybe."

"Go away," a gruff voice said, startling me.

"What?" Emma asked as I looked around in confusion.

"I think someone else is here."

"Of course someone else is here. You're the one hollering. Are you too stupid to realize that you might get attention by doing that?" An older man fazed through the wall of the house and stood outside with hands on his hips. He was in a full set of striped pajamas, complete with a droopy matching hat. A pipe hung out from the side of his mouth, and one of his house shoes tapped the ground in irritation.

"Oh, excuse me. I was under the impression that all the other ghosts had been banished from this house."

The older ghost narrowed his eyes at me. "I remember you. Come back to finish the job, eh? Well you'll have to force me away! This has been my home for nearly a hundred years!"

"Woah, it's okay. I'm not here to force anyone anywhere. I'm just looking for Frank. He used to live here and uhm...then he didn't? He should have come back here though recently. Have you seen him around?"

Emma watched me have a one-sided conversation with a patient smile.

"Yes. You helped capture Frank. I watched the whole thing from the ceiling. Thankfully, you didn't spot me, or else I probably would have been sucked into that terrible portal of doom right along with everyone else! You took my poor Elise that day!"

The familiar weight of guilt crashed down onto my chest. "Yes. I know I messed up! I had no idea what was really happening. I've learned since then that it wasn't right, and I'm trying to fix it. In fact, I plan to save all your friends that we captured that night, including your Elise. You've got to believe me!"

The ghost frowned as if he were considering my words. "Well, don't bring back Arnie. He was so annoying. I admit to enjoying the quiet peace since he's been gone."

A small smirk escaped my lips. "Right. I'll see if I can help him cross over once I free him, so you don't have to put up with him anymore."

"See that you do."

I glanced at Emma who gave me another patient smile, then I turned back to the old ghost. "So about Frank. Have you seen him around?"

"Not since you screamed at him to get into that circle."

"Oh," I said, feeling another stab of guilt. "Maybe he's resting from being captured."

We hadn't had much time to talk after I'd rescued him from Rose, but he was the best lead I had so I'd returned to his original haunt hoping to sweet-talk him into helping me.

The old ghost shrugged. "Not sure. I'll be waiting here for Elise's return."

"I'll do my best."

He grunted and returned into the house, not bothering to use the door.

I sighed and put my hands into the pockets of my jacket. "Well, that was a bust."

"If you weren't talking to Frank, who were you talking to?" Emma asked, her lips pulled into a sympathetic half-frown.

I shrugged and walked past her and out of the backyard. "Not sure who he was, just some other ghost haunting the house. He told me Frank hasn't been back even though it's been like five days since he's been free."

And five days without Brandon.

She hurried to catch up with my long stride as I made my way through the front yard and back onto the sidewalk. "I'm sorry if I was eavesdropping or shouldn't have been listening, but it sounded like you were upset about something you'd done? If I caught it right."

I stopped abruptly and turned to look right into her green eyes, shades darker than Brandon's but still reminding me of him. My sudden confrontation startled her as she widened her eyes and took a step back.

Emma's concerned look zapped away my anger and brought me back to the present. It wasn't her fault that I had been too stupid to realize what I was doing. It wasn't her fault that Frank wasn't there to help me. It wasn't her fault that Brandon was gone.

The only one I could blame was myself, and Emma had been nothing but sweet, supportive, and patient with me.

Instead of telling her off as I'd started to, I closed my eyes and took a deep breath. "Yes, yes. I'm sorry, Emma. You've been a good friend to me. I suppose it wouldn't hurt to tell you what happened here."

Some of the worry seeped out of her expression as her eyes softened. "Maybe I'll be able to help you. Sometimes just venting can help a person feel better."

"I'm not sure that this is one of those times, but I'll try it, and we can see what happens."

"Sounds good."

We found ourselves at a cafe a few blocks away, thanks to Emma's car, sipping at some warm drinks and watching the cold wind blow dead leaves down the street.

"So what happened at that house?" Emma dabbed her lips with a napkin and turned her full attention to me.

Starting from the beginning with the super distracting teacher in history, why I'd contacted Rose in the first place, and ending up with how I'd trapped the ghosts in that house, including Frank, I told Emma the more important bits of the story.

Of course, I left out Brandon, refusing even to put that terrible situation into words in case saying it out loud would make it more real.

"Wow," was all Emma said after a little while. She took another sip of her coffee. "I can't imagine what it's like to deal with these things all the time."

I pressed my lips together and nodded. "You're telling me."

She laughed softly and shook her head. "I don't want all the bad parts, but the fun parts do seem pretty cool. Witches and ghosts. If they exist, what else is out there?"

I chuckled dryly. "I'm not sure you really want to know, even if I could tell you."

Frowning in playful disappointment, she said, "Ah, that's too bad. This stuff is kind of exciting."

"Not so much when you're trapped in a basement with creatures who can control your every move, including whether you are allowed to simply breathe or not." I frowned.

"Okay...that's fair."

We talked about other more normal things for a while and then Emma straightened in her chair. "Oh! I almost forgot. Addy and I are going to a movie tonight. Do you want to come?"

I smiled automatically at the invitation. It was nice to be invited to things without having to position myself so that they had to invite me or risk looking rude, like it had been with my last group of "friends". Then all the pressing fears and pain from the last few days chased away the momentary relief.

I had work to do and going to the movies was not on my long list of tasks. Firstly, I had to find Rose. She might have been a powerful witch and necromancer, apparently, but I wasn't about to let her beat my silly mortal self.

Or at least I was going to die giving it my all.

"What's with the smile and then frown? You changed expressions so fast that it was like you put a mask on your face." Emma watched me carefully.

"Oh, uhm, I did want to go to the movies for a second, but I can't. I have too much to do. I need to track down someone who can help me find Rose. I can't stop to hang out with friends for a fun movie night when..." I swallowed on his name, still unable to admit it out loud, "...some ghosts are struggling in her grasp. Thanksgiving break is the perfect time to focus on it without school distractions and lots of free time to hunt her down."

Emma pressed her lips together in thought and nodded. "I get that, but I still want you to come. I guess that's selfish of me, but you're lots of fun to be around. After all you've been through the last few days, don't you think you deserve a bit of fun?"

I sighed and fiddled with my coffee cup. "It doesn't feel like I'll ever deserve fun again, especially if I can't free those ghosts. If they aren't able to have fun, why should I get to? Not to mention, we just put Steph into the ground yesterday. It doesn't seem fair to keep living when she can't."

"That's a pretty bleak way of looking at it."

I shrugged.

"Well, I'd really like it if you came with us. It's not that I don't like to hang out with Addy, I totally do, but sometimes she can be..."

"A little intense?" I supplied with a sympathetic half-smile.

"Yes." She nodded with wide eyes.

"I know that's right."

"So if you're there, it helps to kind of take off the pressure some, you know? It seems to be more chill if you're around."

I frowned as I thought over her words. A movie wouldn't hurt anything, probably. Plus, it was going to take some time to gather more leads. As it was, Frank's haunt had been a bust. Gryphin was going to ask Mr. Tyler how he'd gotten in contact with Phoenix, and I was waiting for him to get back to me. Meanwhile, Caleb was working through his witchy contacts. Honestly, I was kind of stuck on the Rose hunt for a moment, and maybe going to the movies and doing something different for a few hours would help give me new ideas or a bit of perspective clarity.

"Okay, I'll go."

"Yay!" Emma clapped her hands lightly.

A little later, after having parted with Emma so we could go home for a few hours before meeting up at the theater, I was sitting at the kitchen table, staring at the fridge, and wondering if I could convince myself to eat something. Food had become more of a burden and chore rather than something to be avoided. While my stomach felt hollow and my limbs were weak, I didn't even have the energy to lift a bit of fruit to my mouth. A part of me was patting myself on the back for getting so good at limiting my calories so much that it was easy not to eat. Another part of me was shuddering as it shriveled up in pain, hopelessness, and despair.

What was the point in even living if all there is to it was one pain after the other? Or even if a person had a great, perfect life, there would still be one thing that comes along and shatters it all. All it took was one thing.

I sighed as my head slid out of my hands and dropped onto the table. The pain was all my fault, really. Gran had warned me not to hang out with Brandon so much. I'd gotten too close and too attached and too comfortable. It was also my fault that he got captured. If he hadn't been hanging out with me, he wouldn't have been near Rose at all. The same went for Sarah. I had forced her to take that potion, lured Rose into that private meadow with those glasses, and prevented Sarah from being in her wolf form. Perhaps that would have made a difference.

I wasn't sure what hurt worse—the painful guilt or the hollow space all around me with no one making snarky comments about alivers.

"Hanna?" Trina asked from somewhere nearby. My eyes were listlessly staring at the wall so I couldn't see her.

I grunted.

After a few seconds, I felt her hand sit lightly on my shoulder. "Are you okay?"

I shrugged, still staring at the wall.

"Something tells me you're not okay, but you have every right to be sad. Stephanie seemed like a bright and fun person. The way her body washed up on the shore, and with being able to see her ghost and all of that, it must have been really hard to handle."

I still didn't say anything, not having the energy to tell her about the other things also bothering me. She knew bits of the story about Rose, but I hadn't told her or Mom how dangerous it had gotten with our last confrontation. It was nice to have them care about me, but their overprotection had gotten too stifling. If I were to explain the whole story, I probably wouldn't have been able to leave the house until I was sixty.

"Is there anything I can do to help you? Do you need someone to talk to?"

I blinked a few times.

"Maybe you need someone to talk to you? Where is Brandon? Is he here? Brandon? Maybe you could regale her with one of your amazing stories about living in the 90s."

As she talked, my chest swelled with so much emotion that it flooded into my face, and tears started leaking out of my eyes. That wasn't enough, though, and the feelings pulled my mouth into a sob and made my shoulders shudder. There was too much fear and despair to keep it locked inside, demanding my body express it in a physical way.

Trina gasped, wrapped her arms around my shoulders, and pulled until I was leaning into her, getting her t-shirt wet with my salty pain. "Oh, Hanna! I'm so sorry! I didn't mean to make you feel so bad. Are Brandon's stories really that terrible?"

"He's gone!" I wailed into her shoulder and wrapped my arms around her, so I had something to keep me anchored lest the gale of torrid anguish wash me away.

"What do you mean gone? Did he cross over?"

"No!" I sobbed more, unable to stop crying once it had started. Sure, I'd cried myself to sleep every night since it'd happened, but there was something about having someone there with me that pulled out all the feelings despite the tiny bit of dignity I'd tried to protect.

"No? Where else could he have gone? Did you guys have a fight?"

"It was Rose," I said through hiccoughs. "She took him."

Trina paused for a moment, probably trying to figure out what I was talking about. "You mean like she trapped those other ghosts? How did this happen? When?"

She tried to gently push me away, probably to look into my face, but I held onto her firmly, not ready.

"None of that matters except that she's got him and now he's gone!" I wailed the last part again. My chest heaved with the effort of not dissolving into a puddle and completely losing myself.

Trina made shushing sounds and ran her hands over my hair. "It's alright. Let it out. I know he meant a lot to you, even if he was kind of a dork."

Her comment made me huff a half-laugh, half-sob.

She continued stroking my hair as I let out as many tears as I needed to, which turned out to be quite a lot and for several minutes.

When I was finally able to breathe without sobbing, I sat up, wiped snot and tears off my face, and turned away from Trina in embarrassment. "I'm sorry."

"Don't be sorry. It's okay to have feelings. I'm sorry you feel like it's bad for you to show them." She patted my back a few more times.

I didn't know what to say to that, so I didn't say anything. We sat in silence for a few more minutes, while I tried to clean and massage my swollen face.

"Now that we've let it all out," Trina said, getting up to grab some paper towels from the kitchen and handing them to me. "Let's figure out how to get him back."

I flashed her a timid smile as I wiped my face and blew my nose. "Are you sure you want to help?"

She furrowed her eyebrows as she sat down next to me. "Of course! Although I'm glad I don't have to be the one to listen to his terrible jokes once we do get him back."

"Only if you keep that necklace on," I said and immediately regretted it.

Something flitted across her face, maybe annoyance, but it was gone quickly. "So what's first? I suppose we need to find that witch?"

I put my head back onto the table but kept my face in her direction. The cool smoothness of the countertop felt nice on my puffy and heated face. "I have no idea where she is. She's too powerful and smart. After all, she's older than even Caleb, so probably knows exactly where to hide when she doesn't want to be found."

Trina frowned and rested her elbow on the table with her chin in her hand. "Okay, well, that is a challenge, but we've got more than just us, don't we? Caleb? That werewolf kid? Any other ghosts you can talk to? What about the necromancers? We aren't without help, and some of those helpers are pretty powerful, too. Honestly, I'm surprised Caleb hasn't been able to find her yet. It seems like he'd be pretty good with stuff like that."

I frowned as I thought about her words. "That's true. How weird."

Trina shrugged it off while I tucked it away to think about later. "We've got all these other creatures, maybe it's time we found a witch."

"Ugh, the last time someone said that nothing ended well."

"What?"

"Nevermind. Anyway, yes. Gryphin is working with Mr. Tyler to get a witch's help. I'm just waiting for him to get back to me."

Trina nodded. "Okay. Good deal. I'll get with Caleb and see if I can't put some more pressure on him. Does he know what happened with...your friend?"

I sighed. "Not really. He knows that Steph crossed over and helped with her body, but I didn't tell him all the things that happened that night."

Just like I still hadn't told Trina the whole story. Hopefully, she wouldn't suspect there was more to it. Like the fact that Rose was able to control a vampire, give him strength with her spells, and eat ghosts so she could be even stronger.

"Right. Do you mind if I tell him?"

I shrugged.

She smiled and rubbed my shoulder a few times. "You're not alone, Hanna. We'll get through this together. Everything will work out. You'll see."

Chapter 2

I have no idea how I ended up at the theater later that night. I was like one of Noah's zombies as my body got ready without my mind paying attention to what I was doing. Somehow, I showered, dressed, combed my hair, and got dropped off by Trina who was on her way to somewhere else with her friends.

Addy and Emma greeted me outside, perhaps more enthusiastically than I was ready for. We headed inside chatting about the movie we were going to see. I still felt dazed as we bought popcorn, chocolate, and drinks, gave our tickets to the ticket guy, and found our seats.

Of course, a few ghosts wandered around the place, but I'd grown so used to seeing them all the time that I didn't really think about it until I noticed one sitting in a seat near the middle of the theater as if going to watch the movie with us. It was hard to see many details about the ghost since we'd been forced to sit in the back where there were a few empty seats, but I could tell they at least had long-ish hair and were sharing a chair as an aliver without seeming to care.

The reason why this ghost snagged my attention is that they interacted with the physical surroundings more than most did. Usually, a ghost seemed like they were in their own little world, staring through space, walking around aimlessly, having one-sided conversations with others long gone, or going through random actions that they'd done several times in their lives. Perhaps this ghost was simply watching a movie like he'd done many times before, not really seeing the current movie that was playing for the alivers.

"What are you staring at?" Emma asked from her seat to the left.

"Huh? Oh, nothing."

Addy popped her head around Emma's shoulder where she was sitting on her other side. Her eyes were wide with excitement. "Is it a ghost?"

"Shh!" I glanced around to see if anyone was paying attention to us.

Addy winced and whispered, "Sorry, but is it?"

I gave her a small smile and sat back in my chair.

Addy and Emma giggled together as I shook my head in amusement and allowed myself to eat a few bites of popcorn.

As the lights dimmed and the ads changed into trailers, which were really just more ads, the ghost said loudly, probably because he figured no one could hear him, "Ah, here we go. Finally, something new to watch."

Pushing my lips together in a pensive frown, I glanced down at his glowy-blue head from several rows away. Two thoughts occurred to me then—this was going to be a very long movie if he talked through it the whole time, and his voice sounded vaguely familiar.

I was terrible at placing names and faces out of context, like if one actor was in a rom-com movie and then a few years later I saw him in a thriller, it always took me forever to figure it out. I was even worse with voices.

At various times during the trailers, the ghost made several comments. Some of them were funny but most were annoying.

"Oh, wow. That brick house has aged well."

"Look at that! Computers can do some amazing things nowadays."

"Who would want to watch a movie about *that*?"

"Never would have thought that a space movie about teenagers wielding super-dangerous, hand-cutting-off swords would become such a big deal."

I would have gotten super angry with his comments if I hadn't been so distracted trying to figure out where I'd heard him before. My mind whirled as I tried to place his voice with his face. It was so distracting that I barely paid any attention to the trailers.

But by the time the movie finally started, I'd remembered and felt so stupid that I'd forgotten in the first place. Sure, there were ghosts everywhere, and I'd heard hundreds, maybe thousands talk over the years, but I had spent time with only a few. There weren't that many teenage boy ghosts I'd talked to over the last few months, and it certainly wasn't the one I wanted it to be.

But perhaps the one I needed.

I gasped as the opening scene started, earning weird looks from Emma, Addy, and a few others in front of us.

I sunk lower into my chair feeling dumb and buzzing with energy. Finally, there was something I could do. I'd been looking for that exact ghost earlier that very morning and there he was, sitting in a random movie theater I'd just happened to also be in.

What were the odds of that?

Too bad we were also surrounded by a theater full of people where it would be impossible for me to talk to him without gaining unwanted attention.

I might have been able to focus on the movie and wait out my chance to talk to him with a jiggling knee if he'd just kept quiet, but he was worse than Brandon. Perhaps Brandon would have been this bad if he'd figured no one could hear him.

A small smile perked up my lips for a second as I imagined Brandon sitting next to me, dropping his usual dumb comments.

As it was, it was one of the longest movies I didn't watch. At one point, there was an action scene where a few motorcycles were chasing a van full of the good guys inside. They were shooting at each other and doing stunts, impressing Frank very much.

"Woah! Off the hook!" he exclaimed with a jump as one of the motorcycles blew up. "Did you see that?"

He looked at the people around him, but of course, no one answered his question. "Aw, c'mon! Y'all are a bunch of stiffs! I'm more alive than any of you in here!"

I rolled my eyes, wanting only to tell him none of it was real and either computer graphics or carefully staged stunts.

Finally, the movie ended, and the credits started rolling to some kind of rap song I didn't recognize. People began packing up their stuff and gathering trash as they chatted. The lights slowly grew brighter.

"Not the worst movie I've ever seen," Addy said as she stood, holding her half-eaten bag of popcorn.

"Not the best either." Emma smiled and also stood.

Both of them turned to look at me as I was in their way to exit the aisle.

I pulled my legs up so they could pass by. "You guys go ahead. I'm going to stay here for a second."

"Why?" Emma asked, tilting her head to the side slightly.

"Is it the ghost?" Addy leaned in, at least remembering to keep her voice low. "Can we help?"

"Er, yeah. I just want to have a chat with him. I won't hold you guys up." I smiled awkwardly, hoping they wouldn't get offended.

I wasn't sure how Frank would react to a trio of girls bombarding him with questions, and I needed his help so desperately that I was treating this situation as a delicate one.

Emma frowned and Addy pouted.

"Do you still want to go for ice cream after this?" Emma asked.

"Oh yes, definitely. I'll just be a few minutes. Can I meet you outside?"

No, I didn't want to be tempted by fatty ice cream, but I didn't want to offend them.

They gave me disappointed looks as they scooted past and headed down the stairs. I felt bad, but maybe telling them about the conversation while we ate ice cream would help make it up to them. As I waited for the rest of the theater to empty, feeling like a weird creeper in the back watching everyone leave, it struck me again as odd that I had somehow found friends who wanted to be included in my insane escapades instead of feeling like I had to hide who I really was.

Frank, thank goodness, kept sitting in his seat as people filed past.

My heart was pounding inside my chest with eagerness to contact him and worry that he'd pop out too quickly. I could always summon him back and demand answers, but I was hoping I could avoid all that nastiness.

As the last group of people left the theater, I hastily descended the stairs and plopped myself into the chair next to his.

"Hi, Frank," I said chipperly.

"Jeepers Creepers!" he said, clutching at his chest. "You've got to warn a fella before you do something like that!"

"You deserve it after talking through the whole movie. Do you know how annoying it is when someone does that?" I gave him a flat stare.

He grinned and looked around. "There are few things I get to enjoy in my half-life and pretending I can ruin a movie for a whole room full of people is one of those things. Don't take that away from me."

I shook my head. "Whatever. So how are you here? Did you follow me or something? I went to your haunt today and—"

I had to stop talking because a couple of the movie theater workers came around the wall and were looking to make sure everyone was out. They carried brooms and dustpans, so I figured they were there to clean up.

Frank turned to see whatever it was that had distracted me. "Looks like we've got company."

"Can you meet me in the hall? Hopefully, it'll be pretty clear by now, and I can pretend to be on the phone if I have to," I said in a near whisper as I stood and looped my purse over my shoulder.

Frank shrugged. "Sure. It's not like I have anything else to do. I've been watching movies the past two days, and I'm pretty sure I've seen most of them several times."

I flashed him a grateful smile and headed out of the dark room.

The theater employees gave me odd looks as I passed by, but I pretended it didn't bother me.

The lighting was much better in the hallway, but thankfully not too bright. I'd never thought about that before, but it was probably designed that way on purpose, so no one got overwhelmed after coming out of a dark theater.

My heart had calmed down some after finally getting to talk to Frank, but it began pounding hard again as I saw who was standing in the hallway. Apparently, we'd all been watching the same movie without realizing it.

Andrea, Randi, and a few of their friends I vaguely knew, stopped talking immediately when they saw me step out past the doors and into the hallway.

With a sneer, Andrea looked me up and down. Her face was so disgusted, I had to look down too, just to make sure my clothes weren't covered in dog poop or something.

"What are *you* doing here?" she asked with a curled lip.

I swallowed before answering, hoping I didn't sound too nervous. "I thought I'd come here to watch a movie since that's what most people do at theaters and all—"

She scoffed and sent Randi a pointed look. As for our once mutual friend, she looked torn and uncomfortable. Randi had never been rude to me directly, but it was no surprise to watch her go along with whatever Andrea was doing.

Frank walked through the wall on the other side of me, and he paused as he saw there were other alivers.

I tried to keep my focus on Andrea and Randi instead of staring off into the empty space where Frank stood with hands in his ripped jeans and a scrutinizing expression on his face.

"If I had known they'd let crazy, evil people in here, then I wouldn't have come." Andrea shook her head and turned to leave.

Randi gave me an apologetic, albeit timid, smile behind Andrea's back and turned to leave with her.

"I must have caught the evil part when I was hanging out with you," I said to her back with a dramatic sigh. "Oh well, hopefully, I can get rid of it with only a few exorcisms."

Slowly, Andrea turned back around, her eyes small slits of anger. "Don't flatter yourself. We were never friends. We only kept you around as entertainment."

"And to do your homework for you too, right?" I tilted my head with a sassy bob.

I swear she almost snarled before turning and stomping the rest of the way down the hall with Randi trailing after her like the good little pet she was.

"Brutal. That girl needs to take a chill pill," Frank said as we waited for the hallway to empty.

I sighed, trying to cleanse myself from some of her contagious negativity. "She's just a girl from school. We used to be friends...or at least hang out, but it seems like she hates me now."

"Yeah, well." Frank shrugged. "The older you get, the less things like this will bother you."

I moved to the corner so I could keep a good watch on the hallway in case someone else showed up while I was talking to what appeared to be the voices in my head.

"And you're what? Like seventeen?" I tried not to remember similar conversations I'd had with Brandon.

"Excuse me. I happen to be sixty-seven years old."

I stared at him for a few blinks.

He stared back.

"You do kind of remind me of an old man," I said with a shrug.

"I might have been dead for the last fifty years of my life, but I've still lived every one of them."

"That's interesting, actually. Most ghosts get stuck in their minds and don't even realize they're dead or that time is passing around them. Also, you were one of the hardest ghosts I'd had to work at to command—"

"I'm still angry at you for that," he interrupted with a grumble.

"Fair. I'm sorry. I'll never stop being sorry. I hope freeing you helped make up for some of that."

He stared at me again for a second before answering. "I'll take it under consideration."

"How kind of you. As I was saying, you're kind of a special type of ghost, aren't you? Not to mention, you haven't been back at your haunt since I freed you, and then I find you here without having to summon you. What's up with that?"

"Have you been checking up on me?" Frank narrowed his eyes. "That's creepy, even coming from me."

I sighed. "No. I've been looking for you. That's different. I went to your haunt, and some other ghost named...you know what? I never did catch his name, but he was mad at me for taking his Elise away."

"Oh, that explains why I didn't see Patrick there. He never got caught. Guess you missed one." Frank rubbed the ghostly stubble on his chin as he thought. "Still, it's weird that you were checking up on me."

"I'm sorry. I figured you'd have gone back to your haunt. How come you've been able to get away?" A thought occurred to me that made me scrunch my eyebrows. "Wait a minute. The only way a ghost can get away from their haunt is if they follow me around. Perhaps you're trying to make *me* feel like the creeper when *you're* the one who has been following me around this whole time!"

Frank barked a harsh laugh. "You wish, girlie. Alright, here's the lowdown as far as I can figure out. When you trapped me with Rose, something changed the haunt as it became the crystal. Must have something to do with the spell she casts. Then, when you freed me, my haunt kind of reset. I guess? This building used to be a groovy roller rink that I spent many Saturday nights at. I popped back here instead of back at my house, where I'd been haunting the last fifty years."

I frowned, trying to sort through all the information he'd given me. "So anyone who I get back from Rose will have a different haunt than they had before?"

He shrugged. "So what do you want? You said you were looking for me?"

The anxiety and pain I'd been momentarily distracted from came back, and I took a deep breath. "I'm sure you could figure it out if you thought hard enough. What happened right before Rose left?"

"She gobbled up some ghosts like a rabid cannibal."

"Okay, and after that?"

"Oh, she captured two more ghosts. That naked chick and that other ghost I'd seen around you before." He frowned. "You're wanting to rescue them, aren't you?"

I nodded slowly, trying to push away the despair that threatened to come in and choke me. Again.

"And you think I'll be able to help you?"

"I don't have many other leads."

"Clearly."

I leaned back onto the wall and slid down until I was sitting on the floor with my knees pressed into my chest. As I wrapped my arms around my legs, I rested my forehead on them. Speaking mostly to my leggings, I said, "I don't know where else to start. I've been looking for Rose for almost two months and nothing. She's too powerful for me. I need help."

Frank grunted but was silent for a few moments.

Shuffling sounds and people chatting warned me that others were coming. Soon the cleaning group left the theater and headed into another one. Luckily, they'd been too busy talking to each other to notice me.

"I should get out of here." I sighed and pulled myself up with the help of the wall. "My friends are waiting. See you around, Frank."

After I walked down the hallway a few paces, my heart sliding into more despair with each step, he spoke. "I'll do it."

Slowly, afraid I'd scare him off, I turned around. "What?"

"I'm still mad at you for the whole thing, but you did figure out how to free me, so you know, maybe that makes up for it. And anyway, I might not be the most righteous dude, but I do feel bad for the others that the freaky deaky lady captured."

Relief pushed away the despair, or at least most of it, and I smiled. "Thank you, Frank! I'll help you complete your unfinished business when we're done, if that's what you'd like," at his expression, I changed tactics, "or whatever it is you'd like help with. I'd owe you for sure."

He waved it off. "We can figure that out later. For now, we'll need a necromancer. You don't happen to know one, do you?"

"Uh, yes. In fact, I do."

Chapter 3

Sleep eluded me fiercely that night. After Frank and I made a tentative plan to meet up with Noah, we'd parted ways and agreed to meet up the next day.

I'd gone to eat ice cream with Addy and Emma afterward but was so distracted that I probably had been terrible company. I told them some of what I'd talked to Frank about but not much. I wouldn't have been surprised if they didn't ask me to hang out with them again.

Ever since I'd been kidnapped by that insane vampire queen—perhaps it wasn't fair to call her insane since that was probably in the job description for a vampire queen—but ever since was captured by vampires, entranced by them where they could force me to simply quit breathing if they wanted to, I'd had panic attacks at night, in the dark when all the terrors came flooding back into my mind.

Brandon had been able to keep the worst of it away either by his presence and dumb jokes, or, if it was really bad, by stealing energy from me to become physical for a few minutes, comforting with tight hugs.

But now it was just me.

He was gone, and it was all my fault.

I could have opened my window and called out for the vampire who was probably nearby, but the last thing I wanted was more vampires around, even if Caleb was a good one.

What I wanted was Brandon.

I'd tried summoning him a million times, of course, but it never worked. When I sought him out with my mind like I usually did when summoning a ghost, it was a feeling of vast emptiness.

Like he'd never existed at all.

I wiped tears from my eyes and rolled over in my bed with a huff, glaring at the clock. It was only three a.m. Despite staying up as long as I could, doing homework and cleaning, anything I could think of to keep myself awake and busy, I'd begun to feel sleepy. Yes, I'd felt exhausted for days, but feeling sleepy was an entirely different matter.

However, when I had hesitantly turned out the lights and finally crawled inside the blankets, the sleepy got washed away by my traitorous thoughts.

Just to prove to myself that Brandon had been there, and I hadn't made the whole thing up, I pulled out my phone and typed his name in the search engine. Well, I typed in his first name, cursing myself for never asking what his last name was. I also cursed myself for never thinking to Google him before. I might have been able to learn so much about his life and how he died, all those things that he'd always kept so secret.

Perhaps that's why I'd never looked him up.

It didn't seem like me to want to respect his privacy for such juicy details, but it had never even become a temptation for me to check up on him. His secrets were his own.

Apparently, that rule dissolved when I wasn't able to be around him anymore because I had no qualms about looking him up then.

Obviously, only typing his first name in the search bar would yield too many results to do anything with, so I added the town we lived in and the year he died. I got a bunch of Facebook profiles, several lists of a family with the last name of Brandon, and then pages of obituaries of Brandons either being born in 2000 or dying in 2000.

Carefully, I read through each obituary, trying to piece together what little I knew of his life with the information until I finally found it. Or, at least, it seemed to be the closest one with the clues I had.

Brandon Henry Matthews 1983-2000

Susan Matthews and family regret to announce the passing of their beloved son, Brandon Henry Matthews. Born to Susan and Henry Matthews, Brandon was the oldest of four children. He is preceded in death by his three siblings Shannon Matthews, Savannah Matthews, and Justin Matthews who died unexpectedly only a week prior, and his grandparents, Marvin and Sheila Childers.

The funeral will be held at 6 pm on Sunday.

And that was basically it. No mention of how he died, how his siblings died, why they died so close together, or anything that would have helped me learn more about my lost friend.

I mean, I learned his middle name and his family members' names, but I didn't know what to do with those.

Unless...

He'd told me once that his dad had left when he was eight, but what about his mom? The pain she must have gone through after losing all four of her children within the same week would have been unimaginable.

I Googled her name and began the search, sifting through a bunch of random people named Susan.

Chirps of early-morning birds sounded outside my window before I found anything that seemed helpful. I was grateful for the distraction the research had provided. I'd made it through the whole night without having a panic attack. I'd also gone all night without much, if any, sleep.

But at least I'd been able to breathe.

There was a mention of a Susan Matthews on the tail end of a news article talking about some organization working to help the homeless. The only reason it caught my eye was that the efforts were on a street in our town, where homeless people often hung around. Susan was listed as one of the homeless people expressing thanks for the efforts of the organization. The direct quote was this: *"It's nice to see there are people in the world that still care about those who have lost everything. Most of us aren't homeless because we've chosen to be, merely because life ripped away everything we've ever held dear."*

The article went on to talk about statistics on the homeless and what communities can do to help those in need, but I merely skimmed over that, checking to make sure there wasn't more information about her somewhere else in the article. While it had been written over fifteen years ago, I still hadn't seen an obituary for her despite my hours of searching.

Perhaps Susan was still around. Maybe I could find her and get more of Brandon's story.

I certainly didn't need anything more to do with all my current worries but looking for evidence that Brandon had existed made me feel closer to him. While I was still working on following leads to Rose, clinging to my friend's memory helped me feel slightly better in the meantime.

I got a text from Mr. Tyler later that morning. I'd been able to catch a few hours of sleep as dawn grew across the sky, but I was more than exhausted. As I was slowly pulling a brush through my hair and staring at my sunken cheeks in the bathroom mirror, the music blaring from my phone softened for a second as it buzzed with a text.

Hoping it was good news, I felt some of my tiredness seep away as I opened the text with eager fingers.

I've got two things you might want to hear about. Can we meet for brunch? I'll bring Gryph. You can bring your mom or sister if you want.

My lips perked into a small smile imagining my history teacher feeling awkward at inviting just me to brunch. It was probably weird spending time with a student outside of school like this, especially since I was a girl and he was a man. I didn't blame him for wanting others to tag along with us.

I texted him back agreeing to a time and place, and went in search of my mom. Trina had gone out with someone earlier in the morning, but Mom was sitting at the kitchen table, scrolling through her phone and eating the blandest oatmeal I'd ever seen.

"Hey," I said, sitting down across from her. "Are you busy today?"

"Hey, sweetie." She put her phone down with a smile. "Not until three or so. Why? Do you actually want to spend some time with me?"

The hope in her face both tore at my heart and made me roll my eyes. "Sheesh, Mom. Don't act so clingy, or it'll scare me away."

"My bad." She kept smiling. "What's up?"

"Mr. Tyler is helping me with…ghostly-type things, and he invited us to brunch today to share some information."

Her eyebrows furrowed slightly. "He invited both of us?"

I shrugged.

"Hmm. Okay, sounds fun. Wait, are you sure you don't mind your mother tagging along? It won't harsh your mellow or anything, will it?"

"I don't know what that means, but whatever it is, yes, it probably will, but I don't care. I know how much you like to be involved with my life, and, who knows? Maybe you'll even be able to help me figure some things out. Sometimes it helps to have an old person's perspective."

"I'm not sure if I should be flattered or insulted."

About an hour later, we pulled up to the place Mr. Tyler had picked and got out of the car. It was a perfectly picturesque restaurant one would expect to share a Tuesday morning brunch. There were several outside tables that were probably super nice to use in the seasons when a winter wind wasn't cutting through the air. As it was, subtle white lights lined the building and made it inviting.

We saw Mr. Tyler and Gryphin as soon as we walked in since the place was relatively small. Mr. Tyler waved us over to the table with a wide smile underneath his greying goatee. I couldn't help but notice that Gryphin also wore a pleased smile, but it was easy to assume he was only being polite and not actually happy to see me. After all, I'd seen him only a few days ago at Stephanie's funeral.

Despite spending a fair amount of time with Gryphin in the last two weeks as I helped his werewolf pack hunt down one of their own ghosts, his hotness still threatened to overwhelm me. His hair was soft, gun-metal grey, and wavy with one looping curl that insisted on coming down onto his forehead. With a straight nose, a rigid jawline, rugged chin stubble, piercing forest brown eyes, and abs for days, he was definitely enjoyable to look at. The best part, as odd as it sounds, were the smells of nature that seemed to change each time I was close enough to him. Often, it reminded me of being free in the woods with clear rushing water nearby and a revitalizing breeze.

After I'd lost Brandon and Sarah that night, Gryphin had laid his big fuzzy werewolf head on my body and helped comfort me and ease the choking panic. I blushed slightly as I remembered his close warmth.

"So glad you could make it," Mr. Tyler greeted as we took our chairs around the table.

Gryphin sat to the right of me, and his legs were so long that mine bumped into his as I got settled.

"Sorry," I said automatically and shifted my leg so it wouldn't be intruding into his space.

He grinned and moved his leg closer so they were touching again.

I blushed more as I sent him a small smile.

While Gryphin teased me, Mr. Tyler and my mom were making companionable small talk. Then the server came by and got our drink orders.

Since it was a Tuesday, usually not a popular time for people to gather and have brunch together, there weren't many patrons around, and we had a small amount of privacy. Enough to talk about minor occult things, anyway.

"I assume you've filled your mother on all that's going on?" Mr. Tyler asked after taking a sip of his steaming coffee.

"Yes, she's up to date," I said with a nod.

Well, almost, but there were things I still wasn't ready to talk about despite having piled it all onto Trina's shoulders yesterday. That had been a regrettable moment of weakness, but in some ways, it had helped Trina and I grow a bit closer.

However, I still was back to trying to ignore the whole thing and solve the issue before my feelings decided to take over again.

My mom pressed her lips together as she studied me. "I am grateful that Hanna feels comfortable sharing all these insane things that she goes through, but I also feel bad that she has so much on her shoulders."

Not that I would ever tell her, but it wasn't that I felt "comfortable" enough to tell her these things. It's that I felt guilty not telling her what I could.

Mr. Tyler nodded. "I know what you mean. I'm a werewolf and still haven't had to go through the crap Hanna has had to endure. Honestly, I feel honored that I'm included inside her circle of helpers."

I shrank a little at their praise and wondered how I should react. Gryphin's steady presence next to me, including his leg that rested against mine and his calming vibes, helped me relax a little.

Mom smiled and nodded. "I'm grateful for your help, too. You have no idea how much it lessens my stress to know she's got powerful people on her side who will work to protect her should she need it. After the whole seethe situation," she looked around, making sure no one was listening, and lowered her voice some, "I just wouldn't be able to sleep at all if I didn't know there were people out there watching over my baby."

"Of course. Hanna has also helped us out more than once, and it's our duty to help her," Mr. Tyler said with a friendly smile in my direction.

I squirmed in my chair, feeling weird about all the attention.

Gryphin chimed in. "I'm sure we'd help her even if we didn't owe her anything. It would simply be the ethical thing to do."

Mr. Tyler chuckled and stirred his coffee some more. "Of course we would."

"It's not that I don't enjoy all this weird talking about me as if I'm not here stuff, but can we get on with why we're here?" I asked, hoping I didn't sound too rude but almost not caring.

As Mr. Tyler began to talk, the server showed up with our food. We had to stop and patiently wait as we were served pancakes and sausages. Gryphin had ordered so much bacon, I was worried he'd get a heart attack right then and keel over.

I'd ordered crepes in hopes that they'd be lighter than pancakes and that the fruit would be healthier to eat compared to rivers of syrup. As it was, though, I didn't feel like eating much of it.

"Right, so as I was saying, I've got two bits of news. The first is that Phoenix has agreed to meet with you."

I blinked a few times. "Really? They would do that?"

Gryphin narrowed his eyes. "Are we sure this isn't some kind of trick to lure her into being alone and letting Rose attack again?"

My mom frowned as I winced.

"Wait, what? Rose attacked you?" She turned to look at me with blazing eyes. "Why do I suddenly feel like I'm not as updated as I thought I was?"

Mr. Tyler and Gryphin exchanged uncomfortable glances.

"Uhm, well, it's..." I tried to start telling her part of the story, but that part also led to a worse fact. The familiar panic bloomed inside my chest. It started by trying to get my heart to vibrate its way out of my body and restrict my breathing.

I probably looked like a dramatic teenager trying to get out of telling my mom the truth as I sat there clutching at my chest and wheezing like an asthmatic.

"Hanna? What's going on?" Mom's worried eyes bore into me.

Gryphin's instincts kicked in. He scooted his chair until it was aligned with mine and wrapped his huge arms around my shoulders. As he drew me in, he put his hand on my head and pushed my ear against his solid chest. His breathing was even, and his heart was steady as he cocooned me in gentle pressure.

I couldn't see what my mom or Mr. Tyler were doing as I pressed into Gryphin's blue shirt, but I could imagine their eyes widening in alarm.

"Excuse me, Ms. Sanchez." Gryphin's voice rumbled throughout his body and the calm slowness with which he talked helped ease my breathing. "I'm not trying to... Well, that is to say, this helps with panic attacks. It's probably better when she has soft fur to press in on her, but I figure turning while inside this restaurant wouldn't be a good idea. Not to mention, it would take too long for me to get into furry form. She'll just have to make do with me as I am."

My breathing was becoming more even but still heavy as I battled the emotions I kept trying to force away. His embrace was working to ground me and give me something else to think about as a blush crept into my cheeks. I could feel the strength in his muscles, the steadiness of his heart, and most of all, I could smell the forest pine trees, hear the rushing water, and feel the soft breeze caressing my skin.

It didn't help that I'd seen him naked after he'd transformed from wolf to human form and helped talk to Sarah, but one good thing about panic attacks was that it helped chase away too many other thoughts.

"What's wrong with her?" Mom asked, battling the fear creeping into her voice.

"Looks like a panic attack. I'm so sorry, Ms. Sanchez," Mr. Tyler said. "I had no idea she hadn't told you everything that happened in the meadow, but it seems quite clear now why she couldn't."

At the mention of the meadow, my breathing hitched a few times, and if Gryphin hadn't been anchoring me against his body, I would have fled from the whole scene and ran until my legs couldn't carry me anymore.

"Perhaps the story can wait," Mom said and put her hand on my back beneath Gryphin's arms. "I'm sorry, sweetie. I didn't know…"

"You're not to blame, of course." Mr. Tyler's voice was soft, and it was easy to imagine the sympathetic-teacher eyes underneath those bushy eyebrows. "We'll work through this together. It'll take time, but we'll give her as much as she needs."

"How much can we trust Phoenix?" Gryphin asked, giving voice to some of the millions of thoughts whirling around in my brain.

Finally, my breathing was slowing down to a more regular pace, but I wasn't quite yet ready to leave the comfort of a strong werewolf's embrace.

Mr. Tyler sighed. "I'm not sure, but my instincts are telling me that as long as we take precautions, we should be fine. Remember how they stopped helping...the other person when she started, uhm...doing odd things and then teleported out? Phoenix assured me on the phone that they wanted no part in what was happening, and that if they could, they'd like to help us."

"Why don't they just go to the coven and have them stop her? As far as what I could see, it's probably them who will have the best chances of stopping someone as powerful as her," Gryphin said.

Feeling more embarrassed than panicked now, I slowly pushed back from Gryphin's chest. He let me go with a sympathetic smile but didn't move his chair away and back to the original position around the table.

As if sensing my fragility, no one looked directly at me or said anything, but my mom did grab my hand and held it fiercely.

Mr. Tyler shook his head in answer to Gryphin's question. "They won't move against her, apparently. Phoenix said they're afraid."

My mom swallowed thickly. "I'm not exactly sure what's going on, but if this person is so powerful that a coven, which I assume is witches, is afraid to go against her, then what chance do you guys have?"

Gryphin sighed as he munched on a slice of bacon. "That's a very good question."

"It doesn't matter," I said quietly, my voice sounding as fragile as my lungs felt.

"What, sweetie?" Mom asked, her head tilted toward me, and her eyes were tender, full of worry and love.

I felt terrible making her so much more worried, but it wasn't like I was doing any of this on purpose. In fact, a small logical part of my mind pointed out that my fears of worrying her may have been contributing to the panic that kept trying to take all my oxygen.

"I don't care what the chances are, what the odds are, or what the danger is. We've got to win."

Mom squeezed my hand, and bless her heart, didn't try to talk me out of my insanity for the moment, but I was certain she was saving all that for later.

Quiet descended on our table, and we ate for a few minutes. Our server came by to check on us and fill up coffee cups, but it was nice to take a rest from all the intensity.

"What was the other thing you wanted to tell me?" I asked after reaching the halfway point with my food. The crepes were good, but the richness was starting to make me feel sick.

Mr. Tyler put down his fork. "Oh! Well...don't worry about it. It's not important. I'll tell you later."

Some kind of expression I didn't understand passed between him and my mom, but I didn't have the energy to figure out what was going on.

For the rest of brunch, we hashed out a plan to meet Phoenix, and how we could approach the whole thing feeling as safe as possible and still getting the connection and information about Rose and her coven.

It was a place to start, at least.

As we left the restaurant, Mr. Tyler and my mom were busy talking further down the sidewalk despite the chilly air. I turned to Gryphin, finding it a good time to check in with him.

"I'm sorry we got all wrapped up in my drama, but I really did mean to ask you how the pack was doing. How's your dad?"

Gryphin leaned back against a metal pole that had to have been chilly to the touch, but it struck me then that he never seemed to get cold. Even now he was wearing only a t-shirt and no jacket. There weren't any goosebumps on his arms like there were on mine despite *my* jacket. Mr. Tyler was in a long-sleeved shirt, but also, still no jacket. Maybe being warm was a werewolf thing.

"He's...getting better. Maybe."

I frowned and kicked at a pebble near my shoe. "It must be hard to go through all of this. I feel for your pack. I wish what we'd done had helped more. If we'd been able to help Sarah with her unfinished business, then maybe we could have given your dad more closure, and he'd be able to heal better."

Gryphin shrugged his massive shoulders. "Or it wouldn't matter what we did, and the death of his mate has destroyed something inside of him that can never be fixed."

"Well, that's super bleak."

He sighed and stood up straight, running fingers through his curls in frustration. "Don't get me wrong, H. I really appreciate what you've done for us. We all do, but maybe we're hoping for something that can't be fixed."

"What does Kage say about it?"

"Not much. I suppose we're both biding our time, hoping my dad will pull out of it before another wolf decides he's unfit to be alpha." He sighed. "We always do our best to curb any dissent from the others, but there's only so much we can do when the alpha is...as he is."

Feeling like I should express some kind of physical sympathy, I reached my hand out and rubbed his upper arm a few times. His skin underneath the t-shirt still felt warm, and it was easy to remember what being wrapped up in his embrace had been like.

And I knew I wanted to feel it again.

Chapter 4

After we'd gotten home, Mom had busied herself getting ready for work, and I went to my room, put some music on, and summoned Frank into the heart of my inner sanctum.

"It's about time, space cadet," he said by way of greeting.

I was sitting in my homework chair and gestured for him to take a seat across from me on the bed. "Sorry. My teacher wanted to meet, and since he's the one trying to contact the arcanist, I didn't want to miss it."

"Okay, I can dig it. What did you find out?" He eyed my pink blankets carefully before finally sitting down. My bed wasn't exactly made, but I didn't care. He was a ghost. What did it matter if he sat through a pile of blankets?

I explained our plan to meet with Phoenix and how they seemed to be comfortable with helping us, at least a little.

Frank nodded after I finished. "All right. That's a good start. I still think we should try my plan too, just in case the other one doesn't pan out."

"And this is the one where we need a necromancer? Care to explain why?"

"I'm not sure how much you know about necromancers, but they like to keep their order's secrets guarded closely."

I shook my head. "Boy, do I know about that."

His eyebrows rose in appreciation. "And I'm sure you didn't miss the fact that the witch was surrounded by purple lightning and was pouring it into her vampire goon."

I nodded. "It was hard to miss."

"So, after watching her for a few weeks and after it all went down in that meadow, I'm thinking your witch lady—"

"Rose."

"I'm thinking Rose is breaking some serious rules on both the magic users' side and the necromancers' side. The fact that she had gotten a hold of those necromancer secrets at all is cause enough for the order to pay attention."

I chewed on the side of my lip for a second. "So you're thinking we go tell on her? What will that do?"

He shrugged. "Could do lots of things, and most of those things would at least help us locate her."

"If they share any information with us. They're a tight-lipped group, remember?"

Frank chuckled dryly as I used his own argument against him. "Fair point. Wouldn't hurt to ask, but even if they don't share anything with us, it'll be harder on her to have a whole bunch of others looking for her. While ghosts or whatever can be helpful, necromancers have a whole network of spies and members that can track her down better than a high school student. No offense."

I shrugged. "It's true. I've been terrible at trying to find her."

"Well, luckily you've got me now."

"And apparently a whole order of necromancers."

"It's a place to start, anyway. Oh, and just for the record, I want to make sure you know I'm still upset with you for getting me involved in all of this in the first place. Being a ghost might have been a boring existence, but there was peace in being left alone to stew with my thoughts."

I sighed and rubbed my eyes. "Duly noted. I seem to mess things up a lot."

Frank was quiet for a second as his eyes studied me. It was long enough that I started to feel awkward and shifted in my seat.

"What?" I asked, hoping it would stop him from staring deep into my soul or whatever he was doing.

He pressed his lips together in thought and shook his head. "You were in love with that ghost, weren't you?"

I felt my heart plummet to my toes as I forced myself to take a deep breath and keep my face calm. "What makes you say that?"

"Sweet cheeks, I may have died at seventeen, but I've been around. I know love when I see it."

I forced out a laugh and turned away to look at my phone so he wouldn't see the flush that had burst across my face. "I don't know what you're talking about."

"Right," Frank said dryly. "Of course not. Well, don't add my discontent to your list of worries. I was mostly teasing anyway."

I scoffed, grateful that he'd moved on. "Like I was really worried about your feelings."

He grunted, but we both knew the truth. "There is one other thing I wanted to talk to you about before I forget."

"Okay?"

"Do you remember what you did to free me from Rose's curse?"

I blinked for a few seconds, trying to will my mind to focus on that moment, and only that moment, from that terrible night.

"I...well, I knew from Mr. Tyler's curse there was a ghostly, plasma chain thingy that was connecting you and Rose together, maybe. So I figured if I could break it then the curse would break."

Frank nodded with a frown. "Yes, but didn't you need to use a ghostly knife the last time to break the chain? How did you do it as an aliver with no ghostly knife?"

I considered his questions with pursed lips and drawn eyebrows. "I don't know? All I knew was that I had to free you. If I was able to free you then I could..."

Frank held his hands up to stop my line of thought as my breathing started to hiccough. "Woah, don't take it to the max. Just breathe in slowly. It's okay. You're right. What you did that night helped us then and will help us in the future. As long as you can replicate it, that is. Do you think that's possible?"

I focused on the progress we'd made while forcing myself to take a deep breath in through my nose. I really needed to get a hold of myself if I didn't want to pass out from a panic attack every few hours.

"I think so?"

Frank stood and paced across my carpet a few times while pulling fingers through his long, wavy, dark hair. "This seems to suggest you have the ability to pull your own ghostly spirit or plasma essence or whatever it's called from within inside your body and use to do things outside your body."

"Is that bad?" I watched him move back and forth with raised eyebrows.

He paused and looked at a few pictures I had of my family sitting on a shelf. "No. It's not bad. It may, in fact, be very groovy."

"Let's hope so. Out of curiosity, how do you know so much about necromancers?" I asked, voicing a thought that had popped up. "Most people don't have many interactions with them."

He shrugged. "One of the other ghosts in my very haunted house used to belong to the order. He'd talk about all the time. Super annoying then but turning out to be helpful now."

"Huh. Okay. I guess necroes do have to die sometimes. Just never thought about one being a ghost."

Either Noah didn't have much of a social life during Thanksgiving break or he was eager to meet with me because he had no problem getting together later that same day. After texting Noah and chatting a bit more with Frank, I left my room to ask my mom for permission to go out that evening. Frank was content to wait inside my room, which was odd for me since I'd gotten used to having a certain nosy ghost follow me around everywhere.

As I walked down the hallway, I was surprised to hear the mutterings of a deeper voice coming from the front room.

"This could easily be them, but it might not be. We don't have enough information here," rumbling tones that I identified as Caleb's met me as I rounded the corner.

Mom turned from the couch where she was sitting, and her face flickered from surprise, to guilt, and then forced cheerfulness as she greeted me. "Hey, sweetie. Caleb just dropped by for a second to check in on us. Isn't that nice?"

As for the vampire, his expression was as pleasant and blank as always. He only had about three hundred years to perfect his poker face, and I'm sure he was very good at it. His long legs stretched out in front of him as he sat in the armchair across from my mom. The black slacks he wore were creased with a perfect line down the center. His dress shirt was freshly pressed with two buttons at the top left undone in a way that looked casual but was certainly on purpose. His dark hair was styled with a swoop to the side, and his bright teeth shone in contrast to his darker skin.

"Very nice of him and not at all creepy to see that he's chatting with my mom like y'all are old pals. What were you guys talking about?" I asked, trying to seem innocent as I sat on the other end of the couch.

Mom glanced at Caleb with slightly panicked eyes, but he was as cool as ever.

"Nothing important. Just something your mom saw on social media." He shrugged and sat back in the chair and crossed one leg over the other.

"Right. That makes sense that she'd come to you to talk about it since you're like all hip and up with the times," I said with a sarcastic tone in my voice.

He didn't take the bait. Instead, he grinned that smile that made girls nearly faint at school all the time, including myself at one point. "I'll have you know I work very hard to stay relevant."

I rolled my eyes and shook my head. Turning to my mom, I said, "Don't you have to go to work soon?"

She glanced at her phone and frowned. "I do. I've got a few minutes though. Was there something you wanted to talk about?"

I thought for a second, unsure how much I should say in front of Caleb, but then chided myself for trying to spare his feelings. Using his magic vampire powers, he pretty much kept tabs on me all the time anyway. He might as well find out now that I was going to hang with one of his least favorite people who belonged to one of his least favorite groups.

Of course, they had worked together last week, and while the atmosphere had been nearly tangible with tension, perhaps they'd gotten better at being around each other.

Maybe.

"Is it okay if I hang out with Noah tonight? We'll be back before dark, of course, and we'll be in public the whole time. I just need to ask him some questions about some things I saw from…the other night, and he might be able to help me get some more information I need."

Several things passed through my mom's eyes as she considered my words. She glanced at Caleb before saying anything, and he gave her a half-smile and a nod as if to confirm he'd keep an eye out for me. Like always.

A part of me did feel guilty for putting so many demands on him, but he never complained or acted like it was a hassle. Unless of course I did something stupid that made his life harder. But overall, he seemed fine with watching me all the time.

Perhaps he was bored being an immortal vampire and having nothing else to do. Or perhaps he felt like he owed my grandmother for failing to keep her safe all those years ago and wanted to make it up to her by keeping her granddaughter safe.

Either way, it really was nice of him to stick around. Mostly, it helped my mom's peace of mind more than anything, but I couldn't help but appreciate his gesture all the same. Heck, if it weren't for him, I probably wouldn't be able to leave the house ever. My mom would probably demand I stay home all the time and take a crash course in homeschooling so we could avoid the vampires or werewolves or whatever boogeymen were trying to kidnap me in any given week.

"Are you trying to get more information about Rose? What makes you think Noah will be able to help?" Mom asked, apparently past the concern for my safety as long as my brooding vampire friend would be nearby.

Not to mention the necromancer had also helped us in the past. All on his own, Noah was a passable fighter, even getting the best over Caleb at least once, but he also had some powerful friends that had helped rescue me from a cray-cray vampire queen.

I hesitated, unsure how much to tell her and how much I could go into before dissolving into hysterical breathing fits again.

She must have seen the concern on my face because she scooted closer and grabbed my hand. "Hanna, it's okay. The last thing I want is to upset you anymore than you are. I don't understand the whole situation, and I get why you might not be able to explain it all to me, but sweetie, I can't let you do this on your own. I want to help in any way that I can."

"I know, Mom. I appreciate it. I promise if there is anything that I can think of that you could help with, I'll let you know."

She frowned and moved my hair out of my face with her free hand. "I'd like that. I just wish you didn't have to go through all this. I feel so helpless. It's like I have to let you go into the world to face things all on your own, and all I can focus on is the fear that I wasn't able to prepare you or teach you well enough. And when it comes to the whole occult situation, I *know* I didn't do enough."

I smiled softly and squeezed her hand. "You did your best. Besides, I'm not alone. I have Caleb and Noah and probably at least fifty thousand ghosts who can help me. Even Trina could jump in with an assist now and then."

Caleb grunted his agreement, and my mom leaned in for a hug. "Alright. I suppose I can work with that. For now."

We shared a smile. She might not have been able to help me directly, but just having her support and knowing she loved me no matter what helped go a long way.

Chapter 5

As Frank and I walked towards the restaurant, I felt a surge of guilt for not telling Noah the whole truth in my texts. At first, it hadn't occurred to me that he'd think this was anything else other than a meeting about the occult stuff we were both involved in, but, after seeing his return texts, I'd started to suspect he was hoping it was something else. But by that time, I hadn't wanted to crush his spirits and risk the possibility that he'd cancel on me afterward.

I kept reminding myself I'd said nothing in the texts about going on a date or having any kind of romantic feelings or anything like that. If he'd come to conclusions on his own, that was his problem.

"So how do you know this guy?" Frank asked, mildly surprising me with the chitchat. So far, I'd gotten the impression that Frank was a get-down-to-business kind of guy and didn't care about things like small talk.

"I know him from school. We used to hang out a lot, and I guess now we kind of end up hanging out a lot, but not because we're happy to spend time around each other, but more like we need each other's skills during whatever insanity is happening at the time."

He grunted his acknowledgement and that was it. Perhaps I had pegged him right.

Loud chatter and wafting smells of fried food greeted me as I opened the door and walked in. Frank came in after me, and I held the door open for him even though it probably looked weird to anyone who happened to be watching.

I was getting less concerned about looking weird.

Noah stood from his booth near the window and waved me over. I gave the hostess a polite nod as I moved to meet my party.

My heart sank as I took in his outfit. Usually, he wore jeans, a t-shirt, and his letterman's jacket. But for our dinner, he'd put on nicer jeans (less holes) and a polo shirt that didn't have any wrinkles. It did indeed appear that I'd led him on a bit. Even if it had been accidental at first.

"Hey, Hanna," he said as his eyes flitted down to my outfit. "You look like you're in mourning for something."

I hadn't even taken a second thought to what I was wearing and had ended up in some black leggings and an oversized dark t-shirt, navy or black—I didn't really care.

Shrugging, I slid into the booth, and he sat back down and took a drink of his soda.

"He's right, and scoot over. I don't feel like sitting on your lap," Frank said, standing next to the table.

I sighed and scooted. "Noah, this is Frank. Frank, this is Noah."

Noah's eyebrows rose up so far on his head they were in danger of popping off. "Frank?" He looked around to make sure no one was paying attention to us. "I'm guessing he's one of your...special friends?"

"Yes, he's a ghost. We were hoping to talk to you about some things we need help with."

"Oh, okay." To his credit, he looked only mostly dejected. "Nice to meet you, Frank. Wait...what happened to Brandon?"

Frank sat down next to me and nodded at my friend, even though Noah had no idea. "Nice to meet you. Is he your boyfriend?"

I don't know why I hadn't expected Noah to remember my nearly constant companion of the last several weeks, but it took me by surprise. "He's...gone."

Noah studied me for several seconds, looking at me in a way I wasn't sure I liked. It was somehow a cross between concern, sympathy, and perhaps a tiny twinge of relief. "Did he cross over?"

"Something like that," I said with a shaky breath.

Frank shook his head. "Remember to breathe, girlie."

Perhaps it was because I'd faced reality a few more times recently that the panicked breaths weren't as overpowering. Or maybe I was simply too exhausted to keep up with them. Whatever it was, I was able to keep myself mostly together, aside from the trembling fingers and the thundering heartbeat.

Noah frowned and reached his hand over the menus and across the table. "Hanna, are you alright?"

Not even a month ago, I would have been thrilled to feel Noah's hand around my own and to have him look at me with such concern, but I'd grown in the last few weeks.

Or something.

More because I felt guilt at leaving him hanging, especially after letting him think this was going to be a date, I put my hand in his.

His skin was warm as he wrapped his long fingers around mine, and, while I didn't feel for him as I once did, it was nice to have human contact and warmth.

"I'm okay. That's actually why we're here, honestly."

I glanced at Frank who gave me a thumbs up in encouragement.

"Frank is a ghost that, I'm ashamed to admit, I helped Rose trap a bit ago. Then after some recent events... I was able to bring him back and free him. He's got some inside knowledge about Rose and her...activities we thought you and the order might want to know about."

Noah frowned and opened his mouth to respond when our server came by. Our hands parted as if being caught in an intimate moment, and we greeted her with polite smiles. I ordered a drink, and Noah ordered a heaping pile of nachos for an appetizer.

"Mmm...what I wouldn't give to dig into a pile of nachos," Frank said with his eyes closed after the server left. "You'll have to eat a bunch so I can live vicariously through you."

I gave him a flat look. "Sorry about your luck, pal. You'll have to imagine to be Noah's mouth, because you've picked the wrong girl to eat for you."

Frank huffed and folded his arms across his chest. "I wouldn't want to go anywhere near that guy's mouth."

I stifled a smile and looked back at Noah who was watching me with an amused expression.

"Do I dare ask what that was about?" Noah said, his eyes flitting to the empty space next to me.

"Just a ghost wanting to eat food."

Noah nodded and looked vaguely where Frank was sitting. "I get it, man. Not eating is probably the worst thing about being dead."

Frank turned to me with pursed lips and annoyed eyes. "This guy is in for some fun awakenings when he finally dies."

I gave Frank a one-shoulder shrug. "Yeah, well, not everyone can be as cool as I am."

Frank shook his head and sighed while Noah's eyebrows creased.

"What? Did I say something wrong? Just trying to include the guy is all."

I waved my hand. "Don't worry about it. Frank can be a bit of a grump."

The ghost frowned and looked away from me, shaking his head again. "Can we just get on with this?"

"Right. Okay, so how much do you know about Rose?" I said, looking at Noah.

He thought for a moment, turning his head to the side and letting that brown hair fall into his eyes like I used to love. "Only what you've told me about her. She's some kind of witch who tricked you into helping her catch ghosts and then left town. Wait...did you run into her again?"

I fiddled with the corner of my red cloth napkin. "You could say that. I can't go into the specifics right now."

Or else I'd probably be leaving the restaurant carried out on a stretcher while I gasped for air like some guppy stranded on the beach.

"But let's just say we had a situation where I was able to free Frank, and, during an insane battle with werewolves, we saw some of Rose's moves that we're quite...unnatural."

Frank huffed. "I guess that's one way to put it."

"Basically, she was using necromancer powers as well as witch powers." I leaned in closer as I talked so hopefully no one at the neighboring tables would be able to overhear this absurd conversation. "Have you ever heard of anyone that could do that before? Is that like a thing that next level necroes can do?"

Noah stared at me with wide eyes as our server came back and dropped off my drink. He woke up enough to order a burger and fries after I ordered a small salad that I was probably not going to be able to eat.

When we were alone again, he leaned over the table to speak in near whispers. "Are you seriously saying that a witch was wielding necromancer powers? How do you know?"

"She controlled a vampire, fed him with purple lightning like I saw when you guys raised Steph, and then, when the cost of keeping the vampire alive was too draining, she..." I paused to take a breath and steady myself. "She ate some of her enslaved ghosts and went back to looking completely normal instead of like an old lady."

If we'd been outside, crickets would have chirped loudly, and sagebrush would have rolled across the table before Noah reacted.

"Do you think he had a heart attack?" Frank leaned in to ask me as we both watched Noah for signs of life.

"If he did, I guess he's going to experience the ghost life quicker than we thought."

My words must have woken him up. "Wait, wait, wait a second." He put his hands up as it to stop me from talking some more. "You're telling me this Rose lady you've been searching for is a necromancer arcanist?"

"I guess?" I shrugged.

"That's what it looked like, at least." Frank nodded.

Noah started rubbing his hands through his hair as if there were bugs in it that he was trying to get out with his fingers. "This is not good. Oh, this is really not good."

Frank and I exchanged looks, and he shrugged.

While Noah struggled with his existential crisis or whatever, I turned back to my ghostly friend. "It occurs to me that I never asked you, Frank, what it was like while she had you captured. Were you able to see all the things that were happening, or were you trapped inside the crystal until she needed your services? And if you were trapped inside the crystal all the time, how did you talk to us while Brandon was working on freeing Mr. Tyler?"

Frank sat back in the chair and looked up at the ceiling as he thought through my many questions. "It's hard to say, honestly. It feels a bit fuzzy. I know I didn't get to see all the things she did, that's for sure. Time passed by in weird ways. Mostly, my memories skip around. I do remember when I felt Brandon's presence when he was hacking at the curse chain. I was curious, and strong enough, I guess, to go find out what was happening. There was one time she used me to pull in some more ghosts for her to enslave inside some creepy warehouse, but other than that, I can't say I remember much."

As Frank was talking, the server brought our nachos. Normally, my stomach would have unfurled its beastly head at the sights and smells of that melted cheese and collection of delectable toppings, but nothing stirred.

A small part of me was proud of myself for having overcome the pull of food, especially while having not eaten well for some time. Another part of me wondered if I should be worried. The bigger part was too detached to care.

Noah dove into the nachos as if he needed to stress eat all his concerns away. Frank watched him with hungry eyes while I merely took a sip of my diet soda.

After letting him gobble a bunch of chips, I asked, "I'm guessing from your reaction that this news isn't very good?"

Noah wiped his mouth with a napkin and took a hearty drink. "That's a mild way to put it. I don't know everything, of course, since I'm a mere apprentice, but we were forced to delve into necromancer history to have a base knowledge. There's a whole two-week long session about an evil dude back in the day who sounds a lot like what your Rose is doing."

I wrinkled my nose. "She's not *my* Rose."

"You know what I mean. You found her."

"And helped her a few times," I said with a frown.

"Again, not your fault."

"So what do you know about this dude?"

Noah shook his head and took another drink. "He's bad news."

"Don't you mean was? I hope you mean was," I said, sharing an unnerved look with Frank.

Noah chuckled dryly. "We're not sure, honestly. He could still be around."

"That's terrifying." Frank scowled.

"Maybe Rose has become his apprentice or something?" I said.

"That's not good. That's one thing I'll have to tell David, the order's leader."

I nodded. "I remember."

"He might know something more about her."

"Tell him to explain more about this mysterious dude he's talking about. It might give us clues on how to handle her," Frank said while fiddling with a strand of his shoulder-length, wild, dark hair.

"Tell us more about this bad dude. What kinds of stuff could he do?" I asked.

Noah opened his mouth to explain, but the server showed up with our food. We smiled politely, said "thank you", and resumed talking after she left.

"He did what you described Rose doing. Or at least, that's what it sounds like. He could eat souls to make up for the cost of the necromancer magic. It's one of the worst sins you can do as a necromancer."

"You mean besides controlling life and death? Playing and pretending to be God and all that? There are worse things?" Frank muttered.

"It must be really bad if you guys think it's bad," I said, summing up Frank's point, albeit a bit nicer.

Noah nodded as he reached for the ketchup. "It's so bad. I mean, you're basically consuming a human soul and destroying it completely. It's worse than death. It takes away all the chance a person had to work on their unfinished business and go live wherever it is the soul deserves to live."

"I mean, in some cases that could be a relief," Frank said.

I nodded with upraised appreciative eyebrows. "Depends on the soul, I guess. Would ceasing to exist be better than spending eternity in Hell?"

Noah shrugged and munched on a fry. "I hope we never have to find out. But think about the innocent and good souls. That's such a crime."

"Not to mention, no one should have that much power. That's just...insane. Watching Rose do what she did was truly terrifying. There are costs to the spells necromancers use for a reason." I finally picked up my fork and contemplated the cold chicken on top of the lettuce.

"I mean, it can definitely be inconvenient at times—"

"Says the necromancer," Frank interrupted.

"—but yeah, nature put things like that in place for a reason. With powers like that, it would be hard for any other group to add balance to this kind of supernatural being, and what's to stop them from essentially ruling the world?"

"Certainly not vampires," I said with a shake of my head. "They think they're so powerful. Sure, they are strong, but look at what a necromancer can do to them."

Noah grinned. "Don't let Caleb hear any of that."

"Trust me. I won't."

Frank perked up in his seat. "Wait. You know a necromancer, were-wolves, *and* a vampire?"

"I also know an arcanist, kind of." I turned back to Noah. "Do you think a coven of witches could take out a magic-using necromancer?"

"No idea," Noah said around a bite of burger. "It's possible, but I don't know. They'd have to have inside knowledge about what they were dealing with, and as us necromancers like to keep our secrets, and I'm sure Rose wouldn't tell them, I honestly don't know."

"It's worth a try," Frank said. "So we'll get the order going after her for using this abominable magic. Plus, we'll work with the coven to also hunt her down. I'd say we're making progress."

I sighed, stabbed a piece of chicken, and forced myself to put it into my mouth. "It doesn't feel like enough."

"Oh!" Noah sat up after we'd eaten in silence for a few moments. Well, he ate, and Frank watched him jealously. I mostly poked at my lettuce. "I can't believe I've forgotten this, but y'all distracted me good."

I blinked a few times expectantly.

"David wanted me to let you know we've figured out how you can repay us for raising your friend. He wants to meet with you tomorrow if you can." Noah swallowed and cleared his throat. "Maybe you could even tell him more about what you and your ghost know with this whole Rose thing. This might be the perfect time."

I frowned as I fought the rising dread unfurling inside my stomach. It was true that I owed the order, and I wanted to make good on my promise, but my instincts were warning me that making deals with necromancers was probably not a good idea.

Too bad it was too late.

Chapter 6

O ddly, I slept decently okay that night. Yes, my mind was still trying to feed me the worst-case scenarios of anything I was trying to do, but I was able to fight off the fears better with logic. We'd made progress. There were several people willing to help. It might not have been because they wanted to save one particular ghost but more that they were terrified of what Rose was doing, but hey, it was help, and I was going to take it.

Frank had agreed to come with me to meet the order, but I had a feeling it was more out of curiosity than a desire to help me figure more things out. Mom hadn't been home when I'd left the house that Wednesday morning, but there'd been a note on the counter explaining that she'd gone out shopping for Thanksgiving dinner.

As I read the note, my heart sunk a little. Thanksgiving had been one of my favorite holidays, perhaps even more so than Christmas. I used to love the food and playing board games as a family before going to bed early so we could hit the Black Friday sales at three in the morning. But this year's holiday was sure to be different.

Even if Dad did show up, he wouldn't want to stay long. It was a lot harder to play games with only three people. Not to mention, Mom would certainly be feeling depressed and in no mood to play at all. What was worse, with money so tight, we probably wouldn't be shopping very much for Christmas.

The snarky side of my mind told me that even if we'd had a perfect holiday and Mom and Dad were back together, and Gran was still around, despite being in ghost form, I still wouldn't be able to enjoy it.

There was just someone too important missing.

"It strikes me to ask how you know about other occult stuff. I remember your ghost roomie was a necromancer, but did he tell you about werewolves and vampires and witches, too?" I said to Frank as we waited for Noah to come pick us up for our meeting. We were sitting on the porch in the chilly morning air, and I was only feeling a little guilty for not telling Mom where I was going or waking Trina up to tell her either.

After all we'd been through so far, I should have felt safe visiting with the necromancers. At least, that's what logic told me. Too bad my instincts were refusing to agree.

Frank leaned back and watched the rolling clouds pass above us. "My sister was turned into a werewolf. Her name was Yvonne, and she was only nineteen when it happened."

"Oh, wow. That must have been scary."

Frank's lips pressed together tightly as he kept staring upwards.

"You don't have to tell me about her or anything. It's probably hard to talk about it," I said, not wanting to anger him.

After a few seconds, he took a breath. His ghostly body didn't need the oxygen, and he probably couldn't pull in any if it did, but some habits die hard. "It's been over fifty years. If I can't talk about it now, I'll never be able to."

"Well, you might want to be careful. What if talking about it is your unfinished business? From what I've seen, once you finish that business, you can't really stay here. No matter how much you might want to," I said with a side-smile, mostly as a joke.

"Eh," he shrugged, "I doubt that's it. She was two years older than me and had just graduated high school. It was summer and was supposed to be the best time of her life. Instead, she went camping with friends, got lost, got bitten by a wolf, and came back home a changed person. It was like some kind of fever had overtaken her that left her angry, confused, and super sensitive. The next full moon, I was teasing her as I'd always done but must have gone too far, because the next thing I knew, half her body was changed into something unrecognizable, and her claws were shoved deep into my chest. At first, I was upset that she'd ruined my favorite shirt, but I suppose I should thank her because I've been able to keep it on for the next fifty years."

"Wow," was all I could think of to say after hearing that terrible story.

He shrugged. "Everyone goes some time. I just wish I'd been better equipped to help her with everything. I could have found a...a nearby werewolf pack or something to help her get through it. Instead, I'd angered her, caused her to hurt me, and then she had to live with that pain and guilt for the rest of her life."

I shook my head as my mind struggled to process the whole situation. "You can't blame yourself for that. You couldn't have known."

"Maybe. But I do."

"So then you woke up with your house as your haunt? Was your family still there?" I asked, trying to get a better idea of what had happened to his sister.

He nodded. "Yes, it took me a few days to appear. I'm not sure what happened in the middle, but it was clear my family was never the same."

"Of course not."

"But then a groovy thing happened. My sister's heightened senses allowed her to be aware of me somehow. It wasn't like this," he gestured back and forth between us, "to be sure, but she was able to at least know I was around, and she started talking to me more than we'd ever talked in all our lives."

"Ah, yes. Werewolves seem to be able to sense something about ghosts," I said, thinking about Gryphin's dad.

"Yeah. It wasn't like she could hear me or anything, no matter how hard I tried to talk to her, but she kept me informed about her life until she was married and moved away. Mostly she talked about how she missed me every day and regretted what she'd done, even if it was the animal that had taken over and done it and not her. I was grateful that she'd at least understood that."

"I can't imagine how y'all felt. The whole thing sounds terrible!" I shook my head, trying to imagine how much pain they'd gone through. "And you had to watch them suffer that whole time but were unable to do anything about it."

Frank shrugged again, apparently reaching his quota of personal sharing for the day.

After a few seconds, I said, "Well, thank you for sharing that with me. It must have been hard to open up with all that. I know we haven't known each other very long, and you're only here to help bring down Rose, but I appreciate your efforts. Also, I have to say it's pretty impressive that you've been able to remember all of this so well.

Compared to all the other ghosts I've been around, you seem to have a much better grip on your mind and memories."

He merely grunted in response as Noah pulled up to the side of the road in front of us. I was relieved with his good timing. Not because there was awkward air between Frank and I, but mostly I didn't know what else to say to help ease any of the pain he'd gone through.

Not that there was anything to say that would be that powerful.

"Did they tell you what they wanted from me?" I asked as I sat in the passenger seat of Noah's car while Frank sat in the back, staring out the window, apparently still lost in thoughts and memories.

Noah shook his head as he checked his blind spot and switched lanes. "No. I'm just a lowly guy, so they don't share much stuff with me."

"Oh. Do you think it's going to be something...bad?"

He spared me a glance with furrowed eyebrows. "What do you mean 'bad'?"

"Just...like something that I wouldn't normally do if I didn't have to do?"

He chuckled. "Of course not. What kind of people do you think we are?"

I gave him a wobbly smile and didn't answer the question.

He took us to the same house we'd been to when they'd raised Stephanie from the dead a mere few days ago. It felt like it'd been at least two months to my addled brain, but by normal calendar time, it had barely been a week. It was a large house in the heart of a neighborhood full of other similar houses. The grounds were expansive and immaculate. The main floor still looked like you'd see it in a catalogue for homes—so perfect it looked unlived in.

Instead of steering us to the basement like Noah had done the last time, he took us down the hallway on the first floor into an office which was so cluttered, it made up for the rest of the house looking pristine.

"Ah, good timing," David Fellows, the leader of the necromantic order, said as Noah knocked on the already open door. "I'd stand up to greet y'all, but if you'll remember, that's a bit out of my wheelhouse, so to speak."

He was referring to, of course, the fact that he was in a wheelchair. I was much more prepared to see him again than I had been the first time we'd met, but I was still struck by his appearance. On nearly all accounts, he looked like a very old man—a few strands of grey wispy hair, hunched shoulders, wrinkled skin, and gaunt cheeks. However, like most older-looking necromancers, there was a younger spark in his eyes and a tilt to his mouth that confused my brain about being able to accurately place his age.

I smiled politely and took one of the large leather chairs sitting across from the impressively shiny wood desk. "No worries. I've never been a fancy girl."

Noah chuckled, knowing full too well how casual and sloppy I could be sometimes, and sat in the other leather chair facing the desk.

Frank meandered inside the room with his hands in his ripped jean pockets and started to examine one of the several bookshelves. I hoped he was able to spot something interesting or useful among all the apparent clutter. There were books on the shelves, of course, but also lots of other things—weird disks I didn't know the use for, haphazard stacks of papers, knick-knacks, jars that reminded me of the one they'd used to paint runes on Stephanie's corpse, and lots of other things I could only guess at.

"Thank you for coming to meet with me. I know there's a holiday tomorrow, and it can be a busy season," David said, his voice gravelly but not weak like his appearance would suggest it should be.

I shrugged, unable to refrain from filling in Brandon's usual quips inside my head. He'd have probably rattled off something smart like, "It's not like we had a choice" or something. Perhaps I should have been apologetic for the snarky attitude I'd started to pick up from hanging out with him, but I couldn't bring myself to feel even a tiny amount of remorse.

Except maybe for letting my heart get so attached to the silly kid.

"Well, it's probably good for us to meet, anyway. There are some things we wanted to tell you." I glanced at Noah who nodded at me encouragingly.

"Ah, yes." David also glanced at Noah. "That's quickly become the biggest reason I wanted to meet. I'd like to hear your side of the story. Please, tell me about that night. Don't spare any details as anything small could help us figure out what we need to do next."

As he spoke, Frank cocked his head in my direction, probably watching me in case I started being unable to breathe again.

Somehow, I managed to get through the story without passing out. At one point, Noah frowned, got up from his chair, and sat on my armrest. He rested one arm behind my head and grabbed my hand with the other. I barely noticed as I focused on just putting one word after the other.

I told David as much as I could without getting into details I wasn't sure I wanted him to know. I left out Brandon, Sarah, and Frank. I did explain that I'd been able to free one of the ghosts and gave as much information about how I'd done that as I could remember.

Mostly, I kept the facts I felt like he'd want to know—what Rose had done, the purple lightning, the vampire, the cost of the spells, how she'd counteracted them with eating the souls, and the other magic she performed.

After I was finished, Noah squeezed my hand but didn't move away. I suppose on some level, his presence was comforting in that I didn't feel so alone and like I was going to vibrate with anxiety until my ghostly self left my physical body entirely.

David, his chin propped up on steepled fingers, studied me for a few more seconds. "That must have been quite an experience for you."

"Yeah, I'm pretty sure I need some therapy," I said with a choked laugh.

Noah rubbed my shoulder and both of them had the dignity to not laugh or make light of my comment.

"Pretty sure we all need therapy, pal," Frank muttered, making me perk a small smile.

"You're stronger than you feel, I can assure you." David smiled kindly, reminding me of a wizened grandpa. "You were right to come to Noah with this information. Our order appreciates it, and you can rest assured that we'll do our best to get to the bottom of this matter. If you'd allow us, I'd like you to stop worrying about this necromancing witch altogether and be confident that we can take it from here."

Frank leaned back against a shelf and folded his arms over his chest. "Why does it feel like that's not going to happen?"

I puckered my lips together in thought. "I don't know…"

David put on his most charismatic smile. "I can understand how you'd want to go after this person yourself, especially since you've got some history with her, but that would be entirely too dangerous. You *must* let us more experienced and more powerful people take it from here. You're a Seer and much too valuable to be wasted on trying to clean up necromancer business. Although, I do have to offer you gratitude for your efforts and desire to help us. I know you're a woman of your word and want to repay us for the help we've offered you in the past, but this is not the way to do it. In fact, I've got a task perfect for your skills that would satisfy the debt between us."

I kept blinking as he talked, unsure why my eyes were watering. For some reason, I felt like I'd been chastised or gotten in trouble for something. He'd layered it with gratitude and compliments, but I couldn't help but feel I'd been caught with my hand in the cookie jar.

A few months ago, that would have been more than enough to keep me away from Rose, but now they were dealing with a different me—one who had been hanging out with a slightly rebellious ghost who'd taught me that some things were more important than pleasing authority figures.

Of course, I was also smart enough to play along.

"Okay," I forced myself to say with a meek nod. "I'll let you guys handle it. You'd probably be much better at finding her than I've been."

Noah gave me another pat on the shoulder. "We'll take care of her. You'll see. No need to worry about it anymore."

"It would feel nice not to worry so much," I said, finding truth to say. "So what is the task you've got for me?"

As if satisfied that they'd convinced me to do the "right" thing, David sat back in his chair. "We've got a ghost for you to talk to. We need information from her, and you're just the person to get it."

"Oh, yeah, that sounds like something I can do."

At this point, I was kind of acting on auto-pilot while my mind was still reeling with other things I could do to find Rose without the necromancers' help. In a way, I'd just put a time frame on myself to work harder and faster so I could find Rose first. Not only was I totally out-manned, compared to the order, but I was also definitely out-powered. Perhaps coming to them had been a bad idea.

"Great!" David said with a cheerful smile.

"What kind of information do you need me to get?" I asked, almost paying attention. I really did have to repay them, after all. This way to absolve the debt didn't sound too bad, as long as it wasn't a poltergeist little girl haunting a church that was on its way to falling apart.

"All we need is the location of a necromancer she knew several years ago. I understand that many ghosts have trouble with their memories, but I know you're the right person to get down to the bottom of it."

"I can try?"

"I have every confidence in you."

Frank grunted and shook his head. "The more this guy talks, the less I like him. He's full of contradictions."

"Thank you. Where do I find her and what is the name of the necromancer I need to ask about? It might be important to know their name," I said.

"Of course. You'll most likely find her under the Parkway overpass. Her name is Susan, and all you have to do is merely ask her about Theodore McCutcheon."

"Susan?" I frowned as the name flagged something inside my brain.

David nodded, a patient smile on his face like he was dealing with someone not quite quick on the uptake.

"Okay...I'll get there as soon as I can find a ride. I do have one question though. How did you guys know where her haunt is and that she's a ghost and all that? I get that you might know about someone who died knowing about this particular necromancer you need to find, but how do you know about her ghostly spirit?"

Clearing his throat, David picked up a pen that was sitting on a pile of papers. He fiddled with it as he spoke. "I'm not sure this is relevant to your quest, but I'll explain in case it is. We've tracked down Mr. McCutcheon's associates, Susan being one of them, and hired a Seer to find her. It took some doing and research, but the Seer was able to find Susan. Then things went...south, and we didn't finish our search."

I furrowed my brows, trying to imagine what he meant by all that. "You guys know another Seer? What happened? Why can't you use them to help you now?"

David waved his hand flippantly in the air. "Oh, mostly our paths separated. It's nothing to trouble yourself with. Do let me know as soon as you make contact with Susan. We'd like this matter solved quickly."

Frank and I shared an unnerved expression before I turned back to David and gave him a small nod.

Chapter 7

The rest of the morning went by in a blur after Noah escorted me back home, said a somewhat confusing goodbye where he grabbed me into a tight hug and I forgot to hug him back, and then I ended up sitting on my couch staring at the wall.

"Hey, what's crackin'? You're sure giving that wall a hairy eyeball," Frank said from the armchair.

I blinked a few times. "What?"

Frank said each word slowly so it could reach my addled brain. "Are. You. Okay?"

"How many people in the world do you think are named Susan?"

It was Frank's turn to blink a few times. "Uhm, a lot."

"Yeah, it's probably just a coincidence. The odds are too low," I muttered, mostly to myself. "I guess we might as well make our way to the overpass and check in with that ghost."

Frank nodded. "Listen, I should probably apologize for dragging those guys into this mess. I guess it wasn't the best idea...but then again, maybe it was. You might not be able to get revenge on her yourself, but at least we'll know she'll be caught and punished as she should without putting you in mortal danger. Perhaps I should be saying 'you're welcome' instead of 'sorry'?" He raised his eyebrows with the hopeful question, but after I kept merely staring at him, he shrugged. "Worth a try."

"I suppose my mom, Caleb, and even Noah, I guess, would want me to sit this out and let the 'grown-ups' handle the situation," I said, rolling my eyes up to the ceiling.

"Sounds wise to me. After all, if you're murdered, I'll have to go back to watching those modern atrocities y'all call movies instead of trying to solve crimes against all plasma-dom."

"Yes, how terrible for you if I died," I said sarcastically and regarded him with a flat stare.

Frank chuckled. "You know what I meant. Anyway, maybe you could let the big guys handle Rose. She looks like she's going to be a mess to deal with and having powerful people that can combat her spells and stuff might be good. Not to be rude, but what can you do against an unkillable vampire and a witch that can't be stopped as long as she has spirits to gobble up? If you ask me, we should both stay very far away from her."

"You're forgetting something important."

"And what's that?"

"Without me, they're not going to be able to set any of those ghosts free."

Frank and I stared at each other with mirrored annoyed expressions for several moments.

"Hey, what are you doing?" Trina asked, coming out from the hallway and interrupting our staring contest.

"Just arguing with a ghost. What are you doing?" I said, giving Frank one last squint of my eyes.

"Not much. Studying, mostly. Kinda bored, though." She flopped down onto the couch next to me.

"So you thought you'd come visit your insane sister and see what absurdities she was into at the moment?" I said, probably being a bit ruder than was called for.

Instead of getting offended though, she laughed. "I guess you could say that. You do always seem to have something going on. What were you and the...ghost arguing about? Anything I can help with?"

I had to give her props for kind of, almost, sorta getting close to the topic which we usually avoided—she could also see ghosts if she wanted to take the old family heirloom necklace off.

"Uh," I hesitated, unsure of what I wanted to tell her versus what I should tell her. I already knew that she'd side with Frank on the topic of letting the necromancers take care of Rose while I sat on the sidelines like some not-so-good football player. "Just talking about how we were going to go work on our newest ghostly assignment."

"Ah, okay. I didn't realize you had gotten a new ghost assignment or that that was a thing. Who is the ghost you're arguing with, by the way?" Trina fiddled with her necklace but didn't take it off.

I wondered if she were close to wanting to delve a bit into the world I lived in constantly, but I was afraid to push her in case it had the opposite effect. "His name is Frank. He's actually the ghost I saved from Rose."

"Don't forget you're the reason I got caught in the first place," Frank said with an annoyed huff.

I left that part out for Trina.

"Oh, cool. Nice to meet you, Frank, wherever you are." Trina nodded her head in the direction I had been staring at earlier.

"Eh, no need to be nice to him. He's a bit of a turd," I said, giving him a snarky smile.

Frank rolled his eyes.

"Oh, okay. Sounds like you guys are having fun. Who gave you a ghostly assignment?"

"Oh, only the whole necromantic order. I owe them for helping me with Stephanie, and for rescuing me from the vampires, too, I guess, and that's how they want me to repay them... Say, you don't feel like driving your dear, sweet sister to go check out the underpass where the ghost is supposed to be hanging out, do you?"

Trina frowned. "The underpass? Isn't that where lots of homeless people hang out? It could be dangerous."

I sighed dramatically. "Bah. Why is everyone always so worried about how dangerous everything is? Getting inside a car alone is dangerous. Even walking can be dangerous! Life is dangerous! I should know since I see the ghostly products of dead people all the time."

Trina held her hands up toward me in surrender. "Woah. I can see you're feeling a bit frustrated and angry today. I know you're going through a rough time with...everything, but no need to take it out on me."

I huffed, folded my arms across my chest, and stared at the cute fashion boots I'd gotten a few weeks ago.

"You do seem a bit grumpy," Frank added unhelpfully. "Every time I got grumpy, my mom told me to either eat something or go have a good poo."

His comment surprised me so much, a laugh escaped my angry brooding.

Trina eyed me warily, and I shook my head. "You don't want to know. Fine. Yes, it might be a bit dangerous, but poor Caleb is probably sick of following me around just to make sure I don't skin my knee. If we're going to invite him to come along with us, you have to do it."

A small smile complimented the excitement in Trina's eyes as I mentioned her favorite vampire friend. Hopefully, he was her *only* vampire friend, but I had the feeling he was her favorite friend out of all of them, alive or dead.

"I could do that. I'll text him. Do you want to go now?" she asked, pulling out her phone.

I shrugged. "Got nothing else better to do. Frank? You want to come along or sit this one out? I know you've got lots of amazing movies to watch."

He shook his head. "Ugh, kids nowadays. Naw, it's fine. I doubt I'll be much help on this task, and you can fill me in later if there's anything interesting I should know."

"Alright. Have fun smelling popcorn and not being able to eat it."

He popped back to his haunt while glaring at me.

Trina looked up from her phone for a second. "His haunt is a movie theater? That's pretty cool."

"Yeah, that's one thing I still need to figure out. The first time we met, it was an old, creepy house, but once he came back from Rose's capture, the haunt changed to what used to be a roller-skating rink that he hung out at all the time. At some point, it was changed into a theater so now he gets to spend all day watching new movies, which he hates, of course."

"Weird, but he sounds like a real fun dude."

"He could be worse, I guess. He died young so he looks our age, but he's really, like, sixty and acts it. It's so weird talking to an old man looking like a kid."

Trina grinned and held up her phone to indicate who she was talking to. "I know some of what that's like."

"Right, yeah. I don't know. Somehow Caleb has managed to go with the flow, whereas I'm pretty sure Frank will always be stuck in the 70s," I said, pulling out my phone to check for any notifications.

And that's when all the blood rushed to my face, and my heart started hammering heavily inside my chest.

Trina must have seen the same thing at that moment because she let out a few curse words before turning to me with wide eyes.

Swallowing thickly, I replayed the video, perhaps because I was a glutton for my own punishment. It was done with terrible recording as the person's hand kept moving slightly, the angle was a tad confusing, the theater hallway was badly lit, and a wall got in the way at times. The footage was of me, that was at least clear, and I appeared to be talking to myself. Quite animatedly, I might add.

I recognized it as my conversation with Frank in the hallway, and it was obvious who had taken and posted the video since she'd made no attempt at hiding anything. The caption for the post said, "Proof that Hanna Sanchez is crazy!"

Trina put her phone down and grabbed mine out of my stunned hand. "Don't watch that anymore and definitely don't read any of the comments! You shouldn't give that witch Andrea any more satisfaction."

My stomach coiled tightly as I said slowly, "It already has over two thousand views. Why do that many people care that I'm crazy? That's already more than our whole school."

Trina put our phones on the coffee table and grabbed my shoulders. "Seriously, you can't let this bother you. It'll only be giving her power, and then she'll know you care what she thinks, and she'll try even harder to make you feel bad."

I looked into my sister's blue eyes and saw how much panic was inside them. This situation was probably her worst nightmare had the video been of her. She had worked very hard to become popular at school, including spending a ton of money on clothes and hair styles as she kept up with current fashion. She'd gone to parties and perhaps had done some things that my mom wouldn't approve of just so she could be considered cool by the other kids.

It almost felt like I was seeing this side of her in more detail than I'd ever seen before. Her fear of this very situation happening had probably fueled most of the reason why she kept that necklace on, and I understood at that moment exactly what she was afraid of.

"I thought I didn't care what she thinks." My voice was quiet and soft.

Trina's mouth tipped into a sad frown as tears prickled her eyes. "I'm so sorry, Hanna. Girls can be so mean to each other, but it's okay. You don't have to let this bother you. Or, at least, not so that she or anyone at school knows."

A few tears of my own tickled at the corners of my eyes. "But why would she post this now?"

Trina dropped her arms from my shoulders and rested them in her lap. "I don't know. Have you even talked to her lately?"

"Not since we ran into each other at the theater. She could have posted the video right then, but she waited. Why?"

Before either of us could speculate an answer, my phone buzzed a few times. I looked at her for permission to check my own phone, and she picked it up to see what it was. After looking, she nodded and handed it to me.

"It's Noah. He's safe, right?"

"About as safe as anyone else," I muttered and took my phone.

He'd sent three quick texts all in a row.

OMG! I'm so sorry, Hanna!

Please don't hate me! I didn't mean for this to happen!

I can't believe she would stoop so low!

I frowned and looked back up at Trina, trying to figure out how I should respond. "Apparently, Noah has something to do with this. It sounds like he thinks it's his fault."

Trina crinkled her nose. "Maybe it is?"

Sighing, I texted him back to ask him what happened.

Instead of texting, he called, and the sound coming out of my phone surprised me.

"Hello?"

"Hanna! I'm so sorry! I really didn't mean for you to be dragged into all of this. I know we just hung out this morning, but do you have a minute for lunch or something?"

I looked to Trina for input, but she merely shrugged.

"I don't know..."

"Please? I really feel like I need to clear the air between us. Andrea found out we've been hanging out a bit lately and—"

"You know what?" I interrupted him, feeling my anger flash to the surface. "No. We cannot go to lunch. I'm sick of you and that girl, and I've got work to do for your 'family' so I'm busy trying to get rid of this debt and not have to spend time with any more necromancers."

I didn't wait for his response as I hung up the phone.

Trina raised her eyebrows and gave me an appreciative nod. "Okay then."

"Can we go to the overpass now?" I stood from the couch and went to change my shoes to ones less new.

Trina followed me down the hallway while looking at her phone. "Caleb messaged that he's busy. That's weird, isn't it?"

"Yeah," I said, entering my room and peering under my bed where my shoes usually ended up. "But I mean, it's not really. Most people have normal things and schedules they attend to. It's just weird for him because he's always available to help our family out."

"Yeah...but I don't really feel safe without some kind of protection," Trina said from my door, frowning at her phone.

"I could see if Gryphin is available. He might not be a handsome, brooding vampire, but he's still pretty strong in his human form. Strong enough to at least keep us safe from any crazed hobo who might attack us." I finally located both tennis shoes and took off my boots.

"Okay," she said with a bit of a pout.

"Cheer up. I'm sure they'll be yet another situation soon where we need his help, and you'll get to see him some more." I gave her a knowing smile, and her cheeks colored with a soft blush.

Chapter 8

As we walked toward Gryphin's beat-up van parked outside our house about an hour later, Trina said, "I'm glad to see you're working past this stupid video. Maybe it's a good thing it came out during Thanksgiving break, and everyone will have forgotten about it by the time school starts again."

"You mean in like four days?" I said flatly, feeling more numb about it than horrified.

She shrugged with a sympathetic expression. "Could be worse?"

I thought about everything that was happening and wondered what Brandon would have said about this whole thing. We'd probably get distracted as I had to explain the insanity of internet culture again, but then he'd say something about how this didn't matter. Kids were going to be mean, internet or not. He would probably tell me I'd barely think about it after high school ended and I got on with the rest of my life.

As my chest sunk heavily with the thoughts of my captured friend, I wasn't sure if it was helpful to think about what he'd say in any given situation or if it was more harmful.

Honestly, it probably didn't matter either way since I was sad and angry anyway.

Thinking about Brandon reminded me of the coincidence of the necromancer's ghost and the name of Brandon's mother listed in his obituary being the same. If I was being honest with myself, I was more curious about that connection rather than having any real sense of duty to smooth things over with the necromancers.

"Hello!" Gryphin greeted us as he opened the passenger side door. "Who wants shotgun?"

I waved for Trina to take it as I popped open the sliding door and climbed into the middle seat.

After we'd gotten settled, Gryphin grinned back at me from the front. "So we're going on another ghost hunting adventure?"

The curls of his hair were in fine form that morning, and the one that always found its way to his forehead bobbed with his puppy-like enthusiasm. His excited eyes paired with a strong jaw and bulging arm muscles lured a smile out of my face despite my sour mood.

"I'm sorry to ask you with such short notice." I glanced at Trina who was still taking in Gryphin's presence. They'd met before but being inside an enclosed space with his bubbling energy could be somewhat overwhelming. "We didn't want to go to this part of town by ourselves. It didn't seem like the responsible thing to do."

I didn't mention that he'd been our second pick and that Caleb was busy somewhere doing some kind of mysterious vampire business.

"Cool." He turned around and pulled the van onto the road. "It's good to feel needed sometimes."

We held small talk as we drove to the other side of town. Mostly, I wanted to check in with him and see how his pack was doing after the whole debacle in the meadow. Of course, since it hadn't been but a day since I'd asked him last, there wasn't a lot of change. Tensions were still high among the more dominant of the wolves while his dad still seemed not quite himself.

I was sure that it would help if I could free Sarah's ghost from Rose's clutches, but the last thing I wanted was more pressure to go after her. I had more of that than I'd ever need.

During the drive, my phone buzzed several times in my pocket. At first, I checked it every time, but once it became clear it was Noah spamming me with texts and even a few attempted phone calls, I stopped looking.

Yes, I had something else to focus on instead of that stupid video, but the pain and embarrassment were too fresh for me to face him right now without absolutely saying things I would regret later. It would be best for both of us if I ignored him for a while.

As we pulled up underneath the Parkway overpass and Gryphin navigated his van into a snug parking spot near a concrete pillar, I looked around for any signs of ghostly activity. As I looked, I was immediately grateful for Trina's insistence that we take help and that Gryphin's steady presence would be nearby. Despite the place being near a busy thoroughfare with many people traveling by daily, it was definitely a neglected space.

Graffiti covered nearly any available wall space, and while I could take a minute to appreciate the bright colors of the art, it gave a concerning aspect to the area. There were dumpsters spaced around, but they must not have been emptied on a regular basis. All of them were heaped up with a mountain of garbage that spilled over the sides and piled around the base.

Tarps, tents, and other piles of garbage flowed from the dumpsters in near continuous streams so that it was impossible to tell what had been thrown away on purpose and what was someone's personal property.

Honestly, the depravity of the space surprised me. Sure, I'd been in the car while Mom had driven past here several times but driving quickly past it and actually standing there were very different things.

"Wow, this kind of makes me grateful to live in the commune," Gryphin said quietly as we stood next to his van trying to figure out what our first move was.

"It's really sad," Trina said with wide eyes. "I'm so glad you came with us."

"The city has to know that this is happening. Why isn't anyone doing anything about it?" I said, afraid to walk further into the shadows and step in something so foul I'd never get the stench cleaned off.

"Kind of makes you think..." Trina said, eyeing a nearby dirty diaper.

"Werewolves might be murderous and full of rage, but I swear we'd never let anything like this happen in our communities," Gryphin said with a shake of his head.

Our arrival had gained some attention from a few of the humans populating the area. Some of them had given us glances, some of them had wandered off to somewhere, but the majority kept their dead stares and went on about their business of muttering to themselves or shuffling things around.

"Alright. Well, we can make a note to petition the authorities later. Right now, we need to find a ghost, and as far as I can tell, there are at least ten or so here. Would have been helpful to have a picture or something," I muttered the last part mostly to myself.

The bright blue of ghosts flickered and popped up around us as my mere presence lent strength to the undead spirits. Most of them appeared to be homeless, just as the alivers around us. I spotted a few of them in weird clothes that put them outside the last century.

One lady wearing a dress and a bonnet seemed to be churning some butter, completely oblivious to how the land around her had changed into a concrete jungle and her cows had long since been sold off.

Another ghost wearing a high-end suit from maybe the 20s was walking around, giving a powerful political speech that grew in strength and passion the longer I was nearby.

"Didn't they tell you her name?" Trina asked, her voice quiet in hopes not to draw any attention to herself from anyone alive or dead.

"Yes." I shrugged and shook my head. "Guess that's really the only lead I have. Maybe if I look like a crazy person out here, I'll fit right in and no one will bother me."

Gryphin gave me an encouraging, albeit awkward, smile. "We're here if you need us."

It didn't look like Trina quite agreed and that if she had her way, she'd be back in the van with all the doors locked by now. I also noticed she didn't bother to take off her necklace and help me search, but I wasn't going to push it.

"Susan?" I started out quietly, hoping she'd be nearby and pop up and help me immediately.

Of course that's not how things go in my life.

A few alivers glanced my way, but mostly I was ignored.

Familiar anxiety snuck into my chest as I realized that even if I was able to find Susan and we started up a lively conversation where she had a perfect memory and told me exactly what I needed to know, just our mere connection would alert the other ghosts to what I was. With so many wandering around, we were sure to attract quite a large group of them.

Taking a breath, I walked further into the gloom of the shadows, careful where I stepped. As I worked past the garbage, I noticed a cleared path that made its way around. It was narrow, and in some places there were puddles of questionable liquid, but it was traversable.

Trina clutched her arms tightly around herself, but it wasn't super cold out and she wore a decent jacket, so it probably wasn't because she was trying to warm herself up. Gryphin took up the rear, keeping a watchful eye over anyone or anything that made a move.

"Susan?" I said a bit louder, trying to appear like I was looking for someone alive which was basically the same as trying to look for someone dead.

As I passed by a tent, someone from inside said, "Ain't no Susan here."

Trina tried to smother her surprised squeal, so it turned more into an "eep!"

"Susan? Is there a Susan here?" I kept asking as I walked further inside the tent city.

"You can call me Susan if the price is right," an older guy said from several paces away. He was sitting on a cardboard box and wearing several layers of clothes.

I ignored the comment, but that was probably too difficult for the socially-naïve Gryphin.

"Oh, no thank you," he said to the man with an apologetic nod.

If I hadn't been so keyed up and anxious to get this over with, I might have smiled at his innocence.

Deciding this was getting me nowhere, I didn't care if any of these alivers saw me and thought I was crazy. In fact, there was a video online right now of me talking to myself if they really wanted to learn how crazy I was.

I swallowed my fear and made my way closer to the ghostly woman churning butter. She seemed like the easiest ghost to talk to at the time and had been around a while, so maybe she knew more about the area. There was a chance that I'd be shattering her happy ignorance of being dead just so I could get some information, but that was a chance I was going to take. Plus, it was good for ghosts to face reality, right? Wasn't that the whole point of my existence?

She was sitting partially inside one of those overflowing garbage bins, so talking to her was really going to look like I was insane, but whatever.

"Excuse me?" I said as we approached. "Ma'am?"

The ghost paused and blinked a few times. Then her eyebrows furrowed. Awareness and focus zeroed in on my face.

"What are you doing on my farm? Why are you dressed so oddly? Who are you?" The lady said as she stood and the wooden contraption she'd been using disappeared in its ghostly way.

Her response confirmed my fears that she had no idea she was dead and that the world had changed without her notice. This also meant that she probably didn't realize there were any other ghosts around and wouldn't be able to help me find Susan, but, by that point, I might as well try.

"Excuse me. I'm sorry to intrude. I was just looking for someone," I said, trying to smile kindly instead of like my insides were rolling with anxiety. "I was hoping you could help me."

"Give me the cash in your wallet and those shoes, and I'll help you do anything you want, even fly," the older man hollered from where we'd left him behind.

Gryphin's throat hummed with a low growl I sure hoped the man couldn't hear while Trina gave up being brave and practically glued herself to Gryphin's arm.

I was too distracted to pay much more attention to what the alivers were doing. As the ghost lady looked around, the details of the world started filtering in, and I saw it in her face as the horror and realization struck her.

"Wait... This is not my farm. Where am I?"

I put my hands up in a calming motion. "This may come as a shock to you, but you're dead, and judging from your pioneer dress, I'd say it's been a century or so at the least."

Her eyes stopped darting around the encampment and focused back onto mine. "Well of course I am dead. That foozler Billy shot me in the head."

Gryphin and Trina were still standing nearby, but they'd stopped exchanging words with the older guy. I hadn't paid attention to how that had panned out, but he wasn't coming over here so that was good.

Confusion rippled through me, a pleasant break from the anxiety squeezing my lungs. "Okay, so you know you're a ghost. Why are you surprised to see you're not on your farm?"

She frowned, looked down at the pile of garbage in and through her feet, and put her hands on her hips. "I guess the last time I woke up, there was still a farm here. How long has it been?"

I shrugged. "I have no idea. I guess you probably don't know any of the other ghosts around here, do you?"

She muttered something and shook her head. "Obviously not. What happened to that church bell who told me I was dead in the first place? She promised she would come back and assist me with some unfinished business she kept insisting I had."

"Hold on, you talked to someone who could see you and then wanted to help you with unfinished business?" I asked, eager to hear more about other Seers, even if they were obviously long dead.

"Nearly positive that happened. My memory does not function as well as it did while I was alive," she said, looking around us again. "The future does not look like a nice place to live."

"Well, we don't have to churn butter, like ever, and we've got air conditioning, but right now, I can see how you'd think that." I watched as a person, difficult to tell the age or gender of said person, wandered into the camp from the street pushing a grocery cart full of bags and mostly things that looked like junk to me but were probably valuable to them as they insisted on toting them around all the time.

"Are you going to assist me with my unfinished business so I can go on to Heaven? I am certain to go there since I prayed nearly every day and donated quilts yearly to the local church."

"I'm sure you are," I said, getting nervous as one of the other ghosts was slowly drifting in our direction.

He wore an old-timey swimsuit complete with the black and white stripes, and I spared a thought to wonder where he'd been swimming around these parts. Maybe a pond had been here long ago.

The lady ghost followed my line of sight. "Oh, another ghost! I am unsure if I should be scared or eager to meet one."

"Uh," I turned so I wasn't facing her directly, hoping the other ghost would lose interest. It wasn't long after two ghosts paid attention that all the ghosts in the area would. "Do you happen to know what your unfinished business is? I'm a little busy working with another ghost now and probably should get going, but I do feel bad that you've been waiting for so many years for someone to help you."

"How am I supposed to know what it is? Are you not the ghost doctor?" The lady frowned, still holding her hands on her hips.

"Well, that's a new one. Ghost doctor. Right. It's going to take some time and lots of questions to figure out your business, but honestly, I don't have time right now. I'm so sorry." I took a few steps away from her, hoping she'd get the hint.

She didn't.

"Oh, it is understandable. I will accompany you on your journey until you are available. I have nowhere else to go and nothing else to do. Maybe I could even assist you with your current plight?"

By that time, the guy in the swimsuit was only about ten feet away and looking at me like he was about to figure things out.

"Okay, fine." I didn't bother explaining that most ghosts weren't able to leave their haunt and that only those who hung out with me could and she'd picked the right Seer to stalk. Those didn't seem like necessary details at the moment. "I think you can help me. Let's get back to our van, and we'll talk there."

An idea brewed in my mind as I led Trina and Gryphin back out of the tent city. The guy in the swimsuit lost interest at some point, but I couldn't look back to see exactly when because that would have triggered the exact opposite of what I was trying to do. Thankfully my purposeful walking had deterred him.

As for the alivers around us, someone else was asking about Susan now, but I figured that the odds of them being able to find the ghostly one were too low for me to worry about.

We all let out sighs of relief after we were safely back in the van with the doors locked. It wasn't that the van smelled nice or anything, but it felt a lot safer to breathe inside it instead of out there where more than a few buckets were being used for bathrooms.

The lady ghost settled herself in the seat next to mine while smoothing her dress down and sitting with perfect posture. "This contraption does not require any horses?"

"One of the perks of the future." I gestured to Gryphin and Trina who were sitting in the front seats again and had both turned to look at me for our next move. "This is my friend Gryphin, and this is my sister, Trina. My name is Hanna, and I'm a Seer. That's why I can see you and talk to you. Guys, we've got a new ghost friend whose name is…"

I turned to look at her with expectant eyebrows. "I'm sorry. I didn't catch…"

"Tracy Lindon," she said with an elegant nod of her bonnet-hooded head.

I repeated her name to the alivers who both nodded in her vague direction and mumbled various greetings.

"Did you find Susan?" Trina asked with a wary glance outside again.

"Not yet, but I'm hoping Tracy can help us with that. I was starting to grab attention from the other ghosts, so I wanted to retreat inside the car to prevent any kind of mob from forming."

Gryphin's slim, grey eyebrows raised on his forehead. "Does that happen to you a lot?"

"Enough that I know we need to avoid it, if we can," I said.

Trina winced with a frown, probably feeling grateful for her necklace again. She'd never told me before that she felt guilty for having one when I didn't, but sometimes I thought I could see it in her face.

I turned back to Tracy. "We can get to work on your unfinished business in a bit, but first, do you think you could go out there and find another ghost named Susan? She's supposed to be haunting this same area, and I've been tasked to get information from her for...some friends."

Tracy peered out the window. "What does she look like?"

I shrugged. "Blue and dead?"

"That is not much to help me," she said with a frown.

"I know. I'm sorry. That's why I approached you in the first place, to see if you'd know any of the ghosts and could maybe help me."

"I suppose it would not hurt to go talk to them." She daintily stepped out of the van.

I watched through the windows as she circled around and walked toward the nearest ghost.

"Do you think this will work?" Trina asked, looking back out over the shadowed tent city.

"No idea. I've never asked a ghost to talk to other ghosts before. Honestly, I wouldn't be surprised if she forgot what she was supposed to be doing mid-sentence, or if the other ghosts ignored her completely. I've never seen a ghost confront another ghost and wake them up to their reality without my being nearby. But it's worth a try, I suppose."

"I really don't want to go back out there," Trina said, hugging herself again.

"Me neither."

I kept my eye on Tracy as she wandered around to various ghosts. Obviously, I couldn't hear their conversations from inside the van, but the first one seemed to at least realize another ghost was talking to her. After several exchanges of confused expressions, the strange ghost shook her head, and Tracy moved on to talk to another.

I had to give the girl props for taking this task so seriously and diligently. It could have been the type of person she was, or it could have been her life on the farm and needing to feel like she was doing something productive after all these years of waiting and churning butter that would never solidify.

The second and third ghosts didn't look at her directly, and I have no idea if she got through to them, but the fourth ghost, who was too far away for me to see clearly at first, started following Tracy back toward us.

"Looks like she's bringing someone back," I said, hope and relief blooming in my chest.

"Is it Susan?" Gryphin asked, peering out the window probably more out of habit than any certainty that he'd see the ghosts.

I shrugged. "We'll find out."

As they came closer, I could make out more details from the second ghost, and she looked like any one of the alivers that also haunted the place. She wore a toboggan that held most of her hair in check, but several strands sprung out the bottom in wild ways. Her shoulders were hunched, and she limped a bit as she walked. Several layers of clothes hung off her frame, and for once, I was grateful that someone was dead so I wouldn't have to smell them. It was her gaunt cheeks that pulled sympathy into my heart, and I wondered if she'd died from starvation, being sick, or something just as awful.

I also couldn't help but look for facial features similar to Brandon's. Without being able to see colors, it was more difficult. Plus, I was usually terrible at these kinds of things. Maybe if I had Brandon standing right next to her, and I could compare directly, but as it was, I had no idea.

Forcing the fear that I was forgetting what Brandon looked like out of my head, I opened the van door as an invitation to the two ghosts more than any real need for them to get through the opening.

"Welcome to our Mystery Machine," I said and gestured for them to take a seat inside.

After they were settled, I pulled the door shut and Trina breathed a sigh of relief. Gryphin's amused grin caused a bit of embarrassment to heat up my face, but I tried to ignore it as much as I could. They were used to my odd behaviors.

Speaking of odd behaviors, both the ghosts had taken the two middle seats. To be polite, I moved to the third back row to give them space. This made Gryphin's grin grow even wider, which I studiously ignored.

"This is Susan," Tracy said, turning slightly so she could talk with me. Part of her bonnet went through the roof of the van, and, had it been real, she probably would have had to duck her head in an awkward way.

The second ghost looked nearly as lost being inside the van as Tracy had moments before. Her eyes wouldn't rest on any one thing as they darted around, taking in her surroundings.

"Susan?" I started gently. "My name is Hanna, and these are my friends Gryphin and Trina. We're just wanting to chat with you for a moment, if you have the time."

"Poor dear seems more confused than I was," Tracy said as she rested her hands in her lap and shook her head. "To be honest, I am not certain this is Susan, but when she did not deny it, I figured maybe we could understand more about her together."

"Oh," I said, my shoulders falling slightly. "I'm sorry, ma'am. Is your name Susan?"

"What?" The second ghost's eyes had at least stopped zipping around like they were tracking a fly.

"My name is Hanna. What is your name?"

"Where... What's going on?"

"You're in my friend's van. This is Tracy," I said gesturing to the pioneer lady sitting as calmly inside an old van as a queen sat on her throne. "My name is Hanna. What's your name? Is it Susan?"

She grunted in response, and I followed Tracy's lead and took that as an affirmative.

"Susan, do you know you're dead?"

Trina winced as I got so direct, but I didn't know what she was worried about. It was on me if I botched the whole thing.

"Where are my children? If I'm dead, I should be able to see them," Probably-Susan said, still looking around.

"Your children?" I tried to stifle the bits of excited hope that were trying to form in my chest.

"Oh, my poor dear. Did you lose your children?" Tracy's full lips pulled into a sympathetic frown. "I wonder what happened to mine..."

Feeling bad for both mothers, I reminded myself not to get distracted. Ghosts were super good at getting distracted and distracting others, I was beginning to understand.

"I don't know." Susan looked down at her weathered sneakers. "He was supposed to... I..."

Her eyes widened and she looked up again, searching for something until she found my face. "You're not dead."

I smiled kindly and slowly shook my head. "No, not yet."

"Are you a Seer?"

I nodded again.

Instead of looking relieved or happy that I was there to help her, she narrowed her eyes and glared. "Did *they* send you?"

A heavy feeling started forming in my stomach. "Who?"

She huffed and shook her head. "He said they'd come for me, even after I died. This is the second Seer they've sent, and I don't have to tell you what happened to the first one."

Without waiting for my response, she got up and fazed through the van door.

"Wait!" I scrambled after her, struggling for a second to get the door open and nearly fell out of the van onto a torn muddy tarp. "I want to learn more about your story, not necessarily to help those guys. You have to believe me!"

But she'd gone already, disappearing as ghosts were wont to do sometimes.

"Quiet over there!" Some muffled voice of an aliver shouted. "You're being loud enough to wake the dead!"

Rolling my eyes at the irony of that statement, I retreated into the van and slammed the door shut.

Gryphin and Trina exchanged worried glances.

"What happened?" Gryph asked. "Are we ready to go?"

"Please say yes," Trina nearly whined.

I sat heavily into the seat Susan had vacated and put my head in my hands. "I wish I was better at this. I always say the wrong things."

"I am certain there was nothing different you could have said to alter the outcome." Tracy's voice was kind as she spoke, reminding me she was still there and that I had other things to worry about.

Trina gave me a small pat on the back, twisting herself to reach behind the seats. "I'm sure you're doing your best. There's nothing else you can do."

"I wish Gran were still here. She always knew what to say," I muttered between my knees.

"She was a Seer for a lot longer than you have been. I'm sure she learned the same way you are. Don't be so hard on yourself," Trina said.

"Are you ready to get out of here or...?" Gryphin asked.

Pulling myself into a sitting position, I gave him a wobbly smile. "Let's go. I'll have to come back with a better plan and hopefully more information. We've done enough damage today."

Chapter 9

The evening before Thanksgiving was usually when my mom baked her famous apple pie and prepped her rolls to rise over night, but as I walked into the quiet and dimly lit kitchen, I wondered where she'd gone off to. Sure, she might have had a photography booking, but that seemed unlikely the night before a major holiday.

As I grabbed another bottle of diet soda out of the fridge, I realized I hadn't seen much of her at all in the last few days. Either she was super busy with her business, or she was up to something else.

The divorce hadn't been finalized yet. In fact, I didn't even know if they'd signed the papers to start the whole process, but it was possible that she'd started dating already. If that were the case, I didn't blame her for not wanting to tell us quite yet.

Trina was in the front room watching TV, and she paused it as I sat down on the couch next to her.

"What did you learn from that...wait, was her name Tracy?" Trina asked, a crinkle forming on her forehead as she tried to remember.

"Yes, but I'm not sure what to do next to help her."

After Gryphin had dropped us off at home, I'd sat with Tracy at the kitchen table while Trina had gone to her room to give us privacy. I had asked the ghost any and all questions I could muster to figure out what her unfinished issues might have been. We went through her life's history to start with, and, while it was interesting to hear about the times from someone who was actually there, there were only two things that stuck out—the idiot neighbor who had shot her, Billy, and the two boys she'd left behind, aged eight and ten.

The problem was that since it'd been such a long time ago, they were all dead by now, and I had zero time to go searching for their ghosts, if they hadn't passed on after death.

I dropped my head onto the back of the couch and sighed loudly at the ceiling. "I just have too much to do, but all I want is to go find Rose and wring her neck."

Trina let out a small giggle. "That doesn't sound very menacing."

I shrugged, unable to find the energy to get more descriptive.

Fiddling with her necklace, Trina took a breath. "Do you think maybe...I could help you?"

I sat up slowly and studied her face. Her features were similar to mine, but I always felt they were just a touch prettier with her face a bit more symmetrical and her eyes a bit bigger. This seemed to be confirmed because of how much more popular at school she was than me. Of course, after a recent certain video, perhaps there was another reason I wasn't as popular.

"Are you sure you'd want to do that? It would mean..."

We both looked down at her necklace as she lifted it higher to see more clearly.

"We'll make sure to do it here where no other ghosts can bother me and no one else can see what I am. I can do research with the lady and see if we can find out what happened to her family. Do you think any of that would help you?"

Honestly, I had no idea if it would help solve Tracy's problems, but it didn't matter. Trina was trying to help me, willing to use her powers she was more afraid of than I was, and that mattered most.

I tried not to let the relief of stress form tears in my eyes, but they were a bit shiny as I said, "Thank you. It would help a lot."

At about seven o'clock, I got a text message from Mr. Tyler. I had been working on an English paper for school in the front room, trying to stay away from the quiet loneliness of my own bedroom. Despite my best intentions, the room had somehow become the place where I'd spent the most time with Brandon and being in there now felt nearly unbearable.

Mom still hadn't come home from whatever she was doing, and I'd gotten so worried that I'd decided I'd call her around eight if she still hadn't gotten back. Usually, I felt bad disturbing her at work, but my anxiety was rising too high to not check in with her.

Trina had retreated to her sanctuary, her bedroom, and, while I would have preferred to have her company, or anyone's company for that matter, the loud music pouring down the hall helped ease some of the emptiness. Even if it didn't really help with the task of doing homework.

After the debacle with the necromancers and Frank's plan to tell them about Rose, Mr. Tyler had become my only clear option. Of course, I could try and drill Frank some more in hopes that his memory would suddenly reveal some helpful fact, but that was probably my last resort if this thing with Phoenix didn't pan out.

This is odd timing, I know, but Phoenix has agreed to meet us tomorrow. Would your mom be upset if you weren't home for part of the day?

I stared at Mr. Tyler's text for a few seconds as my brain struggled to put the words into context and then ponder his question. It was wrong to answer without asking my mom first, but based on her different behavior on the day before, one could even question that we were going to have a Thanksgiving dinner at all. However, I was way too eager to get things going that it wasn't even a concern.

I'm sure she'd be fine with it. In fact, if y'all hadn't figured out a good place to meet yet, we could meet at my house. The spell could help keep us safe.

Despite the spell's main function of keeping occult creatures out of our house, Caleb's witch friend had taught me how to invite someone in without causing any issues with the spell. She'd warned me, though, that anyone who I invited in would always be able to get in unless they redid the spell.

I was taking a risk letting Phoenix into the house, for sure, but at least we had assurances that Rose wouldn't be able to suddenly show up again. This made my house even safer than the werewolf territory, and we'd said as much during our brunch planning.

I know Gryphin and I are free for at least part of the day. The commune usually has a big dinner later in the evening, so as long as we are there for that, it should be fine. I'll check with Phoenix and get back with you. The only reason I suggested tomorrow is because I know how eager you've been to get this working, and Phoenix thinks that doing it on the holiday will help prevent the coven from sniffing around.

After sending Mr. Tyler an emoji "thumbs up", it was impossible not to look at the other messages. Noah's frequency had dropped off, but he still hadn't given up, leaving me nearly 45 unread messages for the day.

Shaking my head, I began going through them. They varied between all the same theme which was, in short, he was terribly sorry, wanted to see me, and wasn't going to give up until I said yes.

Too bad I wasn't going to.

At least, not yet.

Eight o'clock rolled around, and I was about to pick up my phone to call Mom when the front door opened, and she sighed loudly as she came inside.

"Oh, hi sweetie. Trina!" she hollered, putting her purse on the hook next to the door. "Turn down that music!"

The familiarity of the situation made me smile as the loud music streaming down the hall was lowered perhaps a tiny smidge.

"I was just about to call you, young lady. You're keeping odd hours these days," I said, setting down my laptop onto the end table and smiling playfully.

"Oh, I'm sorry, sweetie." She flopped into the armchair and looked as exhausted as I felt. Neither of us had been getting enough sleep. "It's just been a week."

"So... I hate to be adding to your stress or anything, but are we planning on having Thanksgiving tomorrow?"

She rubbed at her forehead and sighed.

"I mean, it's okay if we don't have as big a one as we usually do. I was only asking because you usually make pies the day before and clean the house like a mad woman, and since tomorrow is Thanksgiving... I thought that maybe we weren't going to do it?"

"Yes, we're still having it. I've got all the supplies in the fridge. I just haven't had the time... I've been so busy." She laid her head on the back of the chair and closed her eyes.

"We might not be as good at cooking, but we're more than old enough to be able to help. Trina can clean the bathroom. I know how much she likes that," I said with a smile.

Mom's eyes were still closed, but she also smiled at the memories of many years of Trina complaining about cleaning the bathroom. "I'm afraid I will need your help if we're going to eat at any reasonable time tomorrow. Your dad will be here about two to help with the mashed potatoes."

"That's his favorite dish. He loves to make sure it's done right. Uhm, speaking of other people coming over..."

She peeked one eye open at me. "Uh oh."

"Well, it's just Mr. Tyler, his nephew, and that arcanist we talked about at brunch the other day. We're all very sorry to mess up the holiday, but it seems to be the best time to meet."

As I talked, she'd pulled her head up and opened both eyes to listen to me. "I suppose that's doable. Just means you and your sister will have to spend the morning cleaning quickly while I get the turkey and pies started."

"That's fine. Our house isn't that dirty or anything. I don't know why you always worry about having it spotless for Thanksgiving."

She rested her head back down on the chair and shrugged. "Tradition, I guess. Plus, we won't want your visitors to think we're slobs."

"Or Dad to think we've let the house go without him here."

She scoffed and shook her head. "Yeah, the only thing he'll be worried about is if we've kept up with the yard."

"Too bad it's basically winter or else we probably wouldn't have."

"Maybe we'll have to hire Noah to put a bunch of zombies on the task this summer."

I snickered at the image of rotting zombies stinking up in the hot summer heat while mowing and pulling weeds. "Maybe not."

Nighttime found me in my room, avoiding my phone so I didn't see more messages from Noah, laying in my bed, and staring up at the ceiling. I hadn't been able to turn the side table lamp off at nights still, so the room was bathed in a dim yellow glow.

As I tried to will myself into sleep, those nasty thoughts I'd been able to avoid for a few nights came back with a vengeance. The familiar but still scary fears of being kidnapped again bombarded me with multiple scenarios, each more terrifying than the last.

What if Queen Kieran came back? She was still out there somewhere. I tried to remind myself that Caleb was nearly always around, and he would protect me. Flashes of memory went by of seeing him chained with wooden shackles and having been beaten far past what a human could withstand. It didn't help to assure myself over and over that their seethe bond had been broken so that the queen had no power over him now, but the anxiety in me wondered how much that would really help.

Kieran had been strong enough on her own to become queen, perhaps she was still stronger than Caleb, even without the seethe bonds to keep him under control.

Or what if the necromancers decided they didn't like me living my own life and sent a horde of zombies to ransack my house and carry me back to become a spirit-wrangling pet for the necroes? It wasn't hard to remember the awful smells of the zombies or the way they twitched in the grass as I'd walked by.

One of the oldest fears I had showed up too. It had probably been stirred by the events of the day as I had worried about several ghosts at once noticing what I could do. As my mind drowned in an ocean of blue transparent bodies screaming for help, I pushed myself out of bed and paced back and forth across the carpet, hoping the physical movement would bring me out of the terrors of my own mind.

I rubbed at my face with trembling fingers and found I was crying. It had been selfish of me to ask Brandon for help during these attacks. Instead, I should have figured out how to handle them on my own...just in case...

With a wail, I fell down to my knees, clutching my blankets and leaning my head against the bed. A part of me wanted to run outside my bedroom and dive into my mother's warm and comforting bed, but a bigger part wouldn't let me, knowing that doing so would only give my mother more worries.

If I had any chance of doing what I needed to do, I needed to keep my mom thinking I was doing as well as could be expected, despite the meltdown I had at brunch the other day.

Feeling sorrier for myself than I could remember feeling in my whole life, I sobbed into the comforter on my bed, using it to muffle the loud cries as best as I could.

A sound from the window startled me. It was different from what I usually expected to hear from Caleb, more of a longer screeching sound instead of the raps of a few knuckles.

Anxiety told me it was something coming to take me away and that opening my window was a bad idea. Logic told me that Caleb would never let something get as close to my window if it was dangerous, and even then, the spell would keep the monster out.

Besides, I was sick of listening to anxiety.

My legs barely held up as I pulled myself to the window and opened the blinds. Surprise helped keep my cries in check as I saw who was pawing at my window with claws bigger than a kitchen knife.

Forest brown eyes shone in the dim light of my lamp and that grey curl stood out even amongst his thick fur.

A different emotion gathered inside my chest as I opened the window, removed the screen, and made way for the giant wolf to squeeze in through. At first, I was worried it wouldn't work, but perhaps his fur made him look bigger than he was, because he elegantly folded himself in through the square hole and instantly made my room feel cramped.

"Hello," I said a bit shyly as I closed the window against the chilly November night and pulled the blinds closed.

Gryphin dipped his wolf's head in greeting and then tipped it to the side with wide eyes as if to ask me what was going on.

"I..." And this time the tears of gratitude and happiness at not being alone anymore spilled down my face and clogged my throat.

He huffed, wrapped a giant paw around my back, and pulled me into his furry form. We nestled onto the floor in a heap of warmth, and he kept one protective arm over my body. The pressure helped bring me down from the spiraling thoughts and back to earth where I had time to wonder where Caleb was before falling deeply asleep.

Chapter 10

Gryphin was gone by the time I woke up, and I had no idea how he had put me in my bed, tucked me under the blankets, gotten through the window, and closed it again without waking me up. He hadn't been able to close the blinds behind him though. Pale morning light poured into my room as intermittent birds who hadn't flown out for the winter chirped in the bush nearby.

My face still felt puffy from my sobbing attack, and in the bright daylight, I felt embarrassed about Gryphin having seen me in such a state. But overall, I was grateful that someone had been there to hold me tight...even if it wasn't necessarily the person I wanted the most.

After debriefing Trina in the morning of my and Mom's plan, we got to work cleaning and cooking for our guests. As I scrubbed the toilet, because of course Trina refused to, I wondered about how weird it will be with Mom and Dad in the same room for most of the day. It didn't seem right to leave Dad out of the festivities. I had no idea if he'd considered throwing his own dinner party at his tiny apartment, but, perhaps if he had, he'd felt too bad taking us away from Mom on her favorite holiday.

I also thought about the food and sorted through my mind about which ones with lower calories I could eat and which ones I should stay far away from. As a general rule, most Thanksgiving sides weren't healthy, but my appetite still hadn't come back.

Hopefully, it never would.

I had to admit that after looking in the mirror earlier, I was happy to see my legs looked thinner. I was even happier when I put on jeans and noticed they fit looser. If I could keep this up, I'd maybe even get into a size zero. At least Andrea wouldn't be able to tease me about being fat, even if she could tease me about everything else.

Noah hadn't given up his incessant texts and calls, but I still wasn't quite ready to face him. Thankfully my phone buzzed only twice an hour instead of every ten minutes like it had the day before.

I'd finished my cleaning assignments way before Mom had finished with the pies. Trina was still vacuuming the front room as I washed my hands and offered my services to whatever tasks Mom needed done next.

Dad was the first guest to arrive, if one could call him a guest since he'd lived in that very house for several years, and he jumped right in to help with the potatoes.

"Do you mind teaching me your secret potato tricks?" Trina asked, coming to stand next to him as he washed the spuds in the sink. She'd finished cleaning and had been hanging around the kitchen but hadn't offered to jump into anything yet.

I was helping Mom cook noodles for the macaroni and cheese dish we traditionally had while she worked on the green bean casserole.

Dad's bushy eyebrows rose in surprise over his glasses as he looked down at my sister. "You've never shown interest in this before."

She shrugged. "I figure next year I might be on my own for Thanksgiving, and it would be nice to at least know how to make mashed potatoes as good as my dad can."

Mirrored expressions crossed Mom and Dad's face as they looked at her with a kind of pained pride. We hadn't talked much about it as a family, but this was Trina's last year as a student in our home. She had big plans for college and was probably going to be living her best life next year.

"Don't worry," I said, hoping to ease some of the heavy emotion in the room. "You'll have to come home to do your laundry anyway, and a holiday is as good a time as any."

"Speaking of that, it really is time to teach you how to do that yourself," Mom said as she poured frozen green beans into a pot.

I smiled at Trina's pout, and Dad chuckled before starting to explain the best way to make mashed potatoes.

Mom and Dad maintained a pleasant enough vibe between them while we continued to prepare dinner, but once our other guests arrived, things started to get a bit weird.

The doorbell rang, and since Mom was busy stirring the stuffing so it wouldn't overcook, I volunteered to open the door.

"Wow, it smells amazing," Mr. Tyler said. He was wearing something I'd seen him wear several times as a teacher—dress pants, a plaid button-down shirt with the top button undone, and a tweed jacket with those funny elbow patches.

"It smells so good, my stomach growled before we even stepped onto the porch," Gryphin agreed, standing next to his uncle.

Phoenix was nowhere to be seen, but I figured they would probably pop up any second, as that was a thing they liked to do that was both entertaining and slightly terrifying.

"Come in," I said, stepping back and making room.

As Gryphin passed by me behind Mr. Tyler, his eyes met mine with an upraised eyebrow as if to ask how I was feeling. I gave him a cheerful smile that I hoped assured him that all was fine. Although, I did blush a bit thinking about his warmth pressed in around me and enjoying his fresh forest smell.

He must have picked up on the color of my cheeks because one side of his mouth pulled up into an amused smile and revealed a sharp canine tooth.

"Oh! Welcome!" Mom said as she kept stirring the stuffing. "This is Josh, the girls' dad, and you know Trina."

Dad nodded to the newcomers and shot Mom a confused look.

"Mr. Tyler is my history teacher, and this is his nephew, Gryphin," I said, gesturing to them.

"Nice to meet you," Dad said, still looking perplexed but unsure enough of the situation to ask any questions.

"They're here to..." I glanced around the room trying to think of something that would explain why they were showing up and realized that having Dad in the room was going to complicate things heavily. He had no idea what kind of occult things I dealt with on the regular, and I chided myself for thinking this situation was going to work. If he was confused with the wolves here, he was going to be way more surprised when Phoenix showed up.

"Well, they're here to eat dinner, of course," Mom supplied with a happy smile. "We've invited them since they don't really have much of a family at home, and we just thought it would be a nice thing to do."

Dad plastered a pleasant smile on his face, but I could see several thoughts were whirling around inside his mind. The least of which was probably wondering if Mom and Mr. Tyler were dating. As far as he knew, that was the best explanation for this whole thing, and I couldn't figure out a way to let him know it was more of a werewolf/Seer/magic user kind of situation.

Letting him think they were dating was going to be awkward, but at least it was less dangerous than having to tell him vampires and werewolves existed.

"That's a very nice thing to do," Dad said, sounding a bit sad.

"We're also having one more guest." I walked over to the cabinet and started pulling out plates. "Their name is Phoenix and..."

"They're a friend of mine from school," Trina said with a helpful smile. "They also didn't have anywhere to go for Thanksgiving, so we decided to invite them, too."

I gave her a grateful look behind Dad's back and began setting the table for seven people. We'd have to grab a mismatching chair to fit everyone around, but hopefully it wouldn't be too hard to squeeze us in together.

"Oh... I guess I had thought it would just be us family members, but..." Dad looked at our handsome guests and gave a hesitant smile, "I suppose the more the merrier."

As if waiting for a cue, which would so be like Phoenix, a knock sounded on our door. I put down the pile of forks I'd been divvying out and jogged over. Sure enough, Phoenix greeted me from the other side.

"Hey, Phoenix," I said loudly for everyone and then leaned in closer to them to whisper. "My dad is here too. He doesn't know about all the 'real' world stuff, if you know what I mean."

Phoenix, who was wearing a flowy black skirt, black high-heeled booties, and a crop top beneath a warm orange sweater, smiled knowingly. "Ah, I see. I gotchu, girl."

"As far as he knows, you're a friend of my sister's from school."

They grinned as they started to ascend into the doorway, but I held up my hand. "Hold on just one second."

Closing my eyes, I waved my arm in three circles and said, "We welcome Phoenix into our house in full trust."

Understanding twinkled in their eyes as I stepped back and waved them into the house. "Sorry about that. C'mon in!"

If Dad had noticed my odd behavior at the door, he didn't show it. Hopefully he'd been too distracted by watching Mr. Tyler and Gryphin use their overly-large arm muscles to help carry the food to the table.

We finished cooking everything and settled down for our meal. It might have been a tad later than Mom would have preferred, and her hair might have been a bit messier with a few frayed strands sticking out, but overall, we did it. Trina and I also learned how to make a few things, too.

I'd say our preparation for the dinner, despite the late start and last-minute cleaning, was pretty successful.

Dinner conversation stayed mostly lighthearted and in the small-talk range because everyone was smart enough not to mention occult stuff while Dad was there. Mom talked about how well her photography business was going. There was tightness around Dad's eyes while she talked about it, but I couldn't tell if it was because he didn't want her to be successful without him, or if it was because he felt guilty that she'd had to work so hard to pay the bills on her own.

Mr. Tyler and Gryphin talked about the commune they lived in, conveniently leaving out the fact that they were a large pack of werewolves roaming around the forest.

Phoenix didn't add much to the conversation except to dish out compliments on my mom's cooking, Dad's mashed potatoes, and our various outfits we'd worn for the holiday.

When Mom got up to get the pies ready, Dad turned to me while the others were chitchatting. "So...does your teacher come over for family dinners often?"

A couple of emotions floated around inside me, and I wasn't sure which one I wanted to display. First, I was amused that Dad was apparently uncomfortable with the idea of Mom and Mr. Tyler hanging out together, but that quickly grew into anger as the hurt from my dad leaving in the first place reminded me that this whole thing was his fault anyway.

"What? Would it bother you if they were?" I settled for the usual teenage snark and gave him a sassy head bob.

His brown eyes bounced from Mr. Tyler's friendly grin as Trina laid down some gossip about another teacher to Mom's smile as she brought her handcrafted apple pies to the table. "If you'd asked me before today, I would have said it didn't," he muttered, probably more to himself than to me.

"Yeah, well," I said, putting down my fork and hoping I'd stirred around my food enough on the plate so it looked like I'd eaten more than I actually had. "Guess that's what happens when you leave somebody. You've probably already moved on, anyway. How many dates have you gone on?"

The stiffness in his jaw and his silence was enough of an answer for me.

I scoffed and shook my head. Gryphin locked eyes with me from further down the table, and he did that cute puppy tilt to his head to ask if I was okay.

I sent him a much-too-bright smile to let him know I was forcing through the situation as best as could be expected.

"Those look amazing!" I made sure to say to my mom as she cut into the pie and started placing pieces onto small plates.

Trina grabbed the ice cream and caramel sauce and put them onto the table as well. "Mom's pies are the best!"

Mr. Tyler had gathered up a few empty plates and was taking them to the sink. "If they taste as amazing as they smell, we are in for quite a treat."

Dad's eyes narrowed, and he started gathering plates up as well. Trina and I shared an amused look to see him do something he didn't often participate in. "Michelle's favorite holiday is Thanksgiving, and she usually goes all out for it. We've made many great meals thanks to her."

As Dad juggled several more plates than what Mr. Tyler had grabbed, mostly because he'd taken them from people whether they were finished or not, they passed each other. Mr. Tyler gave him a teasing smile he often reserved for his students.

"Y'all are too kind. I just follow the recipe. Anyone can do that," Mom said, a faint blush coloring her cheeks as she passed out the dessert plates.

"Oh, girl. I can't tell you how many times I've tried making a pie, and they never turn out," Phoenix said with the wave of their hand.

Good natured chuckles bounced around the table as we dove into the pie, and everyone was wearing a smile except for my dad.

Which suited me just fine.

Later, Dad had gone to the front room in a sulk and turned on whatever sporting event thing was a big deal on Thanksgiving. Trina and Phoenix went to join him as the rest of us worked to clean up the kitchen.

Gryphin helped me clear off the table while Mom and Mr. Tyler stood at the sink working through the ginormous pile of dishes.

"Is he, like, really crushing on my mom or just putting on a show to annoy my dad so he'll leave soon and we can get to the real reason we're here?" I asked Gryphin quietly as we gathered up dirty forks and half-empty plates.

Chuckling, Gryphin gave me a shrug with one shoulder. "I don't know. Maybe both? I've honestly never seen him flirt much so this is new to me, too. In fact, I kind of always wondered if he was gay since I'd never seen him with any women."

"Maybe he's...not into that kind of thing?"

Gryphin glanced up as my mom laughed a little bit louder than normal. "I'm starting to think that maybe he is. Would it be weird for you if they started dating?"

I considered that question with a pensive frown. "Honestly, I won't know until they do."

"Looks like that could be sooner rather than later."

"It's kinda fun to see my dad so uncomfortable with it."

"That's a bit evil, isn't it?" He grinned big enough to show his bright teeth.

I shrugged. "Maybe, but it's true. He deserves it."

While everyone was still distracted, I lowered my voice even more. "I kept meaning to ask you, but where was Caleb last night? It was a big surprise to see you outside my window."

He picked up some more utensils, carrying several at once in his large hands. "Why? Were you disappointed?"

I let out a friendly chuckle. "Believe me, it's not like that. I enjoyed our time together, and your fur is so soft it feels like it would be worth a million bucks if it was like a coat or something. It's just that I'm used to having him around, and I worry he's doing something dangerous or that if he's off flirting with some chick at a bar while he's supposed to be watching me. If my mom finds out, she'll freak."

"Ah, yeah. He asked me to cover for him last night. I guess he assumed I wouldn't have a problem prowling outside your house in the dark."

"Oh, right. Well, you know what they say about assumptions."

Gryphin tilted his head and gave me a small smile. "In this case, he was right. It was my pleasure, and when I heard you getting upset, I knew I couldn't just sit outside and pretend nothing was happening."

Color rushed to my cheeks as I remembered what a mess I'd been. "I guess I didn't say thank you for that yet."

"You don't need to." His forest brown eyes crinkled at me so kindly, my arms felt an urge to wrap him into a big hug.

I resisted the movement and simply smiled back.

"As for your bloodsucking friend, I have no idea where he went or what he was up to. It's quite possible he had a hot date, but you don't need to worry about your mom getting upset since he at least made sure to cover his place."

"I guess...although I can think of another person who'd be upset to learn Caleb was drinking from other people's necks." I glanced at Trina who was in the middle of a conversation with Phoenix, which Dad appeared to have been trying to studiously ignore.

After we'd cleaned off the table and the dishwasher was stuffed to the gills, we all piled into the front room and pulled out the board games. Dad was still trying to watch the sport's game over our heads as we gathered around the coffee table, but since all of us knew it was time for him to leave and for us to get down to business, we didn't mind the unspoken task of making things more difficult for him.

Phoenix made sure to sit right in front of the TV screen with their tall self and broad shoulders, hopping up to kneel every time it was their turn to roll the dice and move their marker on the board.

After one particularly loud laugh from our group, Dad shut off the TV and stood.

"Well, Michelle, dinner was amazing, as always. It was good to see you, girls. Let's get together again before school starts next week, okay?" he said with one hand on the doorknob.

"Sure!" Trina said brightly.

"It was nice to meet you!" Mr. Tyler stood from the armchair and extended a hand.

Dad hesitated but was man enough to not leave Mr. Tyler hanging. They shook hands, Mr. Tyler much more enthused than my dad.

Grunting with the extra squeeze the lithe werewolf gave him, my dad let go and excused himself out of the house.

We all nearly sighed in relief as one once he'd left, and my mom started putting the board game away. "I'm so sorry about that, everyone. I know you're here to be working on things, but we couldn't just leave him to be alone on Thanksgiving."

I helped stack the fake money into neat piles. "It's fine, Mom. I have a feeling there were more than a few of us teasing him a bit and enjoying it."

"And I live alone so it was honestly a nice afternoon and delicious, too," Phoenix said while patting their stomach with a wide smile.

"It really was delicious," Mr. Tyler agreed as he folded the board and put it back into the box.

"It's a nice appetizer for our dinner later." Gryphin grinned as we settled onto the couch next to each other. "Your mom really is a good cook."

"Well, we helped," Trina said with a mostly-teasing smile and brought a few kitchen table chairs over so no one had to sit on the floor.

Normally, our couch held three people relatively snug, but with Gryphin's broad shoulders, there wasn't going to be room for much more than me on it. Phoenix took the armchair, Trina took the other, and Mom and Mr. Tyler sat next to each other in the wooden table chairs.

"So now that we're free to talk, Phoenix, what do you got for us?" Mr. Tyler took over the authoritative role he was so used to wielding at school.

"I'm afraid that it's not as much as I'd like to give you. I can't even tell you where she lives," they said, looking around our group with a half-frown on their lightly-glossed lips.

"Let's start with what you *can* tell us," Gryphin suggested, the warmth from his arms radiating enough to cross the inch between us.

"How about you start with why you're willing to help us, instead," I said, giving them a skeptical look.

Phoenix winced but nodded. "Fair enough. I'm sorry that I helped her last week. Specifically, to you, William."

They were referring to the incident where they'd locked Mr. Tyler in a bubble for several minutes, rendering him stuck and unable to help the rest of us while we battled a crazed witch and her pet vampire.

Mr. Tyler smiled kindly. "I saw how you reacted to her soul-eating. The wolf part of me might take longer to forgive you, but I appreciate a person who stands up against their friends when a line has been crossed."

Phoenix pressed their lips in a grateful smile. "Thank you. It's true that Rose...crossed a line, and I couldn't stand there anymore and help her."

"I did notice that you didn't turn on her completely and help us," I said pointedly and folded my arms across my chest.

Phoenix looked down at their long fingers sitting in their lap with a frown. "I know, but moving against her so blatantly would get me kicked out of the coven...or worse. Believe me when I say you don't want to make a coven of witches angry."

"Speaking of coven," Mr. Tyler rested his elbows on his lap and leaned in toward Phoenix, "what do they think of Rose's escapades?"

"Yes, well, as far as I know, she's the most powerful witch on this side of the nation with a sizable following, including witches from inside our own coven. The matron doesn't usually like taking the side of one witch or the other. The last thing she wants is a war between ourselves. We have such low numbers as it is." Phoenix looked pained to have to tell us this.

Mr. Tyler shook his head and sat back in the chair. "Well, at least that explains how she's been able to get away with so much."

"What about the other covens? Can't they hold her in check? Aren't there rules and a group of people who are supposed to hold everyone to those rules? If not, it's like a witch can do whatever they want without anyone to answer to," I said, scrunching up my nose in frustration.

Phoenix shrugged, lifted their hands, and shook their head to show helplessness. "The coven is it. We're not united enough to have a council of the coven leaders or anything like that. Witches have tried in years past, but it always ends up in disaster."

"I guess I should have been born a witch," I said sarcastically as I fiddled with the tassel on one of the decorative couch pillows.

"Well, at least a very powerful one," Trina agreed with a shake of her head.

"What about the other witches?" Gryphin said, lifting his head from where he'd been staring at the carpet. "If an alpha was doing such things, all the werewolves underneath him would gather together to take him down. Why can't the witches do something similar?"

Phoenix opened their mouth to answer, but Mr. Tyler spoke faster. "Not always. If they're too scared of failing, or if the alpha is too powerful, sometimes a bad one can be on top for years."

"Yes, that's how the magic users feel right now, as far as I know," Phoenix said with a nod. "If we go up against her and fail, we'll die. Then she'll probably suck in all our spirits to make herself stronger, and no one wants to take a risk and find out what that's like."

"Ugh!" I flopped back onto the couch and flung the pillow to the side. "It's just not fair! Why does she get to do whatever she wants only because she's cheating and eating souls to get more powerful than other people?"

"That's why it's good to be at the top of the food chain," Mr. Tyler said with a frown.

"What about the other supernatural beings? Can't they stop her? Vampires seem pretty strong or even a pack of werewolves? Or even the two groups together? Couldn't we work something out?" Mom, bless her heart, asked as she hopefully looked around the room at each of our faces.

"Even I know that's asking an awful lot, Mom. Though that's a nice thought," I said, sighing.

"We might be supernatural beings, but most of us are still at least half-human, and humans have a difficult time throwing away centuries of history, grudges, and anger to come together and take down a common enemy if it isn't big enough." Mr. Tyler took off his glasses and rubbed his eyes.

"It would take much more than one witch eating ghosts to get that kind of strength," Phoenix added.

"So the alternative is to what? Just let her get away with it?" I stood and moved behind the couch so I could pace back and forth without running into anyone. "That doesn't seem right. I can't just let the necromancers deal with it, even though they said they would, and—"

"Wait a minute," Phoenix said, sitting straighter in their chair. "You told the necroes about her?"

I paused in my pacing to look at them. "Yes. Frank noted that she was using necromancer powers as well as witch powers, and we went to them to see if they had any extra information they could give us, but that whole thing backfired. They didn't tell me a single thing except not to worry and that they'd handle it themselves. Why? Should I have not done that?"

The room erupted into several different conversations at once, and I struggled to figure out which one to follow.

"Who is Frank?" Mom asked anyone who would listen, which was no one at the moment.

"What do you mean 'handle it'?" Gryphin raised his grey eyebrows in concern.

"Ah, yes. Necromancers thinking they're in charge again," Mr. Tyler muttered while shaking his head.

And Phoenix bent over, holding their head in their hands, and cursed up a storm under their breath.

It was their cursing that got the most attention, of course.

"Wait. Why is it so bad that I told the necromancers?" I said, my heart picking up pace in fear of having messed up something important.

When Phoenix kept cursing to themself, Mr. Tyler spoke. "They aren't known for being the most reasonable group. Especially underneath this new patriarch of the order. Well, he's new to me, but I forget how old I am sometimes. I suppose in human years, he's been around a while. In fact...he's been around longer than most necromancer patriarchs. They tend to go through them quickly being that their very magic costs them years at a time."

"Yes, he looks super old, that's for sure," I said. "Wait a minute... How old are you, exactly?"

Mr. Tyler chuckled. "Old enough, but don't worry, being a high school teacher has kept me young at heart."

He said the last part to my mom with a wink, making Trina and I exchange slightly horrified expressions. Maybe my dad hadn't been imagining things after all.

As for Mom, she just looked confused with the whole situation.

"I'm sorry, Phoenix, if I messed something up. I regretted it immediately afterward if that helps," I said, coming back to sit down on the couch, careful not to get so close to Gryphin that we'd accidentally touch.

Although I had to admit that feeling his warmth and security at that moment would have been nice. I was worried about giving him the wrong messages. Having him think I liked him more than a friend would complicate already complicated things.

Phoenix finally pulled their head out of their knees and looked at me. Part of their eyeliner had been smeared and their bright red hair was slightly disheveled on the side that wasn't shaved. "It's okay. I know you wouldn't have done it had you known all the facts. In some ways, maybe it is a good thing they'll get involved. They're so possessive of their magic, they'll want to stifle anyone who is using it that's not a part of the order. Yes, maybe it's a good thing."

"Then why do you seem so upset?" Trina asked, once again playing with her golden necklace.

They sighed and sat back into the chair. "If they do find her, which they might with their considerable resources, they'll kill her right away."

"Okay…" I looked around the room to gauge the others' reactions in case I was missing something. "And that's a bad thing?"

"Only if you want to free any of the spirits she's trapped," Phoenix said, their cool grey eyes finding my own.

Phoenix had been there that night. They knew what I'd lost and what I hoped to get back. They saw what Brandon had said as he tried to reassure me with his last words. They at least understood some of the heartache that was driving me to bring Rose to justice.

The silence in the room told me that everyone else in there also knew the significance of their words.

"So…if she dies, what happens to the spirits she has trapped?" I asked, hoping that what I was afraid of wasn't what they meant.

Phoenix pressed their lips into a line and slowly shook their head. "We don't know a lot about what she's doing. Or at least *I* don't. Rose is using very dark magic, and while there might be darker magic users who understand more, all I know is that there is no way to free the spirits if Rose isn't there to pull them out of the crystal."

Tears pricked my eyes as their words started to sink into my thick skull. The emotion was made even worse by the several eyes of those nearby turning to look at me with worried expressions on their faces. I wasn't sure if they were actually worried about my best friend or worried that I was going to have another panic attack.

The pressure was too much. Gryphin tried to grab my hand as I pushed myself off the couch, but I slipped out of his grasp and ran to my room.

I shut the door loudly, so they'd be sure to understand I wasn't ready for visitors right then. I hoped they'd figure I'd fallen into bed to sob for a while instead of grabbing my backpack and stuffing it with random things I thought I'd need. Without even being sure of where I was going or what I was going to do, I packed a couple of different shirts and pants, socks, underwear, my phone charger, an extra pair of tennis shoes, and the rest of my cash which only added up to about thirty dollars.

As I rushed around my room gathering up the supplies, I had to wipe at my eyes and nose several times. They both kept leaking, but I wasn't in the mood to indulge my body in the crying it wanted to do.

Knowing that the werewolves' hearing was super good, I slid the window open as slowly and quietly as I could. The screen was still popped out because of Gryphin's exit that morning, and I sent him a silent "thank you" as I climbed, careful not to hit my feet against the side of the house or bonk my head.

I had only snuck out of my house once before, ironically to go meet Rose and help her capture a bunch of ghosts, including Frank. My heart hammered inside my chest so loudly, I was afraid Mr. Tyler or Gryphin could hear it.

But no one stopped me as I closed the window carefully behind me, tiptoed through the grass, still wiping at my eyes and nose in case sniffing was too loud, and climbed over my neighbor's fence behind the house so I wouldn't be spotted out front. I'll admit my climbing wasn't the most graceful thing anyone ever saw, but as I landed with a grunt in the other yard, I felt a sense of accomplishment.

I might have had no idea where I was going or what I was going to do, but it felt good to do *something*.

Chapter 11

As I walked down the street that mirrored my own the next row over, I shoved my hands deep into my coat pockets and realized I had no idea what to do next. I'd made sure to grab a heavier coat since I wasn't sure where I'd end up that night and wanted to be prepared in case it was cold.

My thoughts bopped around to different ideas of how to find Rose and stop her plans and prevent her from being killed before I could free those ghosts, and I came up empty, just as I had the past few months.

There was only one lead I could think of that I hadn't squeezed too dry yet, so I shuffled my feet in the direction of the park. As time and chilly air sunk into me, I felt bad for what Mom and Trina would go through once discovering I was gone. I didn't mean to hurt them, but I couldn't sit inside and do nothing while the necromancers killed off Rose and doomed Brandon to a half-existence inside a crystal.

I might not have known what to do or had the ability to do what could be done, but I sure wasn't going to sit around and do nothing. I owed him that much at least.

The park was unsurprisingly quiet for a chilly Thanksgiving evening. I sat on a bench and snuggled into my coat as I mentally summoned Frank. It took a few seconds, and I had to really focus on the clothes he wore and the mental image of him sitting in that movie theater making fun of current movies.

"What's crackin'?" he said while appearing next to me on the bench. "Oh, you don't look good."

"Thank you," I muttered, giving him a flat stare.

"Just saying." The ghost shrugged, his shoulder-length, dark hair framing his face in a way that made me wonder if he'd wanted to be part of a band at some point. Maybe he had been in a band for all I knew, and I'd never asked.

"I've come to a dead end, and I need your help," I said, putting my head into my hands and focusing on breathing.

At least I'd stopped crying at some point.

"You know I'm happy to help any way I can. I just don't know what else I can help with." His eyes looked more earnest than I'd ever seen them, and I was inclined to believe he thought there was nothing else he could do.

I wasn't ready to believe it.

"Tell me every single thing you can think of about your time with Rose. Anything you can think of. You might feel like a detail isn't important or doesn't matter but tell it to me any way. Maybe we can ferret something out of it together."

He sat back on the bench and sighed. "Okay, but only because you've started to grow on me, even with your puffy face."

I didn't respond except to stare at him until he started talking.

"Alright, I'll try my best, but if I say something you've already heard then you can stop me."

My glowering stare must have clued him in that I didn't care about repeats because he shrugged.

"Or not. Right. Well, once you forced me into the crystal's circle—"

I winced and made an apologetic face.

"—which we're past worrying over, and then...as far as I can remember, it was just kind of a blackness? I don't know. Perhaps it was more like being unconscious? I can't remember much except some flashes of light, and then there was that one time she pulled me out to grab some free ghosts for her inside of a freaky deaky warehouse."

"Wait, how did she pull you out? How did you know it was you who should go and not other ghosts trapped in there with you? Could you even feel the other ghosts around?"

Furrowing his eyebrows as he talked, he said, "I'm not sure. I don't think I could really feel the others, but I did have a kind of awareness that I hadn't been alone. And then it was just all of a sudden, I felt a pull, and I was outside in the real world again."

"And what was that like? How much could you do for yourself and how much did she control?"

"Uh... It felt like I had a kind of lifejacket deal on, you know? Like I was me, but there was something wrapped around me that kept me tethered to the crystal. Then when she commanded me to do something, I could only fight so much before I was forced to do the thing. Like maybe the lifejacket took over my body and forced me into the action."

I pressed my lips in thought as I stared out over the park. The swings were moving slightly in the chilly breeze in a way I had to admit was pretty creepy. If I didn't already see ghosts, I'd wonder if one was sitting on a swing or two.

"So can you explain how that felt different or the same from when I... Once again, I'm really sorry, and I promise not to do it again, probably. But was it any different from when I commanded you to go into the circle?"

Frank frowned. "Probably?"

I shrugged with an awkward smile. "You never know when something important might happen."

He rolled his eyes and shook his head. "Ugh. You're lucky I believe in your cause, because otherwise I'd be outta here."

"I appreciate your help."

"Even if it doesn't get you want you want?"

I frowned and looked back at the swings. "It will. We've just got to figure it out, is all. So? Did it feel different?"

"I would say yes to that, but mostly not a lot different. With Rose it was harder to fight off, I suppose."

"Not sure if I should be insulted or not."

"Or she was using stronger magic with the crystal's help? Your commands were more like compels, in a way, if that makes sense. But then it was like each time you commanded me, the compelling got stronger and stronger until I had to obey. With Rose, I had to do what she wanted me to do, no matter who I was or what *I* wanted to do."

"That does not sound fun." I used the toe of my tennis shoe to start digging a small hole in the dirt as I wondered what kinds of things Rose was making Brandon do, or if she'd used him at all.

Maybe he had spent this whole time sleeping in a ghostly way and had no idea what was going on in the world around him?

In some ways, that was a bit of a relief. Perhaps he was merely enjoying an oblivious getaway.

"It wasn't much fun. I have to admit, the most fun I had was when you and Brandon were fiddling with the curse tied to Mr. Tyler."

"Oh yeah." I shifted on the bench so I could hug one of my legs while the other stayed in the dirt. "Tell me about that. How did you get out of there to talk to Brandon?"

"My working theory is that when Rose became aware of something bothering her curse, she wondered what was happening enough for me to use my own will as long as it aligned with hers."

"And how did you know this was happening if you were in a kind of sleep state?"

"Not sure. Just did. I'm sorry, dude. I don't have all the answers."

I sighed and rested my head on the back of the bench. "I know. I'm not trying to be annoying. I'm just…"

"It's fine. I get it. Wish I could be more help."

We fell into silence for a few moments. I had no idea what he was thinking about, but I was playing around with his words in my head, trying to combine them in different ways that would lead me to some ultimate realization, the answer to all my problems, and show me exactly what to do.

It was then that Phoenix appeared out of thin air and scared me so bad I nearly fell off the bench.

"Holy Hand Grenade!" I said, grabbing onto the cool metal next to me.

Frank, excuse the expression, looked as white as a ghost. "…Freaky," he said with wide eyes.

Phoenix didn't look ashamed for their sudden appearance. Instead, they frantically glanced around the park before looking back down at me. "Look, girl. They've just found out you're gone, and I figured I'd pop in here to give you warning in case you don't want to be found. You know how good a werewolf's nose is?"

I stood and looked around the park as well. "Almost as good as their speed."

"I'm not a fan of you being out here on your own," Phoenix said, tossing the long side of their hair over their shoulder, "but I can respect needing to do something. Would you be opposed to me teleporting you out of here? At least this way, the wolves can't track you."

"Wow...that would be...super cool of you! But why are you helping me if you're worried about me being out here alone?" I asked, my eyes continually scanning the park for the telltale sign of a wolf's glowing eyes.

"Let's just say helping a Seer is in everyone's best interest if they're able to get the chance," Phoenix said with a sly smile.

"Fair enough. Frank, I'll summon you in a second. Okay?" I glanced back at the ghost as I took Phoenix's hand, and the world swirled around me like someone had shoved it into a blender and pushed a button.

Once the world aligned itself, I didn't even have time to stop and see where I was before my stomach protested and I barfed into the nearest bush. There wasn't much to bring up since I hadn't eaten a whole lot for dinner, and this time it wasn't even because I was worried about weight. I seriously didn't have an appetite these days.

"I usually give people more warning and break down how to travel by teleportation without getting sick, but we were short on time," Phoenix said with hands on their hips, their kind eyes watching me recover through ragged breaths.

"Lucky me," I managed to wheeze.

"Well, in a way, you are kind of lucky. If we hadn't teleported out of there, those wolves would have found you no matter where or how fast you ran. They're excellent hunters and almost all as good looking as vampires are. Alas, too much hair for my taste, though."

I rested with my hands on my knees and was finally oriented enough to look around. They had brought us to a thickly wooded area surrounding a large cabin. The setting sun pulled long shadows through the trees and cast everything in an orangish glow. There was one gravel road stretching out and meandering into the darkness. As for the cabin, in many ways it reminded me of the werewolves' lodge but without any other structures around it. There was a similar wrap-around porch, and it looked like it had been made by logs stacked on top of each other and molded together with some kind of cement, but this one only had two stories instead of three.

While I took in the surroundings, I mentally summoned Frank. I wasn't sure what help he'd be since I didn't even know where we were, but it seemed like a more secure thing to have him around when I didn't fully trust Phoenix.

It was possible it had been a mistake to go with them.

"Where are we?" Frank asked as soon as he appeared, also looking around at the towering trees above us.

"Where are we?" I echoed his question and felt decent enough to fully stand.

Phoenix did a little twirl in the gravel which was pretty impressive considering how tall their heels were. I was pretty sure I'd have a lot of trouble wearing those around. "We're at the coven's safe house. Isn't it cool?"

A ghost walked out of the woods, through the walls, and into the cabin. Thankfully, it paid us no mind.

"The coolest," I said, sharing a meaningful look with Frank. "It's only slightly haunted."

"Really?" Phoenix jumped on their toes a few times and clapped. "Oh, I'd always suspected so but hadn't actually brought a Seer here before."

"Can't witches sense ghosts?" I asked, remembering when I first went into Rose's shop, and she seemed to realize there was someone else there with me.

Phoenix shrugged their broad shoulders. "Some can. Most can at least feel some kind of presence, but others can't feel anything at all. We certainly can't see them or anything like Seers can do. Magic users' abilities are all over the place, varied as much as our hairstyles."

"Oh, I doubt that," Frank said, giving Phoenix's bright red, half-shaven hair a dubious look.

"So why are we here?" I asked, looking up at the dark windows. "Is it abandoned?"

Phoenix smiled and turned toward the front door. The gravel crunched under their heels, but they had no trouble balancing as they walked. "Oh, it's teeming full of life. It's spelled to look dark and boring on the outside."

I'd started following but then stopped abruptly. "Wait, are there more magic users in there? Is it safe? Is Rose in there? Are you leading me into a trap I'm dumb enough to walk into willingly?"

They turned to look at me with a tilt of their head. "Honey, the last thing we all want is for you to be Rose's puppet. I assure you, I will take you nowhere near her."

"We?" I asked with a gulp as I continued to follow Phoenix closer to the cabin.

"Yes, dear. Everything will be fine. You'll see," they said with a calming voice and opened the door.

Bright yellow light poured out from the opening, none of which had been shining through the dark windows. The air was suddenly filled with loud chatter, laughter, and what sounded like music coming from a tinny record player. As we stepped over the threshold, I was surprised to see that the inside was much bigger than the outside. Vaulted ceilings arched high above us, boasting brilliantly lit chandeliers, and red curtains framed sliding glass door windows that all overlooked a different view. Several people lounged in chairs and couches around the room, drinking out of slim glasses and talking with one another.

As I stepped into the room, Frank slid in behind me quickly before Phoenix shut the door in his face. Everything went quiet as all eyes turned to me. Even the music had stopped playing although I hadn't seen anyone go near the table where the giant gramophone with a golden horn sat.

"Good evening, all." Phoenix sashayed into the room with a brilliant smile on their face. "As you can see my mission was successful. Here she is."

As Phoenix gestured to me like I was some big prize, I resisted the urge to curtsy or bow or something just as dumb, and, instead, merely smiled awkwardly. Several pairs of eyes studied me so intently, I felt naked with all my secrets laid out bare in front of these strangers.

"These ladies are freaky deaky," Frank said, looking around the room. "And those doors are even worse. Does that one lead into the *middle* of the ocean?"

I took a second to glance at the door he was referring to and was surprised to see it completely underwater, and a couple of lazy fish floated past.

One woman emerged from the crowd, standing from where she'd been lounging, and set her glass onto a nearby table. From the looks of her, I was surprised she was able to stand on her own at all. Her skin was wrinkled and saggy, her eyes somewhat cloudy, while her grey hair was twirled atop her head in a tight bun.

"She is *very* young. Poor thing," the lady said, her tone confusing as I wasn't sure if she was mocking me or genuinely feeling sorry for me.

"And I have to say she's been through it already." Phoenix gave me a sad pout.

"Yes, but she will be safe here." The stooped-shouldered lady extended her hand toward me once she was close enough. "Welcome to our coven house. I'm the matron, Cordelia. And you are Hanna?"

I stuck out my hand slowly, feeling more and more like I'd fallen into some kind of magical trap. Her skin was soft but eerily chilled. "Yes, nice to meet you, maybe, depending on what you want with me."

Cordelia laughed as she let go of my hand, and most of the others in the room followed. "Oh, you're going to be a delight to have around. I can already tell."

I frowned and glanced at Phoenix, wondering how mad I should be at them or if I should only be mad at myself for trusting them.

"Let me guess, you've got some kind of ghost problem. You need me to talk to one of your former magic users and pull information out of them. There was no one else up to the task, despite the fact that I'm super inexperienced and don't know what I'm doing half the time, which is also part of the reason I'm finding myself in the heart of a witches' coven with no idea if I'm going to be locked away forever."

Cordelia laughed again and flicked her hand. At her motion, the music started playing again, and she said loudly, "Oh, it's nothing like that, dear. We're only here to help you. Let's relax first, though, shall we? You seem very on edge."

Frank had wandered back to my side after having studied a few more doors. "The vibes in this room are all over the place. I can't help but feel like we've stumbled into a den of vipers with pretty wigs and fancy shoes."

"Here, dear. What would you like to drink?" Cordelia asked as she gestured toward the long bar stretching across the left side of the room. The countertop was a white marble, and all kinds of different shapes and colors of bottles sat upon it, sparkling in the bright lights.

Frank and I followed her as Phoenix left us in the matron's hand and went to talk with some other people in the room. The laughter and chatter resumed, but I still felt in a spotlight of sorts as, at any given moment, at least two others in the room were darting glances in my direction.

"Oh, um, I don't suppose you have any Diet Coke?" I asked, feeling dumb and childish, but also not wanting to lose any of my senses by drinking alcohol or risking my mom getting madder at me than she already was going to be.

Of course, that was if I made it out in one piece.

"Let me check," Cordelia said as she stepped behind the bar and waved her wrinkled hand with long, black nails.

Several of the bottles shook for a second, and I was worried a few of them were going to crash to the floor, but as they stilled, one familiar-looking bottle of Diet Coke wormed its way out from among the collection and flew toward me.

I managed to get my hand up just in time to catch it and found it was chilled perfectly. "Neat trick."

"Groovy," Frank agreed with an appreciative nod.

Cordelia smiled and flicked her wrist again. A decanter of something poured into a small glass as a few ice cubes floated out of somewhere and plopped into the liquid. The drink floated to her as if happy to obey, and she clutched at it deftly.

"Let's find a nice place to rest, shall we?"

I dutifully followed her away from the bar and deeper into the room.

As we walked, Frank shook his head and said, "We should probably get out of here. The odds of this being a completely safe place seem pretty low from where I'm looking."

Hoping the crowd was loud enough to cover my voice, I whispered, "And how do you expect me to do that? Even if the door is miraculously unlocked and lets me out, how do I even know where to go after that? I have no idea where we are or if we're even still in the same country anymore."

Frank shook his head as a passing woman gave me an odd look to which I returned with a shaky smile. "The woods might be safer than in here."

"We don't know that. I feel like this is the closest I've ever been to finding Rose right now. Maybe they'll help."

As I finished speaking, Cordelia whirled around and sunk into a cozy armchair. Her eyes twinkled in amusement that probably meant she'd caught me talking to the ghost, but she was kind, or savvy, enough not to say anything.

Feeling dumb, I sat in the other chair close by and plastered an awkward smile on my face.

Frank looked around with a huff as the closest chair was several paces away. "Guess I'll sit on the floor like the undignified and unappreciated ghost that I am." He settled onto the yellow accent rug next to my feet and kept mumbling to himself.

Cordelia returned my smile with a graceful one and took a small sip of her drink. The ice clinked inside. I took that moment to look around us some more.

I still hadn't opened my own drink, more because I was having a hard time trusting a bottle that had moved on its own rather than not being thirsty. In fact, after yakking into the bushes outside, I probably did need to at least rinse out my mouth.

"This place is amazing," I said, looking outside another door that displayed a bright beach with swaying palm trees and calm, whispering waves.

"No, magic is amazing. This is just a sample of what some of us can do." Cordelia swirled the drink around in her glass as her deceptively sharp eyes went around the room, assessing. "Being in a coven is both like having a large magical family and a bit like being in a large magical mafia. Give me a moment while I cast a silence spell around us so no one can listen in."

I watched with wide eyes as the matron's surprisingly steady hand moved around in a few circles and waves while she chanted softly. There was a dampening feeling like my ears needed to pop when she finished. I could still hear the others in the room outside of our bubble, but they sounded far away.

"Okay... Seems like a shame you have to do that among your own coven," I said, glancing first at Frank, unsure of why she was doing this, why I was sitting here afraid to drink an unopened bottle of diet soda, and why I was even there in the first place.

It seemed clear that the matron had been expecting me, and Phoenix was supposed to bring me in. Maybe the whole story about the werewolves smelling me out hadn't even been true. Guess it was convenient for them that I'd ran away.

I was really dumb sometimes.

"See, while we try to operate as a democracy with a council, allowing people to have a voice as much as we can, sometimes there are situations where the matron must step in and make the choices herself. You know, for the good of the people."

"Right," I said, half-listening while I watched Phoenix chatting with some other magic users. Most of them were as vibrant in style as they were, but I was surprised to note how many looked like regular people I might pass by in the grocery store.

Cordelia sighed, drank the rest of what was in her glass, and set it down on the table between us. "I'm afraid Rose is going to be one of those things I need to deal with myself."

"Uh oh. We've heard this before." Frank shook his head, his dark wavy hair swaying.

My eyebrows pulled up my forehead in realization of how this connected to me. "Why is that?"

"Phoenix saw what she can do, but luckily, they are one of the good ones. If some other arcanists here saw what she can do, they'd beg her to teach them the old magic. As much as I am all for magic users' rights, I know that we can't run unchecked around the human population doing whatever it is we want. Despite our magic, the humans simply outnumber us far too much. We'd be slaughtered like we were when Rose was a child."

"The Salem witch trials, you mean?"

She nodded and continued to look around at her flock of magic users. "To be honest, I'm sure there are several inside this room right now who are loyal to Rose. They'll have already told her you're meeting with me. And I'm not sure if that is worse for me or worse for you. You can drink that, by the way. I assure you it's safe."

Her half-smile was confusing with the last bit of info about Rose she had just dropped. Was I in danger?

A snarky piece of my brain, probably related to Brandon, answered, *When am I not in danger?*

Deciding I was better off with whatever poison might be in the drink than continuing to have puke-breath, I opened the soda bottle and pulled in several gulps.

"Why would me being here be bad for you?" I asked after feeling the refreshing cool liquid seep into my chest.

"Rose has a thing against Seers." Cordelia shrugged. "I don't personally know the whole story, but I do know that she hunts them. We've had to save one or two in the past. They are rare and helpful, after all."

I frowned, fear and anger mixing inside my chest. Words from Queen Kieran's mouth as Gran searched through the vampire's memories floated back to me. "I think she killed my grandmother for a pair of glasses that allow one to communicate with ghosts."

Cordelia turned her attention to me and placed a warm palm on my knee. It was the first time I'd seen any kind of emotion besides frustration or nonchalance cross her face. Her lips pressed into a line as she looked at me. "I'm sorry you had to learn about that. We'd dispatched several witches to stop her, but we were too late. Rose knew exactly where your grandmother lived and was gone before we could track her movements."

Distrust swirled around with the fear and anger in my heart. "I'm sure you would have found a way to stop her had she actually gotten the glasses from my gran."

The skin around her eyes tightened slightly, but that was her only negative reaction. It was enough to confirm that while she might have been trying to do something good, her desires would come before any good deeds, if it came down to it.

"Hanna, that's a very valuable tool. I'm not going to lie to you. We'd love to have it in our possession, but we're not going to kill someone like your grandmother over it," Cordelia said with another kind pat to my knee before sitting back up.

"Why do I not fully believe that?" Frank pushed his lips out like a suspicious duck and shook his head.

"Right. Well, if that's true, it's a bit reassuring," I said with a wavering smile. "I guess."

"But your grandmother was still murdered," Frank pointed out, much to my annoyance.

Cordelia said, "I can't promise that all us magic users are good people. We're like any group—we have good, bad, and most are somewhere in the middle. But I can promise that while I'm still matron of this coven, we're going to do what we can that's best for the coven. This includes not letting any one individual have such power."

"Wait a minute," Frank said, scrunching his face in thought. "Didn't Phoenix say the coven was too afraid to make a stand against her? What did they say?"

Cordelia watched me with a curious expression on my face as I listened to Frank's questions before responding to what she'd just said. It was a look I was used to getting from others who didn't realize there was a ghost around, but it stung slightly so close to the recent video Andrea had posted about me being crazy.

I still needed to figure out how to handle that whole mess.

"Uhm, sorry. I don't mean to be like...doubting you or anything—"

"Except we do, very much," Frank interrupted.

I kept talking, ignoring his truthful comment, "—but Phoenix said something about the coven not wanting to take a stand against her. That maybe she was too powerful or something?"

Cordelia frowned and looked out at the others still having a good time around us. There was a particularly large group laughing and enjoying themselves. "Well, here we come into an issue with trying to have a democracy kind of situation. The council voted against doing anything to stop her. For one, they felt she wasn't a threat to us because she is only trying to help the cause of magic users."

"Wait...wouldn't helping the witches get stronger mean more threats to humans which means there would be a battle?" I said, frowning as I tried to sort through all of these confusing details.

"I tried to explain that to them, but they didn't listen. That's why I told Phoenix that they're too afraid to move against her. She is very powerful. Perhaps one of the most powerful of us all, but you're right,

Hanna. If she keeps going down this road, she's putting not only this coven in danger, but all of us magic users in danger."

"So what are you going to do?" I asked, fiddling with the cap of my soda bottle.

"And why do you need Hanna here?" Frank asked as he studied the matron.

"I have plans that I can't discuss here with you, but Phoenix has told me you've gotten the necromancers involved?"

"Yeah… Sorry about that." I winced. "I knew it had been the wrong thing to do right after I did it."

"The necromancer leader is about as trustworthy as the coven's leader," Frank said with a pout. "Why can't we find any leaders who we know will make good choices?"

"It is an unfortunate complication, but that just means we'll need to move fast. Usually, I would perform a tracking spell, but as Rose hasn't been among us for many years, I don't have anything of hers to use for it." Cordelia steepled her long fingers together as she considered our next moves.

I thought for a second before an idea hit me like getting pooped on by a seagull at the beach. "What if she carried something of mine with her? Would that work?"

The matron turned to me with sparkling eyes and nodded. "We could work with that."

Chapter 12

Not a half-hour later, we were standing in a different room inside the space paradox that was the coven's safehouse. We'd left the larger room, the one I'd nicknamed "The Room of Requirement", after Cordelia had motioned to two other magic users to accompany us.

The four of us alivers stood around a table while Frank kept back behind my right shoulder. I still hadn't told any of them there was a ghost with me, but it didn't seem to be something they needed to know at the moment. It might not have been that powerful of a secret, but I felt justified in keeping it since I knew for certain they weren't telling *me* everything.

Spread before us on the table was a large map of the world. It was so big that it allowed for details of all the countries and their provinces. Also on the table were several candles and a silver necklace with a palm-sized heart in the center.

"Leah, please place silence wards around the room," Matron Cordelia said, nodding to the third witch who had joined us. She was shorter than me with chin-length blonde hair and intelligent blue eyes.

"Okay. It'll just take a second," she said, picking up one of the candles and doing some odd movements I didn't understand around the room, focusing several seconds on the doorway.

Phoenix caught my eye while we waited and gave me another apologetic smile, but I merely looked at them with a blank expression. Obviously, they were feeling guilty for luring me here under false pretenses. I wasn't ready to forgive them yet. That all depended on why I was here. Like the real reason I was here, not the runaround Cordelia had given me so far.

I did have to admit, though, it felt good to be able to help and feel like we were finally making progress. Maybe the whole thing wasn't as hopeless as it had felt while sitting on that cold bench in the park.

After encircling the room twice, Leah returned to the table and put the candle back, giving the matron a nod. "Silence spell placed."

"Excellent. Thank you. We may now speak openly without worrying that others can hear us. I've chosen you all here because I can trust all of you completely while I can't afford that same luxury to every coven member, sadly. And a generous thank you to Leah here, for traveling from the mid-west coven to add some extra help. Our families are old friends, and I'm glad I can depend on her," Cordelia gave Leah a friendly smile.

The small witch nodded back to her graciously.

"Not a good sign if the coven matron can't trust her own members," Frank muttered over my shoulder.

I was getting sick of his Debbie-downer comments, but I wasn't in a place to tell him to be more optimistic nor was he wrong.

"We're going to attempt a location spell to find Ann Good, or Rose as she is known to some. The reason we haven't attempted this before now is because we didn't have any personal items of hers, but Hanna here," Cordelia nodded her head in my direction, "has got something we know is at least on Ann's person. Now, this spell may have trouble with the fact that this particular something happens to be some of Hanna's hair, so it may locate two places for us, and hopefully one will be this room. We'll know that's Hanna here, and the other location will be wherever Ann is, or her bag is, at least."

Excitement grew inside my chest. It would be nice to find Rose and stop her from hurting more people, of course, but I was way more interested in those crystals and getting the ghosts out.

Leah frowned and studied me for a second. "Why does Ann have some of your hair?"

"Er," I glanced at Cordelia to see what I should say but after she nodded, I turned back to Leah. "I'm a Seer and apparently, she needs Seer hair to do her ghost-binding spells. I was dumb enough to give it to her before I understood what she was doing."

Leah's eyes widened for a moment, but she didn't comment on my stupidity, only nodded.

"No one blames you for falling for her tricks," Phoenix said with a kind smile. "We've all been there a time or two."

"Fair enough," I said, still not ready to return their smile.

"Hanna, if you wouldn't mind?" Cordelia asked, handing me a pair of scissors she'd gotten from a nearby desk's drawer.

I took the scissors from her with trembling fingers and smoothed out a lock of hair. "How much do you need?"

"It doesn't need to be much. A few strands will do," Cordelia said as she reached over for the necklace and popped the heart pendant open.

I took a deep breath hoping to steady my fingers some before I snipped off four strands of hair, all about three inches long. On an average day, my brush pulled out more than that, so I wasn't going to miss it. Unlike the several inches I'd chopped off for Rose—my shorter hair constantly reminding me of my naive dumbness.

Cordelia put the hair inside the pendant, closed it securely, and grabbed the necklace by its clasp. Moving to the center of the map, stretching her wrinkled arm to reach, she held the necklace aloft and began chanting words I didn't understand.

Leah and Phoenix joined in with her, and I stood there feeling kind of useless. At least I'd been able to give the hair.

Glowing light started inside the pendant and grew softly outwards until it was difficult to even look at the necklace. The chain moved in slow circles at first, but with each round, its circles grew bigger. Cordelia moved the necklace slowly over the map, eventually covering over all of it before starting again.

The matron's eyebrows furrowed in concentration as all three continued chanting. The necklace spun so fast I wondered if it was going to liftoff like a helicopter, taking the old witch with it.

Suddenly it stopped and stilled, completely calm over a part of the map I didn't know. It was green and lacked the roads of a city, so I assumed it was a forest area.

"That's Hanna," Phoenix said, peering over where the necklace had stopped.

I tried to get a good look of where we were in case I needed to escape and run away for some reason. It was difficult to see much with everyone crowding around and making me feel like I shouldn't be trying to find out where we were, but I could at least tell we were still in Virginia, even if it was several miles away from town. Definitely wasn't within walking distance, but I could get a ride from an app or find a bus or something.

Cordelia nodded, and they picked up their chanting again. The necklace followed the same pattern of glowing and increasing in its spin for several more minutes. It kept going back to the woods, but Cordelia pulled it away each time as if it was a bad kid trying to get at a candy bar. Finally, the spell must have figured it out and stood rigidly still over another location.

We all leaned closer over the map to see where Rose was potentially hiding out. I was surprised to see it was relatively nearby, considering she could have been anywhere in the whole world. Instead, she was somewhere in the middle of West Virginia. Despite our states being neighbors, I hadn't traveled through there very often and couldn't remember much about the area.

"Hmm," Phoenix said, using their finger to trace the highway we'd need to take to get there. "Looks like a six- or seven-hour drive."

"Why can't y'all teleport there?" I asked, studying the map as well.

"We can only teleport somewhere we've already been, and driving doesn't count. We need to have put our foot down on the soil. Have either of you been nearby?" Cordelia asked as she looked at each of us.

"I've been to a gas station somewhere in the middle there, but it's been a while. I couldn't say for sure where we'd end up, and then we'd be without a car," Leah said, her voice high-pitched and small, like her frame.

Cordelia nodded. "It's best that we drive there. Hanna, are you up for a road trip?"

I tried to covertly glance at Frank who only shrugged as if he had nothing else better to do—which I guess he didn't, then looked back at the matron. "Yes. I want to go, but we should get going right away. If my family finds out where I am, they'll come for me, and I'll probably be grounded for the rest of my life."

The matron smiled with half of her mouth. "I agree."

We left it unsaid whether or not I was in their safehouse as a guest or a prisoner, but I wasn't sure if I wanted the answer.

An hour later, we were piling into a glamorous RV that had been parked out back. I'd been shown to an elegant bathroom where I showered, changed into a different outfit from the backpack full of clothes I brought, and wished I'd thought to grab my toothbrush.

Frank had grumbled about needing some alone time and not wanting to spend several hours on the road for no reason, so I agreed to summon him again when we got to where we were going.

The time alone had given me space to think, but it wasn't something I welcomed. I felt guilty for leaving my family, Gryphin, and Mr. Tyler like that. They were probably worrying about me so much, My mom was getting more wrinkles and grey hair from all the stress. I truly didn't want to give her that worry, but I had other things I wanted more.

I'd shut off my phone mostly to conserve battery life so it would work if I needed it for something important, but also so I wouldn't have to see all their frantic messages, or risk them being able to track me with an app.

No, it wasn't kind, but like I said, I had other things I wanted more. I'd deal with the fallout when I got back, and even if I was grounded for the rest of my life, at least I knew I wouldn't have been alone.

It was all going to be worth it. That's what I kept trying to reassure myself, anyway.

"Wow, this is nice," I said, as I climbed up the steps of the RV and looked around. "I could get used to this magic where stuff is bigger on the inside."

Phoenix giggled from behind me as they also climbed into the RV. "Right? It's one of my favorite spells... Well, besides the one where I can eat whatever I want and never gain weight."

I turned to them with big eyes. "There's a spell for that?"

"Sure," they shrugged one broad shoulder and settled into the front passenger seat. "We might as well use magic to do important things like be able to eat as much cake as we want."

"Wow. That would be...amazing." I shook my head, just thinking about the relief from my worries of being fat all the time.

As Leah and Cordelia boarded the RV and stacked their bags into one of the cabinets near the door, I took a few minutes to explore.

The RV was the same shape as it would normally be, narrow and rectangular, but it was much bigger than it would be with regular physics. Despite being narrow, it was still a good fifteen feet across, more like a trailer than an RV. There was a full kitchen, complete with a full-sized oven and fridge. Although, I wondered if magic users even needed kitchens or if they could simply magic themselves some food.

There was a table that could easily fit six with chairs instead of benches, and a large front room area with a couch and two armchairs. All the furniture matched with a dark-stained wood and red, nearly magenta, fabric. Even the kitchen chairs were upholstered with the same look. In the back were three fully equipped bedrooms, each with a queen-size bed, large closet, and its own bathroom.

Leah was settling into the driver's seat, adjusting it several times so she could reach all the pedals and controls, as I walked back to the front.

"This is much nicer than having to fly the whole way on a cold and super uncomfortable broom," I said, finding that I could remember to make some jokes when the prospect of seeing Brandon in a few hours was, perhaps remotely, possible.

The three magic users laughed way harder than I expected.

"Oh, girl, we got rid of brooms a long time ago," Phoenix said, waving their hand as if shooing the prospect away.

"Yeah, vacuum cleaners are much more comfortable," Leah added with a grin.

Cordelia, who was seated in one of the opulent armchairs, again nursing some kind of small-glassed drink, shook her head with a smile. "Y'all are going to put weird ideas in her head. To clear the record, we don't fly on brooms. We use the coven's personal jet, of course."

"Right. Of course."

"Okay, take a seat. We'll be on our way now," Leah said, glancing back at me with a pleasant smile and pushing the start engine button.

I nodded, decided Cordelia had the right idea, and plopped down onto the other armchair. It felt a bit stiffer than I'd expected but was still comfortable.

After listening for a few minutes while the others engaged in small talk, sometimes speaking about different issues in the coven, I found myself drifting off to sleep where I dreamed about flying through the cool night air with a sturdy broom beneath me and a black cat sitting behind.

Chapter 13

We pulled up to a rest stop somewhere in the heart of West Virginia as the light of dawn peeked over the hills. After climbing out of the RV, we all stretched and took in the cool morning breeze.

"We're going to need to redo the spell again," Phoenix said quietly so nearby travelers wouldn't overhear.

It was early morning, but still the day after Thanksgiving, and there was no shortage of other travelers getting gas or walking inside the store and back.

Cordelia nodded. "Yes. We need to get more specific as to where she is. That's one reason I don't like using that big map, but we had to be sure she was still in the country."

Leah went to the front of the RV and started doing some movements I didn't understand. When she saw me looking at her oddly, she flashed a smile and said, "Just putting gas back into the tank," as if it was the most normal thing in the world to use magic for that.

I was beginning to think being a Seer wasn't nearly as cool as being a magic user.

"Okay, we'll meet back here in five and do another relocation spell," Phoenix said, eyeing the gas station's store. "I've got a date with a doughnut."

"That sounds amazing," I said, surprising myself. Perhaps getting to actually do something in the direction of helping Brandon had stirred some of the base functions of my body.

Cordelia nodded at Phoenix and went back inside the RV while I followed them into the store, grabbed a chocolate milk and a fresh-ly-baked doughnut, and paid with the wad of cash I'd stuffed into my pocket.

Once we were back inside the RV, we gathered around the kitchen table where Cordelia had spread out a smaller, more specific map of West Virginia that Phoenix had gotten from the store.

I sat on one of the chairs, out of the way, and happily drank the cool, refreshing milk as it washed down the doughnut I probably should have regretted eating but didn't quite yet. The next time I weighed myself on the scale might change my mind, but I was hoping I'd done so well lately that a single doughnut shouldn't be too bad.

The arcanists repeated their relocation spell, using the same pen-dant which still had my hair in it from last night. Dawn crept in through the thin curtains and for the first time in a while, I felt a bit of...not happiness exactly, but contentment without the overshad-owing darkness that had followed me around like my own personal gloomy cloud the last week.

It took a couple of tries for the spell again, since it kept wanting to point out where I was and not where Rose was, but it finally pinpointed another location other than the one we were at.

"Mmm," Phoenix said with a frown as they looked closer at where the pendant had stopped. "Hard to tell what's there, exactly, except for a bunch of greenery."

"Which is pretty much the whole map." Leah pulled her lips to the side in thought.

"Well, guess we'll drive there and see." Cordelia shrugged. "I don't like going in blind, but there's not much else we can do."

"It might help to put a transformation spell on the RV, so we're a bit more inconspicuous," Phoenix said, still staring at the map.

"That's not usually your style," Leah said with a teasing smile.

"Well, I didn't say it had to be ugly. Maybe like a bright red Ferrari or something," they said with a flip of their hand.

Cordelia shook her head with a smile while Leah chuckled and said, "That sounds more like it."

"You guys can really change an RV like this into looking like a smaller sports car?" I asked, wondering how hard it would be to become a magic user.

"Sure. It's easy." Phoenix shrugged and looked around the large interior. "Although...this spell might take two of us."

"Let's find a more secluded space to park, and then we'll change it." Cordelia folded up the map, almost as neatly as it had come out of the package.

Phoenix got into the driver's side this time while Leah went back into a bedroom, perhaps to catch a quick nap. Cordelia also went into the other bedroom she'd spent most of the night in already, so I crawled into the passenger seat.

"Alright, let's be real," I said after they had pulled out and gotten back onto the interstate. "When do you guys start threatening me to help you or lock me into a room so I can't escape, thereby turning me into your coven's personal Seer?"

Phoenix barked out a laugh and shook their head, the long side of their bright red hair waving. "So that's why you've been giving me the cold shoulder. Why do you think we're going to do any of that? It's not like I kidnapped you. In some perspectives, you could say I rescued you."

"Except when you showed up, the coven was expecting me. How did you know I ran away and didn't want to be found quite yet?" I gave them a pointed look and then went back to studying the oranges and browns of the year's last fading leaves.

West Virginia was a huge area of rolling mountains with trees everywhere, as far as I could tell from our interstate drive. Sure there were houses and small cities and stuff, but mostly, it was trees and hills.

"It's true that the matron wanted to meet with you, but that doesn't mean I didn't rescue you, either," Phoenix said with a sly tilt to their eyebrows.

I rolled my eyes. "Fine. So if I hadn't wanted to come with you? What then? Would you have kidnapped me?"

"Nah, honey. I can be quite persuasive if need be. You can't tell me you wouldn't have been interested in coming to meet the matron, especially if it helped you get more answers about Rose." Phoenix gave me a pointed look before turning their gaze back to the curving roads.

I sighed. "Fine. Yes, I'm sure I would have come with you anyway. I'm just so used to having everyone want something from me, I expect you guys to show your true colors at any moment. What about when all this is over? Will y'all let me go home to my family without locking me up in your basement?"

Phoenix rolled their eyes. "No, of course we won't lock you up. What do you take us for? Vampires? We're much more subtle than they are."

"Right. Because that makes me feel so much better."

"I didn't say that to make you feel better. It's just the truth." Phoenix smiled blandly.

We drove for a while, chatting about regular things like school, my family, and Phoenix's part-time job as a barista mostly because they loved coffee so much and wanted something to do rather than needing a job for the money.

The more we talked, the more I felt like Phoenix was pretty cool. I still wasn't ready to trust them with all my secrets, but they were pleasant enough to spend time with.

"So can I ask how you got involved with Rose? I mean, at what point did you think her plans were a good thing? Did she come to you and say, 'I really want those Seer glasses and if you ever see them, come get me?'" I asked at one point, finally putting words to part of the distrust I felt for them.

Phoenix pressed their lips in a regretful look while still keeping their eyes on the road. "Yeah, I'm sorry about that. It wasn't quite that condensed. As you grow older, I think you'll realize that relationships are hardly black and white, no matter what we want to think they can be as the dumb humans we are. Rose and I have been friends for many years. We'd both done research together and learned about the glasses. By the way, most of being a magic user is research. If you don't like putting your nose in a book for long hours, being a magic user is not for you."

There were lots of things I wanted to respond to from their comment, but I tried to stick to the important bits. "What did you learn about the glasses? Why does Rose even want them anyway?"

"Well, thanks to me, whatever she wanted to do with them, she's probably already done," they said with a wince.

"So you don't know what that was? I assume it was to talk to a dead person somewhere? But what would be so important that she'd risk popping into werewolf territory and battle it out to grab them? Or, if my memory is working right, which it doesn't always do, I think that's what she was after when she came for my grandma. I think she killed her for them. Did you know she was a killer?"

"Wow," Phoenix rubbed the back of their neck while shaking their head, "you sure know how to ask the hard questions. I don't know where to start. Let's go back to the black and white thing. Life just isn't that way for a normal human, and it's even more complicated when you start involving things like supernatural creatures. Is it murder to kill a zombie? What about a vampire?"

"Zombie, no. Definitely not. They're already dead and should probably get back to being dead."

"But vampires are already dead, too. So that's not murder? If I staked your vampire friend, wouldn't that be murder?"

"How did you know I have a vampire friend?"

"Doesn't everyone? Besides, it's my job to keep track of attractive men," Phoenix said with a side-smile.

"Right. Of course. So yes, it would be murder to kill a vampire, but if you do it in self-defense or if you know killing the vampire will save others, it would be okay. I think?"

Phoenix gave me a pointed look. "See? It's not so black and white. Yes, I knew Rose had killed people, both regular humans and supernatural creatures. Did I know about your grandmother specifically? No. I didn't."

"What about all the other Seers she's supposedly gone after? Did you know about them? Cordelia seems to know. I only know because we possessed a vampire queen who'd done research on Rose, which I still don't know why she did. But anyway, yeah. Did you know about the Seers?"

"I knew about some of them, yes."

"Why does Rose have it out for them? What's her angle there?" I fiddled with the lid of my empty chocolate milk bottle and stared out the window, wondering if I should be worried she'd come for me next.

Honestly, she wouldn't have time. I was coming for her.

A few splatters of rain started tapping on the windshield. The RV's wipers automatically responded, going up and down to clear the water. I hadn't even noticed the clouds coming over the morning sun as we'd traveled.

"Part of it was the glasses. I'm not sure what happened between her and your grandmother, but she was probably trying to threaten her life to get the answers she wanted, and then lost her temper."

"There was a gunshot. She wasn't even murdered by a cool spell or anything," I said, knowing I sounded psycho, but the candid talk with Phoenix had lowered my walls.

"Rose liked to use a gun because it usually fools the cops into looking at a human situation. Mysterious spells cause more issues, even if they are less traceable. Guns are so widely used, and they get overlooked more and more."

"I guess that makes sense, although it's stupid and horrible." I shook my head, thinking about the daily shootings I read about in the news.

"The other Seers probably met similar fates. If she has any kind of vendetta against Seers specifically, she never shared it with me. In fact, as far as I can see, she needs them for their hair to complete her ghost spells. It would make more sense to keep one alive so the hair would keep growing instead of killing one for only a limited amount of hair."

"Ugh, how can we talk about all this so calmly? It's super weird."

"Agreed," Phoenix flashed me a smile, "but life is super weird, especially for people like me and you. So do you think killing Rose would be murder? We'd save all those souls she would eat in the future to keep herself powerful and anyone else who would have been murdered for getting in her way."

"Depends on if she takes all those spirits with her," I said, shaking my head. "In one way to look at it, she's super old, so she should be dead already anyway. We'd be restoring things back to their natural order."

"In that case, I should probably be dead too." Phoenix glanced at a sign and flipped the turn signal on to get off the interstate.

"Oh, well. Right. How old are you?"

"Not as old as Rose but still getting close to one-fifty," Phoenix said, shooting me a teasing grin as they pulled the RV over onto an empty road.

The others came out of their rooms when they felt the RV slow to a stop and the engine shut off.

I followed Phoenix's lead and got out, making sure to grab my backpack just in case it got transformed with the RV.

Cordelia's greying bun bobbed on her head as she stepped out of the RV and looked around. "This will do."

It was mid-morning but there were grey autumn clouds crowding the sky. Even though the rain had stopped, the sun was still a muted white. Chilly air tried to claw its way into me, but my jacket did its job, at least in the places it could cover. I was glad I was wearing jeans though and not some leggings or a thin dress.

"How close are we to Rose?" Leah asked as she climbed out, carrying a purse as big as a beach bag.

"We know this is the exit to take, but beyond that..." Cordelia shook her head and shrugged.

"Wow, this relocation spell isn't much of a science, is it? Too bad y'all don't have a spell that can use the GPS to show us exactly where she is," I said, taking a slow turn around to look at the rolling mountains covered with those emptying, skeletal trees.

"Well," Leah said, taking the pendant out of her giant bag, "we do have this. It'll point us in the direction to go, a lot like a compass."

"And it doesn't yell at you if you go the wrong way," Phoenix grinned.

"Alright, let's transform the RV into something less obvious and get going. Hopefully, we'll have the element of surprise, and Rose won't be expecting us." Cordelia gestured to Leah to start the spell.

Leah put her bag onto the gravel, tucked the pendant snuggly into her jumpsuit pocket, and pulled out a candle and a hunk of some twisted root-looking thing. After lighting the candle, she started doing those weird arm movements and chanting as she slowly encircled the RV. Phoenix joined in the chanting and motions. After several rounds, but in between one blink and the next, a bright light flashed, and the ostentatious RV turned into an unassuming SUV.

"Wow, that's some magic right there." I blinked several times, trying to adjust my eyes from seeing spots.

Leah put the items back into her purse and rested for a moment, putting her hands on her thighs and bending over. "And it takes a lot of energy, too."

Phoenix didn't look as tired. I guessed it was because they were merely the assistant and not the primary caster of the spell.

Cordelia smiled kindly down at Leah even though she couldn't see her expression. "And we're grateful for your gift, sister."

Leah waved it off with a weak wrist before climbing into the passenger seat of the SUV with wobbly legs. Phoenix was there to spot her in case she fell.

Cordelia slid into the front seat while Phoenix and I climbed into the back. I couldn't help looking around inside trying to see if there was any indication of what had once been the RV. I didn't know what I was looking for, but it would have greatly amused me if there was a bunch of miniature furniture in the back. But alas, it all looked like a normal SUV.

The gravel cracked and crunched underneath our tires as Cordelia led us onto the center of the road and down into the countryside. There wasn't much to see beyond the trees and an occasional trailer or small house where someone had found some flat land within all these mountains. Leaves cluttered all over the sides of the hills and ditches, danced across the road, and sometimes tapped on the windows.

Leah got the pendant out again and held it up high enough to let the chain decide where it wanted to point. At first, it tried pointing at me several times, but after Leah gave it a stern talking-to, it began angling toward another direction. It wasn't necessarily the same way the road was going, but since there weren't many turn offs, we kept going down the gravel path in hopes that it would turn eventually and lead us to where we need to go.

After several minutes of travel, I began to wonder out loud. "Not to like diss your method or anything, but how will we know when we're close? It doesn't seem like a good idea to drive up to the place in open daylight."

Phoenix turned from where they had been looking out the window. "The pendant starts to vibrate the closer we get. As soon as it hits a certain stage, we'll pull over, probably take an awful walk into the soggy woods, and assess what we are going into. But I appreciate where your mind is. It wouldn't do just to drive up to whatever place and expect to maintain the element of surprise."

"Okay...and then what? March in there and demand that she let the ghosts go and stop doing dark magic? One of my ghost friends would be going crazy at our lack of planning right now," I said with a pang in my heart. Brandon would have hated how haphazard we were being with this whole thing.

"We have a few tricks up our sleeves," Cordelia said with a quick smile in my direction before she went back to driving.

"She's right about one thing though," Leah said, still holding the pendant aloft. "We'll probably have to imprison her at the least. She'll need to be given a trial by her peers, and then we'll enact whatever punishment the council deems appropriate."

I frowned. "Didn't you say that the council was afraid of her? Or perhaps even on her side? I don't see a trial doing much good."

The muscles around Cordelia's eyes tightened at my questions, but it was Phoenix who answered me. "I'm sure you must be worried that she will escape and come for you, but I assure you, we'll keep you safe."

"And all the ghosts she has and wants to enslave? Will they be safe too?"

Phoenix nodded, their smile feeling slightly condescending but perhaps that was my own fears projecting that into their look. "Yes, they'll be safe. We'll make sure Rose won't cause any more damage or pain."

I gave them a nod of understanding but couldn't help the titters of anxiety and concern that flitted through my chest. I wasn't sure if we were prepared for what we'd need to do or even if any of us could ethically do it, but one thing was sure. We needed to rescue those ghosts and stop Rose from eating more and do it before the necromancers closed in on her. They might not have had the location spells that the coven had, but I was certain they had contacts and means to get what they wanted.

I was reminded, momentarily, of the task I had been given to find a ghost for them, but that was going to have to wait. If they wanted the information bad enough, they'd just be grateful to get it, even if it came a few days later than they wanted. Once I got Brandon back, he and I could track down Susan, help Trina with Tracy's ghost, and we'd all get what we needed and wanted.

After another forty-five minutes of driving, the terrain not changing much except perhaps more trees and less residences, Leah put her hand up, and Cordelia pulled over nearly into a ditch. The road had long since became dirt instead of gravel, and we'd gone over so many bumps, I was worried about the car giving out on us completely. Sure, they probably could have magicked anything they'd need to fix it, but still, it was jarring.

"We're close," Leah said, her arm radiating with the pendant's vibrations.

"We'll go on foot from here. Tuck your pants into your socks if you don't want ticks. They might be out more in summer, but I wouldn't risk it. Also, make sure your phones are on silent," Cordelia said as she shut off the engine and opened the door.

It was nothing short of an obstacle course to get out of the car at the weird angle it'd been parked and back out onto the dirt road. We hadn't seen another car in some time, so I wasn't too worried about getting ran over.

We gathered together, Leah with her big purse over one shoulder, looking slightly better for the rest she'd had, Phoenix with their sequined backpack that had appeared from nowhere that I'd seen, and Cordelia with tall hiking boots she hadn't been wearing until just that moment. I put my backpack onto both of my shoulders and gripped the straps tightly.

"Before we go, can I ask why you're letting me come? I've half expected y'all to dump me off somewhere and tell me to sit like a good dog until you come back to pick me up," I asked, causing Phoenix to give me an amused smirk.

"Someone has got to make sure we free the ghosts correctly, right?" Cordelia said with a glance in my direction before taking note of where the pendant was pointing us toward.

Of course, it was straight into the woods.

"Plus, we'll protect you. We might not be as strong as vampires or as agile as werewolves, but we're definitely just as sexy and full of surprises." Phoenix gave me a pointed look with upraised eyebrows.

"I'm sure you are," I muttered mostly to myself as the others started off into the woods, stepping over the ditch again and crunching onto the dead leaves.

Chapter 14

The trek through the hills and trees was not super enjoyable on that cold November afternoon. We had to climb a few of the hills, sliding down leaves and mud. Despite it all, Phoenix handled it like a pro in their heels while I struggled in my tennis shoes. Even Cordelia's elderly body seemed to be stronger than she looked.

It didn't help that I'd only eaten a doughnut for the whole day and barely anything the week before. My head started to feel floaty and detached as my legs trembled and my stomach flopped angrily. I forced my body to continue anyway.

We didn't talk much, mostly because we were concentrating on making our way through the woods as quietly as we could. The whole point of walking, as opposed to driving right up to the place, was to keep the element of surprise.

Leah took the lead, following the pendant as it pointed in the direction for us to go, looking like some kind of tiny, metal puppy on a leash.

Excitement bubbled up through my exhaustion. I was going to finally confront Rose after weeks and weeks of feeling guilty for helping her and days and days of anguish and pain.

She might have underestimated me the last time we met, but I'd learned a lot since then, gotten a few more friends, and understood more about the insane things she was doing. We weren't going to let her get away with her villainous ways anymore.

And, if everything went well, I could be talking with Brandon in no time.

Thinking about him reminded me that I'd agreed to summon Frank when we reached our destination. He probably wanted revenge on Rose nearly as much as I did.

Still staying quiet, I mentally summoned him, picturing his long, dark hair, his Led Zeppelin t-shirt, and his distressed jeans. It took several seconds of focus before he popped in next to me, his hands on his hips as he surveyed our surroundings.

"Uhm, out for a hike in the woods, are we? What's crackin'?"

I was trailing behind the magic users, so I didn't feel too weird about responding physically to Frank's comments and questions. I shot him a shrug and gestured toward the magic users who were walking in front of me, talking quietly to themselves and navigating our way through the forest.

"Ah, it strikes me as amusing that you're going on a witch hunt with some witches. Do we have any idea of what we're walking into? This could be a super bad idea. Rose probably knows she has your hair and that these coven witches can track that. We know enough about Rose by now to know she is smart."

I gave him an annoyed look.

"What? I've had a lot of time to think while waiting for you to summon me like some kind of ghostly servant."

Chewing on my lip, I looked around at the trees rising above our heads with scraggly arms and fingers. Suddenly everything looked a lot more ominous. He was right. Of course Rose knew we could track her with my hair. She might not have understood how much I wanted Brandon back, but she certainly could figure out I would come for her at least for the family heirloom glasses she stole.

Just as I caught up with Phoenix and was about to tap them on the shoulder and voice my concerns, Leah stopped.

"I think it's up that hill," she said quietly, pointing with her free hand, the other still holding the pendant up. The necklace was sticking out ruler-straight and vibrating frantically as if it was excited as I had been moments ago before Frank crushed my dreams.

"Guys, I've been thinking..." I said, causing Cordelia to turn to me with an inquisitive eyebrow. "Wouldn't Rose know we'd do this very thing? She could be expecting us."

The three magic users looked at each other for a second before all three sets of eyes landed back on me.

"You may have a point," Phoenix said, their mouth tilting in a half-frown.

"Are we walking into a trap?" Leah asked, her eyebrows furrowed and gaze returning toward her matron.

Cordelia considered our words for a second and then looked back toward the hill. "Perhaps. But let's crest the hill and see what we can see. We'll test for wards and decide what to do from there. We've already come this far, and Rose has underestimated me in the past. I won't let her do that again."

Unease tickling my stomach, we tried to ascend the hill as quietly as possible. I slipped a few times on the wet leaves, earning concerned glances from Phoenix, but I ignored them.

Frank had no trouble walking, of course, with his feet going through the leaves to find the solid ground. It was odd that his feet could go through leaves and trees but land on the earth beneath them—another one of those weird ghostly rules of existence.

At least he didn't leave drips of plasma behind wherever he went. That would have been terrible to deal with.

As we neared the top, we all crouched low, trying to see over the hill without being seen ourselves. There was some good cover in the brush, but it would have been better during the warmer months when there was more greenery to cover us up.

"Looks like an innocent old lady's trailer in the middle of the woods," Leah said, stuffing the pendant into her pocket, and crouching down next to a wide tree.

Our hill overlooked a small, flat area with a road that snaked away from a neatly trimmed slanting yard surrounding a double-wide trailer with an overbearing garden. Statues, garden decorations, gnomes, pinwheels, and one large fountain were set around the trailer, and had there been a full garden of flowers to accompany it, the scene might have looked more friendly than creepy. As it was, chills were skittering down my back.

"Seems like a faraway place to live for an old lady all out on her own," Phoenix said, eyeing the scene.

"I can sense at least three wards in place," Cordelia said, her eyes bouncing from the trees, to the road, to the trailer, and back again.

Leah nodded, placed her purse onto the ground, and rummaged around for a few moments before finding a candle and a bundle of some kind of dried plant with white flowers. She set the candle in the leaves, which lit seemingly by itself as she crushed the plant in her fingers and sprinkled it down over the flame. Then picking up the candle, she brought it to her lips and blew toward the house.

In a flash that had me checking my eyebrows, the fire spread out, encircled the area like a big dome, and then dissipated as quickly as it had come.

"Nothing like a giant flash of fire to announce our arrival. Wouldn't it have been just as easy to trip her wards and risk that exposure?" I asked, sinking into the cold ground to sit down instead of continuing to crouch. My legs were burning so badly, it didn't matter if I got my pants caked in mud.

"It's a risk, to be sure, but it also dispels anything protecting the house, not just alarms signaling someone has trespassed, but anything that could have harmed intruders. As long as she doesn't visibly see it, she won't know her protections are gone," Phoenix said, watching the house below for signs of movement.

"Right. As long as she didn't see a bright light big enough that it was probably visible from space, we'll be fine," I muttered, earning an amused look from Leah as she put the candle back into her bag.

Cordelia stood, making sure to keep next to a wide tree, and shook her legs out. "Under normal circumstances, I'd advise us to wait here until it got dark so we could sneak in better, but as we're racing against the necroes and their night-loving pets, I say we go in now."

Phoenix nodded, stood, and helped Leah and I stand as well. "No time like the present."

"This could still be a trap." Frank shook his head.

"Now, time for trick number one," Cordelia said with a smile and nodded at Leah.

"Oh, I do love this part." Phoenix smoothed down the side of their hair that wasn't shaved with a grin.

"What part?" I asked, wondering if I should get more worried.

Leah pulled out four vials of liquid from inside her bag and handed them one-by-one to Cordelia who spoke a few words over each vial before giving them to us. I stared up at my vial, bringing it to eye-level so I could better inspect it. Whatever was inside looked like water, clear and empty, and probably full of microbes that were going to take over my body and make me a slave to the coven for the rest of my miserable life.

Once we all had one, Cordelia popped the top on hers and threw it back like she was a college girl downing shots at a bar. She swallowed and simply disappeared.

Leah and Phoenix followed her lead, Phoenix flashing me a teasing grin before winking out like a glitch in the matrix.

"Far out..." Frank said with an appreciative nod. "Maybe y'all won't come join me as a ghost after all. Thank goodness. I don't want to have to put up with you lot for the rest of eternity."

"Go ahead, Hanna." Cordelia's disembodied voice floated to me on the wind. "It won't hurt and will wear off in about twenty minutes."

"Yes, so hurry up before we run out of time," Leah said from somewhere nearby. "These aren't easy to make, and I only had enough for one dose."

I shook my head in disbelief as I popped the cap off my vial and poured it down my throat. It only burned a little, kind of like swallowing a wad of toothpaste, and my body tingled as the transformation took over. In awe, I lifted my hands and couldn't see anything. The world around me looked the same; I was simply missing from it.

"Okay, try to stay together. Rely on your hearing more than your sight. Hanna, if things get weird or dangerous, I want you to run. Got it?" Cordelia said.

I nodded before realizing no one could tell. "Got it."

Leah grunted her agreement while Phoenix let out a happy, "Mmmhmm."

Leaves crunched below our invisible feet as we moved over the crest of the hill and began our descent. Bushes moved out of our way, dried out weeds from the summer bent down under our weight, and hidden sticks snapped as we passed down the hill.

"Okay, so y'all are louder than a herd of elephants. Couldn't they do some kind of silent spell as well?" Frank asked, keeping a sharp eye on the ground to make sure he could follow us by our footprints.

I was doing the same because I certainly had no idea where anyone else was.

Once, I slipped on a muddy patch of leaves and only caught myself by grabbing onto a nearby tree trunk.

"Shh!" Someone hissed somewhere in front of me.

"Oof, sorry," I whispered, struggling to pull myself onto my feet again.

It was much easier to be quiet once we made it to the lawn, but lots harder to follow their footsteps. Looking for footsteps of flattened grass, I did my best to keep up with the group, surprised at how quiet they were when not having to worry about as many crunching leaves.

Of course they were still scattered around the lawn, but it was easier to avoid them than it had been in the woods.

Nothing had stirred at our approach, the trailer still looking the same with no old witch hobbling out to yell at us to get off her lawn. The wind brushed by, picking up the leaves for a dance and turning a few of the pinwheels in sporadic movements.

"You know, this wouldn't be a bad place to live, if you think about it," Frank said as we approached the trailer. "No neighbors bothering you, nobody walking past your house on the sidewalk, and the quiet whispers of the trees. Yeah, I could see myself settling down here to live out a quiet life in my old age."

I couldn't really respond without making sound, but my heart did go out to him. Poor kid died so young, he didn't even get to choose how he wanted to live his life. Perhaps his unfinished business was relaxing in the woods, rocking on the porch, smoking a pipe, and waiting for an errant deer to come onto his property so he could shoot it and have meat for the winter.

Once we got to the front yard, I stopped, unsure what everyone else was planning. Were they going to go in through the front door? That seemed too easy, somehow. But it would be dumb to climb into the window when an arcanist could just pop open a lock at the front door.

It was neat that we were invisible but like...I had no idea what the others were doing or planning to do. If it weren't for grumpy-old-man Frank, I would have felt very alone as I stood in the crunchy, leaf-covered grass.

After a few moments, there was a soft popping sound, and the front door eased open. Shrugging to myself, I hurried to get past the front door before someone closed it on me.

"Hey!" someone, sounded like Leah, whispered harshly as I made my way through the doorway and bumped into something solid that I couldn't see.

"Sorry," I whispered as loudly as I dared.

I slowly, very slowly, shut the door behind me, easing it closed and hoping everyone was inside that wanted to be. The house was brightly lit compared to the dull, cloudy autumn day outside. Nearly almost all the lights were on, reflecting off the polished hard-wood floors, and presenting a cheerful front room with light green furniture, a neatly set coffee table, and a side table with plants like one might find in some fancy magazine. A delicious smell also welcomed us into the house that reminded me of a mouth-watering soup, with bread to dip, and a cinnamon muffin to chase it down with. Soft music even played from a speaker somewhere that was some kind of classical song with string instruments and no vocals.

Everything was quiet, aside from the background music, as we stood and tried to figure out what to do next. Or at least that's what I assume everyone was doing. Mostly, I was looking for signs of move-ment.

"Well, this is definitely not what I'd picture if someone said we'd be going to a witch's house. You can stay here. I'll check out the other rooms," Frank said as he walked through the wall toward what I assumed was the kitchen.

I heard faint footfalls as the others moved around. No one said anything in case there was anyone nearby. Unsure of what to do and waiting for Frank to come back and report what he'd found, I turned around on a whim and tried the door, just to make sure we were able to leave.

It was locked.

I jiggled the handle again, not caring about being quiet. It didn't matter how many times I turned the lock, the handle, or the deadbolt, the door stayed firmly and unequivocally shut.

Frank came back as I turned around, fear clutching my chest.

"So the whole place is empty. There's three bedrooms, two bathrooms, the master having a quite sizable jacuzzi bathtub, but no people. Or ghosts for that matter," Frank said, looking around the front room with hands in his pockets. "If it weren't so perfectly creepy, this place would be really nice."

"We're stuck, you guys," I said in a normal-volumed voice, no longer worried we'd get caught for breaking and entering.

We'd clearly walked right into a trap like a bunch of lemming strolling off the edge of a cliff.

"What do you mean stuck?" Phoenix said with a strained whisper from somewhere near the happily crackling fireplace.

"The door won't open. Locked or unlocked. It's stuck," I said, trying the door again to make sure I wasn't being a dumb blonde and messing it up somehow.

It still didn't budge.

"Let me try a window," Leah said as I watched the two latches on the front window snap open. Despite being unlocked, the window didn't move at all. "It's stuck, too."

"Groovy," Frank said with a frown and nodded his head. "Just what I wanted to hear."

A huge sigh came from the couch as an impression of someone sitting on it appeared without being able to see the someone. "I should have realized she'd cast this spell. Wow, I'm an utter failure as a matron.

I've led you guys right into this. I suppose the Rose supporters are right. She's smarter than me and should be running the coven."

"Ugh, don't say that," Phoenix said as another indention was made on the couch. "Even if she is smarter than you, which I don't agree with, it doesn't matter. Brains aren't as important as heart when it comes to leading a coven. Can you imagine what kind of havoc she would cause if she had influence over so many magic users? We'd be at war with the humans before you could blink."

"I'd never follow her, and I know the matron of the mid-west coven wouldn't follow her either, so not only would she bring a war of humans, but she'd bring a war of covens. Phoenix and I could have realized we were walking into this spell, too, but we didn't. This isn't all on you," Leah said from still nearby the window.

I made my way to the armchair and plopped into it. "Frank says the rest of the house is empty, if you guys were worried about that."

"Who's Frank?" Phoenix asked.

At the same time, Cordelia said, "Of course it's empty. We're trapped inside a picture."

"Wait—what? A picture?" I said, my face curling into confusion which no one could see.

"Yes." Cordelia sighed again. "It's a transformation spell. It must have been set on the porch or even the threshold of the doorway. Once we walked in, we were effectively put into a picture. It was a good spell choice on Rose's end because it didn't need to 'see' us and didn't need wards to protect it. And we're trapped until she decides we're not. Even more fun, if something happens to the hard copy of the picture, wherever that is, that same thing will happen to us."

The room was quiet for a few seconds as my slow brain took in her words.

"So..." I finally said after a bit, "how do we break it? How do we get out?"

Cordelia's third sigh sounded more like an inhaled sob. "We don't."

"But I've seen you guys do some amazing things, and you're the matron of a whole freaking coven!" I didn't mean to yell, but it was hard not to feel panicked. "Surely you can do something to get out of it!"

Her only answer was a few wavery breaths.

"If we weren't invisible, would she be able to see us inside the picture?" I asked, trying to wrap my mind around the whole thing.

"And also, since she's trapped a ghost, is the picture now haunted? Am I visible inside the picture as a super cool scary shadow or is my presence as nonessential as ever?" Frank asked, taking a seat in front of the fireplace with his butt on the hearth and his knees high enough to comfortably rest his elbows.

"Like she said, the only one who can let us out is the one who cast the spell," Leah said, sounding slightly annoyed by my inability to accept our situation.

"Or if someone managed to get a hold of the picture," Phoenix added, their tone softer and more thoughtful. "And Hanna has a point. We still have about ten minutes of invisibility. Rose might not realize she's caught us yet. Maybe we can use that to our advantage, somehow."

"Yeah? How?" Leah challenged.

"Well, if she's planning on burning it once we're trapped, that will keep us from being burnt for a time, at least," Phoenix mused.

I rolled my eyes, probably acting sassier than I would have if they could have seen me. "Great. So we've got ten minutes to live. Awesome."

"Shall I try popping out of here and go to my haunt? Or maybe you should try summoning another ghost here who might be able to get a message out there about us?" Frank asked, his lips pulled into a thoughtful pucker.

"Time enough for you to explain who Frank is," Phoenix said, apparently having not forgotten my mention of him.

"He's a ghost that Rose had trapped for a while, but I was able to set him free the last time I saw Rose. He's hanging out by the fireplace wondering if how much of spell will react to ghosts."

Cordelia cleared her throat. "Why didn't you say there was a ghost here? We can use that."

I rolled my eyes again. "If I told you every single time I spotted a ghost, I'd never shut up. I'm a Seer. Who else do you think I hang around with all day?"

"You seem to be forgetting that not every Seer can keep ghosts with them. Ghosts can't usually leave their haunt, remember?" Phoenix said, finding some snap to their voice after all.

I probably was speaking to the matron of a witch's coven too harshly, but yeah, I'll admit it, I kind of blamed her for our situation. How could she have let us walk into such a simple trap?

"Oh, right. Sorry. I'm feeling..."

"I'm sure we're all feeling similar frustration and worry," Leah said, her voice softening in a type of apology.

"So how can Frank help us get out of here? He wants to try popping back to his haunt to see if he can leave, but even if that works, will I be able to summon him back? I'm not sure it's worth the risk if he gets free without any kind of plan first," I said, asking questions and answering Frank's at the same time.

Cordelia's voice sounded more stable and less nasally the more she spoke. "Ghosts are essentially beings in another dimension able to exist in ours in some ways while working beyond the rules in other ways. Seers have the power to see beyond this dimension to communicate with ghosts. It sounds weird but makes sense if you think about it."

I nodded unnecessarily, but it was hard to stop using body language just because no one could see it. "Right. I'm with you so far... I think."

"So a ghost also messes with normal spells focused on working within the realms of our dimension. The picture spell is not used often because it interacts with another dimension. It has to place objects into something that's 2D and physically exists in our normal realm. The spell doesn't take into account something from an entirely different dimension."

"She's going to use up all our time just trying to explain this to us," Frank muttered as she continued talking.

"If a ghost was able to be transported into this place from where we were, theoretically, the ghost may be able to travel out again to the physical place and not necessarily have to go back to the haunt. I have no idea how your powers work, Hanna, but we could theorize that as long as the ghost is near the picture where you are stuck, he should be able to exist outside his haunt. Maybe."

"So you've wasted a bunch of words just to say that you think he'll be able to leave and go exist in the real world next to the picture? What good will that do? And if I eat something from the kitchen in this dimension, will that mean I'm technically eating paper?"

Cordelia took a second to recover from my abrupt change in questions. "Yes. It's helpful because he could investigate what's happening outside, perhaps even make contact with the coven so they could help us. At the very least, he could see where the picture is being held so we can start to form a plan."

"Ugh, we need to get better at this planning thing," I said, folding my arms and staring at the ceiling.

Phoenix sighed. "I've forgotten how frustrating teenagers can be. Just follow what the matron says, alright? She knows what she's talking about and is smart enough to figure out how to get us out of here, if anyone is."

Cordelia murmured a soft, "thank you," and sniffed again.

"Well, it's not really up to me. Is it? Frank?" I asked, turning back to look at him where he still sat by the fire. "Do you feel like going on a field trip?"

"Better than sitting around here with you boring lot," Frank said, standing, and dusting off his pants despite the dust not being able to stick to them.

"He says he'll go. What exactly do you want him to look for and how exactly does he get out of here when we can't?" I asked, turning back where I thought Cordelia was sitting.

"Just go through the wall. It should pop him back out of the picture," Cordelia said.

Phoenix jumped in. "Look for anything that can give us clues. Where the real picture is being held, if anyone is watching it, and anything else he can see. Also, try to go as far away from it as he can go, so we know the limits."

"Won't he only go outside like where we were before we walked in here?" I asked, taking a peek out of the window, noting that it was still the dreary autumn afternoon scene.

"We can't be sure exactly when we walked into the trap, but it's got to be nearby. If he ends up outside like we were, he should keep walking until the terrain changes," Cordelia said.

I frowned. "This doesn't make any sense but whatever. Frank, you heard her. I have no idea how far away you'll be able to get from me without having to go back to your haunt. If I don't hear back from you in ten minutes, I'll summon you back here. If that doesn't work, well then, I guess we're screwed."

"Awesome. See you in a bit." Frank gave me a half-hearted wave before walking directly through the wall to the outside.

Silence descended on us as we waited. I fiddled with my fingers, wishing I could see them enough to check for hangnails.

Phoenix coughed awkwardly. "Perhaps we should be working on a plan B while we wait. What else can we do? How can we use this invisibility? If we had longer, we might be able to use it, but as it is, we'll run out and be present inside the picture in a mere few minutes. That's not nearly enough time to get someone to prevent Rose from seeing we've fallen into her trap...even if someone has coincidentally been in the same place the picture is and can teleport there to help us."

Leah sighed. "There's not enough time. What do you think will happen once she realizes we're in the picture?"

"Oh, I don't think you'll have to worry about that," a voice said as the front door opened, and a figure stepped inside. "It was quite clever to use an invisibility potion, to be sure, but too bad for you, I have excellent hearing."

My eyes widened as I turned to the door, and, once I saw who it was, my body had several instinctual responses. The first was my heart began pounding in my chest in such a way I was afraid it would bounce right out. The second was blood rushed away from my face, perhaps in fear. The third was that my hands balled into fists, and I had to forcibly keep my legs from jumping up so I could punch her in the face.

Chapter 15

None of us spoke, probably frozen in fear and shock, hoping we still had the advantage of being unseen.

Although it was obvious she knew we were there.

Perhaps if we'd been able to see each other, we could have coordinated some kind of attack, but as it was, we stayed in our seats, barely daring to breathe.

"Now now, don't go all silent on me. I know there are three magic users and one young Seer visiting me in my cozy cottage. Aren't you relieved I picked this picture for you to rest in instead of something more dangerous? I'm sure you wouldn't enjoy hanging around with a bunch of tigers. Even in paper form, they can leave some nasty cuts," Rose said as she shut the door behind her and looked around the room as if she knew where each of us was sitting.

She looked as elegant as ever, her blonde hair piled neatly atop her head with no strand out of place, a flowery blouse, pressed jeans, and black booties. In fact, she looked like she fit right in with the perfect photo, model good-looks and all.

Leather creaked as one of the magic users stood up, and since Cordelia spoke first, I assumed it was her, "You do realize moving against a matron will bring the whole coven in on you. It'll only be a matter of time before they hunt you down."

The ice in the matron's voice surprised me.

Rose laughed, her head tilted back in an endearing way that made me madder. "Oh, so they'd use the location spell and end up somewhere similar to this? I'm so scared."

"Let us out, and we can avoid the whole mess," Phoenix said, also standing if I could judge from more couch leather creaking.

"And you. You were my friend. I have to say the betrayal hurts, even if it's not surprising," Rose said, shaking her head.

"I can't stand by and let you devour souls. Your friendship meant a lot to me, and watching you turn to darker magic has been more painful for me than my apparently expected betrayal has hurt you." Phoenix's voice was low enough, it almost felt like they were growling.

Rose pouted her ruby red lips. "Aw, poor Phoenix. How sad for you. Without your conscience, you'd be free to do what you'd like. Do you want me to fix that for you?"

A popping sound disoriented me for a second and then Rose grunted, grabbing something in front of her. "Are you that stupid? This is *my* spell!"

Her fingers looked like they were wrapped around something nearing the size of a coffee cup but judging from the height of it and some choking sounds, I was willing to bet she had a hold of someone's throat.

"Leah!" Cordelia shouted.

"Let her go!" Phoenix yelled at the same time.

Jumping up, unable to sit there while this insanity was going on, I charged toward Rose, letting fury fuel my steps.

Rose merely lifted a hand, and I was frozen—unable to move, unable to put my foot down that was still raised into the air. Though I was grateful that at least my vital organs were able to function or I would have keeled over right there.

"I suppose you simply don't understand the situation," Rose said into the heavy silence.

The only things I could hear were ragged breaths around me and some gurgling from Leah. Rose must have frozen us all.

"You are my prisoners. You are under my complete control. You're only still alive because I will it. Why do you think it's possible to rise against me inside my own spell? Truly pathetic."

She pushed forward with her hand and released Leah's neck. There was a thunk and several scuffling sounds that made me think Leah was scrambling away from Rose as fast as she could.

"Until I can figure out what to do with you, I've only come to tell you that all your plotting will be for nothing. You might as well enjoy yourselves, take a nap, eat some snacks, and ponder your sad existence as you stare out the window at the rain. In the meantime, I'm going to use my newfound knowledge to prepare for the incoming necromancers and enjoy syphoning all their souls. Did you know that eating a necromancer soul, one that can control other souls, is about as delicious as a soul can get? It'll be fun to see how many I can nab."

With a smirk, Rose left the cozy scene through the door again. Once the door shut behind her, several thuds clued me in that everyone was unfrozen and probably as sprawled out on the ground as I was.

Finally able to move, I jumped up and ran to the door. Knowing I was dumb but too hopeful to deny it, I jiggled the handle in hopes that she'd been forgetful enough to leave it open.

Of course, she hadn't been, but if she had and I hadn't tried, then I would have been really extra dumb.

Panting, I turned around, leaned on the door, and smacked my head back against it a few times. "I can't believe this."

"I prefer to stay positive, if I can," Phoenix said while we watched their hand flicker back into existence, "but she's beginning to beat it out of me."

In a matter of seconds, our bodies were all visible again, mine appearing last since I'd drank the potion last. Cordelia and Phoenix were crouched down next to Leah who had backed up against the far wall. She was upright and breathing, but it sounded labored and harsh red marks surrounded her throat.

"It's alright," Cordelia said, wavering her fingers over Leah's neck and chest. "Just focus on breathing."

Slowly, Leah was able to get back in control of her lungs, and while the marks didn't go away, at least she'd stopped coughing and wheezing as much.

Cordelia and Phoenix helped Leah get up and find a more comfortable place on the couch. Once she was situated, Phoenix started pacing back and forth in front of the window. They ran their fingers through their hair over and over as they muttered to themselves.

Cordelia stayed next to Leah, held her hand, and rubbed her back.

As for me, I kept staring at the ceiling as if it would suddenly break over our heads into a million pieces, taking the spell with it.

"In all the centuries magic users have been around that pictures have also been around, you guys have never figured out a way to break this spell?" I asked. "It seems laughable that something so simple feels so dooming."

Phoenix paused in their pacing long enough to give me an icy glare. "That's not helping. This kind of spell hasn't been used much since the seventies and was usually cast on humans, not fellow magic users."

Their anger at me didn't do anything but fuel the rage I was already feeling. "Well excuse me for being a stupid human with no understanding of spells and crap. We can't simply give up and roll over just because Rose tells us to. There's got to be something we can do!"

Cordelia gave Leah's hand a squeeze before letting go and walking toward me. As she drew nearer, I wondered if I should brace myself for a good smack.

Instead, she hugged me.

Maybe she'd been appointed matron, or however that worked, because she was compassionate and knew that grumpy teens just needed hugs.

Whatever the reason, it eventually worked to relieve some tension. After a few seconds, my body relaxed, and, while I didn't hug her back very well, I didn't push her away either.

"If there's one thing I've learned from my many years of being alive, it's that bad things usually get better. Life isn't as bleak as it feels when we're in the heart of it," Cordelia said into my hair before releasing me and grabbing onto my shoulders.

"So how are we going to get out of here?" I said after clearing my throat a few times.

"We may not know how right this second, but the way will become clear." Cordelia smiled and rubbed my shoulders a few times before turning back to Phoenix and Leah. "Who's up for baking some cookies?"

Hours or only half-hours later, I had no idea, we were sitting around the dining room table in our perfect homey magazine picture eating cookies that tasted real enough to me and drinking cool glasses of milk.

All in all, there really could have been worse places to be locked up.

It was kind of fun, in a I-need-to-be-distracted way, to watch Leah, Cordelia, and Phoenix chat about different things that had happened with the coven members lately and hear some interesting stories from Leah's coven.

I worried about how much my mom and Trina were worrying. Last time, they'd gotten tangled up with the necromancers, thanks to Noah's help, and came to rescue me from the dungeon of a vampire queen. This time, being stuck inside a magic user's picture seemed a lot more hopeless, no matter how daunting it had been to infiltrate an entire vampire seethe.

At least it had been in the corporeal world.

"Oh! I forgot to call Frank back," I said, suddenly sitting up and interrupting whatever Phoenix had been saying.

Cordelia furrowed her eyebrows and looked down at the half-eaten plate of cookies. "Uh oh, we seem to be experiencing some of the side effects of the spell."

"What are you talking about?" I asked, shuffling my thoughts around so I could focus on Frank and getting him back.

"Part of this spell, which is probably even more scary than the fact that we're trapped, is that we start to become part of the picture," Phoenix said while shaking their head as if to clear it from cobwebs. "If I start wanting to cut my hair into something 'normal' and change into some manly pants or something, you know we've got a problem."

"Well, one good thing about all of us being in here together is that we can keep taking turns helping the others to focus. Being trapped in here alone would be a difficult struggle to keep on task, to be sure," Leah said, dusting her fingers from the cookies and getting up to put her glass into the sink.

Fighting through a weird fog, I was finally able to picture Frank in my head with his jeans and his t-shirt and his long, dark, wavy hair.

"Did you forget about me?" Frank popped in, sitting on top of the kitchen counter, his legs crossed with an annoyed look on his face. "For being your only hope out of here, you sure took your time."

"Honestly? Yeah. Apparently, that's part of the spell in here. If we stay too long, we're going to become part of the picture," I said, interrupting whatever Cordelia had been saying.

The magic users looked at me for a second and then figured out I was talking to Frank.

"Is he back?" Leah asked.

"What did he learn?" Cordelia added.

I looked at Frank expectantly so he could answer the question.

"I see y'all are visible again. It's much easier being able to see what I'm talking to," Frank said, hopping off the counter and coming toward the plate of cookies. "I bet those smell amazing."

"That's rich coming from a ghost who no one can see," I said, rolling my eyes.

"Hey, you can see me."

"Whoopee."

Frank turned away from the cookies and frowned. "I can see you're in a fine mood. Did you eat a cookie or three? I think you could use it."

I kept glaring at him until he started talking again.

"Alright. Fine. So the spell must have started once we'd walked into the house because as soon as I stepped out, I was somewhere else entirely." He took a seat on a barstool next to the island since all the dining room chairs were taken.

"Okay, what did you see?" I asked, mostly for the benefit of our audience so they could follow at least half of where our conversation was going.

"Basically, a tiny metal room. There was a big garage door at one end, but other than that, there were no other exits or entrances. You may be happy to know your picture is inside one of those lady magazines with pictures of rooms and decorations and stuff."

"So happy to know that," I said flatly. "It sounds like a storage unit."

He shrugged. "At least you're not stuck in a horror picture. That's got to be nice of her. Maybe she's not as bad as we think?"

"She enslaved you and ate several of your ghost friends. Is that not bad enough? Oh, and while you were gone, she paid us a little visit saying she was going to keep us here until she could figure out what to do and then she choked Leah." I gestured to the blonde witch who rubbed at her neck with the memory. "So is that not bad enough for you?"

"Wow, glad I wasn't here for that." Frank gave Leah's neck a glance and shook his head. "Okay, she's as bad as you want to label her. Well, as far as I could see, the place was empty except for a few boxes that contained mostly candles and clothes. It was dark, but I couldn't go too far away from the magazine, and you, I assume. Fun fact, though. There were three other ghosts in there, and they seemed excited to see me."

I frowned. "Okay... So it's a haunted storage unit with a random *Home and Garden* magazine. How are we supposed to work with that?"

Cordelia chewed on her lip as she took in my words. "Does he know where the storage unit is?"

"No idea, and the ghosts there were sent to guard the magazine." Frank scooted up on his stool so he was nearly on the edge. "Apparently, Rose can leave a crystal in a place, summon the ghosts that are contained in there, and then leave, basically giving them a temporary haunt."

"Oh. So that's how your haunt changed once I freed you. The crystal must become like a haunt itself. That's pretty cool to know, at least. Still not sure how it can help us right now though," I said with a frown. Somewhere in the back of my mind, I wondered if Brandon's haunt would get changed too, but I didn't take the time to pursue that line of thought.

"The other ghosts had an idea," Frank said with a sly twist to his mouth.

"They did? Why didn't you say that in the first place?" I gave him an annoyed glare.

"You were too busy being a surly teenager." Frank's teasing grin did nothing to make me feel better.

"So...what did they say?"

"They watched her cast the spell inside the garage. They think they know how to break it."

"I have several questions, but one of them is why didn't you come right back here and let me know all this instead of waiting for me to summon you back? Were you stuck outside the picture?"

"Yes, exactly. I couldn't get back in. Eventually, I just went back to my haunt, figuring you'd call me when you needed me. It sucks feeling used like this." He sighed dramatically.

Rolling my eyes, I turned to Cordelia and filled her in with what Frank had said.

The matron nodded. "Interesting."

Turning back to Frank, I asked, "So how do we break the spell? Are they even able to move against Rose since she's captured them?"

"She only instructed them to alert her should someone come into the garage or something happen to the magazine. Even as her slaves, we only have to obey the direct commands. And one other cool fact, I guess your presence inside the magazine is strong enough that even being near the picture has strengthened the ghosts."

"Oh, right. I can do that. I also know that a ghost can take energy from me enough to be able to touch and manipulate material items. Will they need to do that to break the spell?" I asked, trying to think through things while my brain felt like taking a nap.

"Just because they watched her cast the spell, does not mean they know how to undo it," Leah pointed out with wobbly smile.

"That's fine, because we do," Phoenix said, their grin moving into something more confident.

"Wait, first, what did the ghosts think would break the spell? They will wait for you to get back before trying anything, right?" I asked, feeling a wave of concern.

Frank's reassuring nod started out strong but slowly waned. "Well, I'd hope so. I do have to say that I don't really know them at all, and they did seem pretty young..."

"Do you smell that?" Leah asked, furrowing her eyebrows.

"Did we leave the oven on?" Phoenix looked toward the innocent-looking steel appliance.

"Oh, that might be them trying to get y'all out," Frank said with a worried look toward the front room. "What did you say would happen if they set fire to the paper?"

"She said we'd all burn down with them! Please tell me you didn't let them think lighting the picture on fire was a good idea!" I said, my eyes widening as the smell of smoke grew stronger.

Cordelia cursed and stood from the chair as if she could somehow stop it. "Tell him to go out there right now, put the fire out, and instead, roll up the whole magazine, and dip it into some pure water mixed with turmeric."

"Where do you suggest we get turmeric?" Frank asked, his face scrunching up in confusion.

Dark smoke started billowing out of the front room and into the kitchen while the air felt dry and very, very warm.

"Go tell them to stop lighting us on fire! We'll figure out the rest later!" I urged Frank, covering my mouth and nose with my shirt in hopes it would help me breathe better.

"Right, because I'm just the errand boy," he said, muttering under his breath as he walked through the front room and back out the door.

"Hurry up, hurry up, hurry up," I said, standing from the table and going to the sink to see if the water would still run.

It did, but it was super-hot to the touch.

Phoenix and Leah got underneath the table, finding better air to breathe, and after messing with the sink and coughing like an elderly lady who had smoked her whole life, I followed their lead and sunk onto the floor. Cordelia was crawling toward the back door in the kitchen, probably in hopes that it would somehow miraculously open and let us all out to safety.

Hissing and cursing, Cordelia pulled her hand back from the doorknob. It must have been too hot to even check to see if it was locked.

The heat sunk into my clothes, sweat dripped off my forehead, and we all grouped together into the corner that seemed to be the least affected by the fire, as far as we could tell.

After a moment where I was sure that Frank had left us to melt into bloody popsicles, a whooshing, sizzling sound erupted, and we were all soaking wet. But I didn't even care because at least the smoke and heat had stopped trying to murder me.

Chapter 16

"Well..." I said, blinking water and smoke out of my eyes and standing.

The picture had been doused, judging from what I could tell. The fire had burnt up most of the living room, basically closing us off into the dining room and part of the kitchen. It was weird because the walls came in and ran through the house in odd angles and places, keeping us locked into the spell. One wall cut through the dining room, almost hitting the table but ended at the kitchen island. Another wall started in the middle of the kitchen sink and sliced through the room, so we only had use of half of it.

As for the walls themselves, they only looked singed. Water flowed off the counters, pooled onto the floor, and dripped from the curtains. Somehow, it managed to drain away until things were only mostly wet.

"If that fire had lasted any longer, we'd have been burnt up," Phoenix said, bending down to help Cordelia stand.

Leah scrambled to help the matron as well. "Doesn't look like the water they used was mixed with turmeric though, since we're still inside the spell."

"I'm not surprised. They probably used the closest water they could get to. The odds of having turmeric nearby in a storage shed seem pretty low." I pulled my jacket off and draped it onto the back of a chair. Droplets of water fell onto the floor from the sleeves while I wrung out the bottom half of my t-shirt.

"On the other hand, if the shed has supplies from which Rose used to make the spell, there could be other things they might find, maybe even turmeric," Leah said pinching her shirt at the top and trying to fluff it dry.

"If I were a smart magic user, I would not keep the ingredients needed to undo the spell next to where the spell was being kept. Maybe that's just me, but..." I plopped down onto the chair with my jacket, relieved to see that the water seemed to be evaporating quickly, probably because we were inside paper.

Phoenix nodded and helped Cordelia sit into a chair and sat down in the one next to her and beside mine. "Fair enough. It's probably not nearby. At least we didn't lose the cookies."

They gestured to the plate in the middle of the table that looked a bit soggy but was drying by the second. If this had been a real world, the cookies would have been a crumbly mess, even dry, but inside the photo they retained their size and shape.

"Dang it, I lost my backpack," I said with a frown and a glance toward where the front room used to be. "I'll summon Frank back in a second so he can update us on what they're planning to do. I don't like being stuck somewhere dependent on ghosts to get me out. They aren't the most reliable creatures, even if their memories work decently. I've been thinking, though. We must have been sent inside the spell once we'd set foot inside the house, but how did that work if the paper is in a storage unit somewhere?" I asked, pulling my phone out of my jacket pocket and inspecting it for any damage.

"I lost my bag of supplies, too," Leah said with a pout.

"Did you have any turmeric in there, by chance?" I asked, giving her an ironic smile.

She shook her head. "No. Didn't have that, but there were lots of other things that could come in handy."

Cordelia patted her hand that was resting on the table as Leah sat in the seat across from Phoenix. "It's okay, dear. Once we get out of here, we can teleport back home and grab the things we need."

"So one reason this spell fell out of use fifty years ago is because of the way you have to set it up." Phoenix shifted in their seat as they answered my question. "You have to put the trigger of the spell somewhere different than the paper you're keeping the target in. I'm not sure why, but whoever invented the spell had to work out some kinks to get it to work, and one of those kinks was that the paper and the trigger have to be in separate places."

"Probably because it would be unlikely for a person to step on a piece of paper as the trigger. At least magic users would know better, and humans would probably simply step around the paper, in most cases." Leah ran her fingers through her drying hair, trying to keep it from becoming frizzy, but without a hair dryer it was likely a lost cause.

"Maybe. At any rate, the trigger point and the paper are kept in separate places. Oh, I just had a thought. Maybe it's because the paper could get sucked into the paper spell, too. That would cause a whole weird world of paradoxes inside the spell, and, not to mention, making it much more difficult to end the spell for whoever was casting it," Phoenix said.

"I suppose that makes sense." I shrugged. "Well, whatever. How are we going to get our ghosts to grab some turmeric if they can't leave their haunt or leave me?"

"Forgive me if I'm asking something dumb, I'm not sure how the ghost rules work exactly, but could one of them carry the paper around while they go somewhere to get the turmeric?" Leah asked, still trying to smooth out her hair.

I blinked a few times and scrunched my eyebrows as I considered her words. "You might be onto something. If they keep me with them, then they can travel outside their haunt, and if they use up my energy instead of their own, they can safely materialize and hold onto the paper, thus carrying me with them. It's kind of genius, actually."

Leah smiled and blushed under my compliment.

"If they're material, though, will they be able to go through walls and say...through a storage shed door?" Phoenix asked.

"Yeah, they'll have to do things the old-fashioned way." I finally decided to turn on my phone. Perhaps if Mom was using her location app to find it, she'd see it pop up where the picture was instead of where we'd traveled to trigger the spell.

"So if they're somehow able to open the door from the inside, perhaps one could go through the door and help from the outside. Unfortunately, that will trigger the wards Rose has likely placed around the storage unit." Cordelia tapped her shriveled fingers on the table.

"That probably wouldn't be good. I bet she'd teleport there right away and figure out what was happening." I sighed. "Great. Another plan shot in the foot before we can even get started."

"I feel like I'd be happy as long as they don't set fire to our paper again." Phoenix raised their eyebrows and shook their head in incredulity.

"Right?" Leah chuckled.

"What if Rose is distracted with something else that is more important than the wards on her storage shed?" I asked, waving my phone around to find some service.

Phoenix sat back in their chair and crossed one arm over their chest and rested the other on their chin. "Hmmm... That may give us a better chance of escaping, but what could we use that would be enough of an important distraction?"

"I bet the necromancers finding her would be a good distraction... Too bad we don't know how to get them a message or where to send them," I said with a side-frown, still waving my phone around.

"You know there isn't going to be service inside a witch's spell, right?" Leah asked, her eyes following my phone as I waved it.

Sighing, I turned it back off to conserve battery and put it down onto the table. "Yeah, I was just hoping for some kind of miracle."

"Let's summon Frank back and see if they have come up with any ideas," Cordelia said.

"That don't include lighting our picture on fire." Phoenix gave me a pointed look.

Nodding, I closed my eyes and pictured Frank again in my head. I must have been getting better at it with him because it didn't take long before he popped in next to the table.

"Wow, this place looks different," he said, eyeing the wall that went halfway through the kitchen.

"What do you think happened when we got set on fire?" I asked, giving him my best sassy teenager head bob.

"Hey, it wasn't me! I told you, those other ghosts are young, impulsive, the older two girls are as snotty as you."

I rolled my eyes. "I'm a downright peach, and you know it."

It was his turn to roll his eyes.

"So we're guessing y'all didn't find any turmeric inside the shed?" I asked, glancing at the three magic users who were attentively listening to my half of the conversation.

He shook his head. "None. We did find a couple spiders, though, if that helps?"

I gave him a flat look. "We're thinking that if one of y'all can use my energy to carry the paper around, then your haunt will be portable and can go find some turmeric."

"Kinda smart but still not sure where to go to find that. Even if I went to a store, I don't exactly have a bunch of cash on me to buy it," Frank said, pointing out another flaw in my plan.

I sighed and put my forehead onto the table. "Plus, if y'all opened the storage unit door, we're pretty sure it would set off wards that would summon Rose. We thought if there was some kind of distraction at the same time that was more urgent, it would at least delay her for a time."

Frank shrugged. "Could work."

"Frank pointed out that he wouldn't know where to go to find turmeric, and even if he did find some in a nearby store, he didn't have any cash to buy it. It wouldn't work for us to give him money as he wouldn't be able to take it out of the spell with him," I said, informing the magic users of yet another kink in our plan.

Leah's shoulders slumped while Phoenix let out a frustrated sigh. Cordelia sat motionless as she studied the wood grain in the table or maybe the cookie crumbs sitting in front of her.

"Let me tell you, dealing with those ghost kids is getting quite frustrating. I get the feeling they've been stuck inside that crystal for a long time. All they do is ask me dumb questions about the outside world and stuff that's happened since they died," Frank said, walking over to the kitchen sink and examining where the sink ended and the wall began.

"I wish we had a magic user on the outside that could help us," Phoenix said with another sigh. "It would be so much easier to go places and get things. It must be terrible being a mortal and stuck with these kinds of restraints."

"Yeah...being a magic user is sounding more and more fun the more I hear about it," I said, my head still on the table as I stared at the wall.

"A magic-using Seer would be a formidable force, to be sure," Leah said with a nod. "How do you feel about taking some lessons? It's not like we have anything else to do."

"As much as I'd love to learn more about it, I can't just sit here and wait for Rose to figure out her nefarious plans. We've got to do something. We're almost there. I can feel it," I said, slowly lifting my head off the table and wondering why it suddenly felt like it weighed a hundred pounds.

Phoenix pulled their lips to the side in thought. "I agree with you, but I can also feel the spell's pull on me to either go exercise for two hours or go take a nap. It's very distracting trying to think of ways to escape while having to also battle these side effects."

"Why do you think we made cookies?" Leah nodded to the plate on the table.

"Too bad there isn't any turmeric at the movie theater," Frank said, turning away from the sink and facing the group. "Then I could just grab some and go find the...nevermind, I have no idea where the storage shed is."

"Yeah...that doesn't sound like it will work, but I appreciate the effort," I said dryly, resting my cheeks on my hands and probably making a silly, frustrated face. "The spell is telling me to go clean something. My mom always cleans when she's frustrated or sad. I guess it's picking up on that gene."

Cordelia suddenly looked up from the table and locked her eyes on me. "The bottle of soda."

"What?" I darted a glance at Phoenix in case this was some kind of old-person delusion the matron was susceptible to.

Phoenix shrugged with upraised eyebrows.

"I had them keep the bottle, just in case. You accepted that as a gift from me, so it was technically yours," Cordelia's eyes were lit with excitement that stirred some hope in my chest.

"Okay..." I said, waiting for her to get to the point.

"And they can use that for the location spell. Luckily it targets you where the picture is stored, not where the trigger was. That's another reason the spell has fallen out of use. If a magic user had an item to do the location spell, then it was easy to find out where the picture was being stored."

"And then with the location, they can tip off the necromancers to come cause a bigger distraction so our ghosts can do what they need to do without interference from Rose, theoretically," Phoenix said, catching onto what Cordelia was thinking.

"Yes! There are risks, to be sure, but at least it's a better step in the right direction." Cordelia nodded. "If we're lucky, we can escape before any real damage has been done and stop the necromancers from killing Rose, keep her from consuming anymore souls, and free the ghosts she's enslaved."

"I hate to be the wet blanket here, but how are the ghosts going to get the turmeric that fast? And I thought we were the only magic users you completely trusted. Do you have anyone you can contact you trust for sure?" Leah asked, still fiddling with the back of her hair.

"And how would you contact them?" I frowned, looking down at my phone. "I was clever enough to discover we have no service here."

"Well, there is one way that I don't often feel right using and, since I avoid it, I forget about it. As a matron, I have a special connection to my coven members which means I can do a small spell to get in contact with them, no matter where I am. The problem is it's not very pleasant." Cordelia looked past us into the kitchen. "Perhaps we'll have a knife nearby we can use though. If we're lucky."

"A knife?" My eyes widened as Phoenix stood and went to search the surviving cabinets and drawers.

"Oh man, things are about to get serious if the old woman asks for a knife," Frank said, moving out of Phoenix's way even though it wasn't strictly necessary.

"What are you going to do?" I asked with wide eyes as Phoenix came back with a small paring knife they had found in one of the drawers.

"I don't usually recommend witches to use blood magic, but sometimes there's nothing else we can do," Cordelia said as she took the knife from Phoenix.

"But who are you going to contact? How do we know we can trust them?" Leah asked, her eyebrows furrowing in concern.

"While Rose has been smart in her recruiting, and there are several witches I suspect of turning to her side, there are some that I'm not sure about at all. We'll just have to hope fate is on our side. If not, we'll still be stuck in the picture."

Leah nodded, but her lips were pressing together in uncertainty.

While chanting unintelligible words, Cordelia pressed the blade into her palm. The cut wasn't deep, but as the blood pooled into her hand, she closed her eyes and chanted some more. After doing that for a few seconds, she opened her eyes and looked down into the puddle cupped inside her palm. I couldn't see anything inside but wasn't surprised at my lack of skills.

"Peaches, can you hear me?" Cordelia asked, looking intently into the slowly growing pool of blood in her palm.

"Peaches?" I mouthed, looking at Phoenix with an amused frown. It was easier to feel a bit more personality when hope was starting to churn inside.

Maybe there was a way out of here.

After explaining what Cordelia needed the mysterious Peaches to do, she ended the spell and dumped the pool of blood into the sink. In some miracle, the fire hadn't destroyed the faucet and we were still able to get running water.

We hadn't been able to hear Peaches's side of the conversation, only the matron had been able to hear their words, but judging from Cordelia's responses, it seemed it had gone well.

We'd instructed Frank on what to do and who to look for so he could grab the turmeric and more water from Peaches while the necromancers hopefully opened the storage shed door and triggered Rose's wards themselves. That conversation drew me to asking where the ghosts had found the water to douse the picture earlier, and Frank told me it had been a half-empty discarded water bottle.

Frank left to update the other ghosts with what we were going to do and to wait for Peaches to, hopefully, do the location spell, tell the necromancers where the hideout was, and then for everyone to arrive. Without knowing how far away the storage unit was from everything, it was impossible to say how long it all would take.

"So what do we do now?" I asked as Phoenix helped Cordelia sit back into her chair, and Leah used some paper towels left on the counter to wrap around the matron's hand and clean up any of the blood splatters that had made it onto the table.

"Well, if we had any beds, I'd suggest a nap," Cordelia said, looking longingly at the wall where the hallway to the bedrooms had been.

"Anyone up for a game of two truths and a lie?" Leah asked with a shrug of her shoulders.

Chapter 17

It was refreshing to feel hope instead of the miasma of angst and depression I'd been enduring, but the feeling had a terrible effect on how time flowed. Or maybe it was simply the fact that we were trapped at a table waiting for something to happen, because time just felt. so. so. so. slow.

After playing as many word games as we could think of more times than I kept track, we started to doubt whether this Peaches person was going to pull through. Before the fear came back in too strongly though, I got whiff of a spicy-orangey smell.

Phoenix lifted their head at about the same time, and I followed their gaze to the corner of the room that looked a little different than the rest of the walls and ceiling. It was colors of things were blending together like a watercolor painting.

"Is it working?" I asked, my heart starting to beat excitedly.

"We'll know in a few minutes if we're going to drown or be set free," Leah said, following our gazes.

We waited and watched. I barely dared to breathe as the watery look spread and sloped down the walls. Then in between one blink and the next, I was inside a cramped room with fluorescent lights overhead and a metal door that was shut tight.

Several things happened at once with our arrival. First, Frank and the three ghosts with him cheered and applauded. Well, Frank mostly just half-smiled in his unemotional, grumpy-old-man way while the three younger ghosts cheered and clapped.

"Yay! It worked!" One of the girl ghosts hopped up and down. It wasn't hard to notice the older two were twins. They were both wearing identical clothes except their multi-layered tank tops were different shades. The jeans they had on were low-waisted with big belts and wide legs. On their feet were platform flipflops which I didn't realize were a thing but must have been popular at some point. They both had long straightened hair, which based on the blue hue of their ghostly forms, had to have been light, probably blonde, in life.

The third ghost was a younger boy, perhaps just hitting the teen years. He jumped around like he was at some kind of punk-rock concert. It was too bad the bright dinosaur shirt kind of ruined the effect even if the small skater shoes didn't. "Yes!"

As the four of us shuffled around to have space apart from each other inside the suddenly confining space, me being the only one trying not to step through a ghost but finding it nearly impossible, we realized there was another person inside the shed with us and they were certainly not dead.

"Holy—" the deeper voice said, startled by our sudden appearance.

The ghosts had managed to dip the picture into a water basin which was a weird orangey-yellow color, I assumed from the turmeric, in the corner of the room.

From my experience with Brandon, any time he made one part of his body material, the effect would slowly spread from that point to throughout the rest of his body. As we appeared, whoever had done it, had gone right back to being a ghost because none were physically visible.

Well, except to me, of course.

"Noah?" I asked, peering around a shelf as he bumped into a pile of boxes after being startled. "Is that you?"

"Hanna?" He squinted his eyes as he righted himself and brushed off any dust from his lettermen's jacket. "What are you doing here? What happened? Who are they?"

His eyes widened as the three magic users crowded in behind me. I was first to come around the shelf, and the others followed, looking curiously at the junior necromancer who had apparently been tasked to investigate the shed on his own.

"These are friends," I said with a gesture over my shoulder. "We can explain later, but right now we need to get out of here. Rose could come by and check on her shed at any moment, and you do not want to be here when she shows up. Did the order send you? And can you three please quiet down?!"

I yelled the last bit in the direction of a darker corner where no one but me could see three chatty ghosts with an impatiently annoyed Frank. They'd all kept chattering to themselves in excitement, but I didn't have the mental space to focus on their words.

I did catch a few comments of how they'd triumphantly picked up our picture and put it into the orange water the necromancer had brought with him. I couldn't tell if they were more excited about having helped us or having terrified the necromancer sent to help us.

Noah's eyes widened at my outburst, but he had been around enough to figure out what was happening. Instead, he nodded, answering my question while continuing to glance at the strangers behind me. "Yeah. Rose is actually outside already, and so is the order. David told me to come in here while they kept her busy."

Blood rushed out of my face and hammered throughout the rest of my body. "Rose is here?"

At the same time, Phoenix cursed from somewhere behind me. "Matron, what do you want us to do? Should we teleport back to the coven, get spell supplies, and come back here?"

"I have another travel bag packed ready to go back at home," Leah added hastily.

"We have to make sure they don't kill her!" I said, not waiting to see what the matron advised doing and pushed past a baffled Noah, climbing my way to the rolling metal door.

"Wait!" Noah grabbed my arm and stopped me short. "Don't go out there! You could get hurt."

"Noah, if they kill her, the ghosts that she has enslaved will all die or disappear," I said, taking a second to speak calmly and intently so he understood how important this was.

"And even if they don't, she could be eating other souls right now to keep in the fight," Cordelia said, standing alone next to me as I assumed Phoenix and Leah had teleported back home to prepare for battle.

Even as we talked, I could hear thumps and shouts and perhaps a zombie moan or two. The scuffle must not have reached the specific storage shed yet because all the chaos sounded muffled. I needed to get out before they reached us so we wouldn't be fish in a barrel, waiting to be slaughtered.

"If you go out there, you might die. There are maybe millions of ghosts, but only one you. Don't you think that should mean something?" Noah said as fear, concern, and something heavy filled his eyes.

"Not to me it doesn't." I pulled my arm out of his grip and Cordelia helped me unlatch the door and pull it open. I wasn't sure how much help she was actually giving me with lifting it, but the thought was nice anyway.

The hallway was empty, but the sounds of fighting were louder, perhaps only a few yards away. I got my few first sniffs of the now-familiar smell of zombie corpses and wondered how well they would fare against the witch and her vampire pet.

Frank kept the younger ghosts inside the storage shed, and I recalled him later telling them to stay behind and keep low, in case Rose started eating ghosts and they happened to be the ones closest.

Noah caught me once more as we stepped out of the small unit, and this time it was by the shoulders. He shook me lightly as he stared right into my eyes. "Hanna, it means a lot to me. More than I've ever been able to say. Please, *please* don't go out there. Have the magic users teleport you somewhere safe and leave Rose up to us. I'll make sure they don't kill her, and you can set the ghosts free once she's in our custody. I couldn't handle it if something happened to you."

Cordelia was joined with Leah and Phoenix, both carrying big bags of spell supplies and the three of them had hurried past us down the hall. The old matron spared one look back for me but must have decided they didn't need my immediate help.

I mean, what was I going to do against Rose, anyway? I had no idea, but I had to at least try.

I knew I didn't have the time but couldn't help myself from snarling at Noah with a sarcastic bob to my head. "Well, thanks for the sentiment, but I'm sure Andrea would be upset to hear any of that."

"She's dead, Hanna."

"Yes, I'm sure. Now let me... Wait. What?" I asked, finally processing his words.

"She's basically a zombie I'm trying to keep alive every day. I have to be near her to cast the spell. The order tasked me with the job because we can never let her father find out the truth of how we botched her resurrection spell. They don't always go as smooth as Stephanie's went." Noah's hazel eyes bore into mine and his fingers dug into my shoulders almost painfully.

"Okay, well," I blinked a few times, "that sucks, and it's actually super funnily ironic that she's a zombie based on all the times she's judged me, but why are we talking about this *now*?"

"In order for me to be close to her every day, we needed a ruse. That made being her boyfriend a simple choice, and it was simple until you. We got closer and..."

I glanced behind him as someone snarled nearby but still couldn't see any of the conflict. "Look, Noah. Can we talk about this later? I've got ghosts to free."

"No, not if you die."

"Thanks for the confidence."

"Listen, Hanna, I want to be with *you*. When I saw that strange vampire come to homecoming, I had to take the chance to dance with you. It felt so good to be able to talk how I wanted. I just—"

"Noah," I said, interrupting him and looking him right in the eyes. "I'm grateful for our friendship, but *please* can we talk about this later?"

He dropped his hands from off my shoulders and the fire ebbed out of his eyes. "Alright. But I'm coming with you."

I didn't bother with a vocal response but simply jogged down the hallway, trying not to breathe the growing smell any more than I needed to, turned the corner, and skidded to another stop. I had no idea why I'd thought I could make a difference in a battle between a small horde of zombies, their controlling masters, three magic users that seemed to be momentarily distracted with their supplies—perhaps getting together a rather large spell— and a vampire fueled by a necromancer witch.

Rose stood on one end, zapping purple electricity into her brutish vampire friend or slave, I didn't really know, as he battled zombies. He tossed them like they were ragdolls and smashed their heads together, and they erupted into mush like rotting Jack O'lanterns.

There were three necromancers controlling the horde of zombies, and as soon as one of their pets fell, they raised another to take its place. Where all the dead bodies were coming from, I had no clue. One of the three was David, and, despite still being in his wheelchair, he was as powerful as the other three, if not more so, as he raised two zombies to every one that the others did. I vaguely recognized the other two necroes but didn't spare time to remember their names.

Cordelia smashed something in a bowl with a pestle, Leah held a book open and was reading or chanting from it, while Phoenix stood guard, making sure the two of them weren't disturbed.

I stood there in awe of the battle and tried to figure out what to do. If I distracted Rose, she might be taken down and killed. If I distracted the necroes and was successful, somehow, Rose might get away or have time to swallow a soul. And I definitely didn't want to distract the magic users as they were hopefully constructing a spell that would capture Rose and put an end to this madness.

Noah grunted as he took a few steps toward the battle and zapped his own purple energy into one of the nearby zombies that had lost a leg. With the necromancer's infusion of power, the zombie pulled itself up and began hopping toward the vampire, but what it was going to do when it got there, I had no idea.

Then my eyes landed on a discarded bag a few paces behind Rose. Perhaps she had been carrying it when she popped in to check on her storage shed but had tossed it aside when realizing she needed to defend herself from the zombies.

Perhaps that bag was the only thing keeping her here in the battle when she could have easily teleported out.

"Noah," I whispered harshly and got close enough that I hoped he could hear me over all the snarling, grunting, and wet, gory sounds of bodies being destroyed. "Keep her distracted. I'm going to see if I can free some ghosts."

He darted a glance in my direction. "Okay. I'll try."

I told myself I wasn't using his feelings for me to work on my own priorities, but I could worry about that when I was safe inside my own bedroom with plenty of time for the anxiety of the day to sink into my head.

After I was far enough away from him that Rose wouldn't immediately spot me, I hoped, Noah hollered out. "Hey! Crazy lady! Did you eat your Wheaties for breakfast, or would you rather feast on bloated zombie flesh?"

She only spared a quick glance at the apprentice necromancer with a lip snarled in annoyance and then went back to focusing on her pet vampire. If there was a way to sever her focus on the brute, then maybe he'd be taken down by the zombies. Some of them carried wooden spikes, and when one was dropped, another zombie picked it up.

The effort of keeping the vampire strong was starting to take its toll on the usually elegant witch. Grey streaks spread throughout her light hair, and the skin on her arms crinkled like wadded-up paper.

Worried that she'd start to summon the ghosts, I decided to forget about being sneaky and sprinted toward the bag. I slid on my knees for the last few feet and stopped worrying about what was happening around me as I ripped open the leather canvas and was happily satisfied to hear the clinks of crystals and see their soft pink surfaces glittering inside.

"What are you doing?" Rose's shrill voice reached me over the chaos.

I turned to her with an evil smile and pulled a crystal out. My hair was wrapped around it, the ends sealed with wax.

Rose kept her arms outstretched, still pouring purple lightning into the vampire, but her eyes were panicked for a second. Then as I watched, the features of her aging face changed into something more sinister and triumphant. "I don't know what you think you're doing, but I appreciate the help."

The last thing I saw from her was a wink before I was bombarded with ghostly bodies. I couldn't count how many she had summoned, but it felt like it was the contents of the entire bag. There were so many, I couldn't see through to the battle. It was even worse when they started to solidify and held me down to keep me from messing with her crystals.

There was probably a way to set the ghosts free when messing with the crystals, but Rose had either forgotten or hadn't understood how I'd set Frank free. When that had happened, I hadn't needed the crystal.

All I had needed was my hand.

Two ghosts formed physical hands and arms as they pushed me onto the cold tile while three others grappled with my kicking legs. I didn't recognize any of them even though my eyes darted across each ghost I could see, searching.

Determined to free as many as I could, whoever they were, I focused on the one holding my right arm down. He was an older man when he'd died wearing a farmer's hat, a plaid shirt, and some worn jeans, but not like he'd bought them that way, more like he'd earned them that way. As his body solidified, his skin turned from the blue transparency of a ghost to a sun-kissed dark hue.

He was grunting as he held me down but also grimacing as he uttered apologies. "Sorry, miss. Just doing what I'm told. It would help if you'd stop moving around so much."

The other ghosts were talking and shouting as well, and if I had focused on all of it at once, I would have easily become overwhelmed. So I only focused on the farmer.

"Shift a bit to the right, and I can set you free," I said through clenched teeth.

His thick eyebrows crunched together, but he did as I instructed, still following Rose's command to keep me secure but also placing his chest right above my hand.

It was easier the second time, probably because I knew I could do it. Tingles radiated from my fingers as I pulled my spirit out of my body, or at least that's what it felt like was happening, and grabbed onto the spell's lock. It was harder to yank on the chains since I didn't have much room for leverage, so I mostly just squeezed it, hoping they'd burst under the pressure.

And somehow it worked.

Both the ghost and I gasped as the plasma chains fell away from his body. Immediately, he backed up and ran hands all over his chest and stomach.

"You did it!" he said, relief filling his eyes.

"Yes, now tell the others to come hold down my arm one at a time so I can free them too," I said, turning my attention to the other ghost who held my left arm.

It was a middle-aged woman with her hair done in a tasteful bun and wearing a tight-corseted dress from somewhere in the Victorian age, maybe. I really wasn't an expert on those kinds of things, although maybe I should have been since I dealt with many from different periods.

"Move over a bit," I said to the woman.

She glanced up to where the farmer guy had gone and turned to look at me with a nod. Scooting over, she placed the middle of her chest over my hand, and I did the same thing again—pulled a part of my spirit out of my body into the ghost world, clamped down on the chains, and squeezed with all the power I could. It took a bit longer since my left hand wasn't as strong as my right, but I was finally able to do it.

She sat up in marvel as she checked herself over much like the farmer had done. With twinkling eyes, she said, "Thank you," and disappeared.

Two ghosts moved in on my arms and there were still so many of them, I couldn't see anything of what was happening around me. Judging by the sounds, the zombies and vampire brute were still going at it. I was worried Rose would start to gobble the ghosts, or perhaps already had eaten some while I wasn't able to watch.

Hurrying, with my heart hammering in my chest, I convinced the ghosts to let me reach into their bodies and smash the chains. One after the other, one side after the other side, I extended, squeezed, and broke chain after chain.

If Rose could feel what I was doing, I didn't know. I assumed she did, feeling certain I was running out of time.

Each of the ghosts seemed relieved and grateful to be released. I had no idea how long any of them had been captured except for the ones I'd doomed. I saw a few familiar ghosts, including the first one that had been haunting my history class, but didn't stop to chat with them as I set them free.

There was only one ghost I had eyes for.

As I worked, the ghosts around me lessened and faded until I could see more of what was happening. It was about that same time that Cordelia and Leah, shouting and chanting together, threw something at Rose.

With a grunt, Rose got the vampire to toss a zombie at the same time, intercepting whatever the magic users had thrown at her. There was a shattering sound, a puff of pink smoke, and the zombie froze in mid-air. They thunked onto the ground with a sickening crunch, emitting another wave of the awful smell.

Both of the magic users and I gagged while Rose laughed.

"Are you forgetting I know exactly what spell you were doing? Do you think I'm that dumb?" Rose taunted, continuing to pour purple lightning into her pet.

She didn't look as much aged, so I feared she'd eaten a ghost while I hadn't been able to watch, and I prayed with all my heart that it wasn't someone I knew.

Cordelia and Leah exchanged glances but didn't look like a couple of defeated magic users who had just spent several minutes casting a spell that would only end up on a poor, helpless zombie.

"That's why we made two," Phoenix said from the other side of the room. They must have gotten over there while no one was paying them any attention. Without hesitation, they threw another bottle at Rose, too quick for her to react.

I knew enough about vampires to understand that if he had been free to move on his own, he would have been fast enough to catch it. However, since he was under Rose's control, he could only react to what she wanted him to react to.

The bottle soared through the air, smacked into the ground right in front of Rose's feet, and a bright pink plume of smoke enveloped her until she was as frozen as a statue, her mouth open with snarling anger.

The vampire pet froze as well, but didn't appear to be freed, only mimicking what his master was capable of telling him to do. As the zombies brought him down, stabbing him in several places with wooden stakes, I felt a surge of pity for the poor guy, not knowing anything about his story and if he was a willing participant or only a slave like the ghosts.

During this chaos, I kept freeing the ghosts, trying to get rid of as many as possible. While the zombies brought down the vampire, I found myself face-to-face with Sarah, the alpha's mate who'd died while gambling on magic to help her become a mother.

"Sarah! I'm so sorry you were caught! Let me free you," I said in a hushed whisper.

Smiling kindly at me, apparently no longer required to do Rose's bidding, she nodded. "It's okay. I know it wasn't your fault."

The ghosts had retreated some and given me space enough to stand. All of them were going back into their blue forms, no longer being forced to do Rose's bidding.

After pulling myself up with an inelegant grunt, I pushed my hand into Sarah's chest and felt the satisfaction of pulling off the cursed chain.

"You might want to get back to your alpha. I know things haven't been going so well for him," I said with a smile.

She nodded. "Thank you, Hanna."

And she popped out, back to her haunt, before I could ask if she'd seen Brandon.

I was glad I'd been able to help her and fix some of my crimes, but the relief was overshadowed with anxiety that slowly elevated to panic with each ghost I encountered that wasn't the one that had become my best friend...and perhaps something more.

After their job was done, the zombies stilled and stood like creepy Halloween decorations while awaiting further orders. The necromancers closed in on the frozen Rose carefully, but the magic users reached her first.

Turning to David, the leader of the necromancer order, Cordelia put herself between him and Rose. Phoenix and Leah stood on either side of her, their postures not quite relaxed enough to indicate they trusted the order.

"Thank you for the assistance. Without your help, we surely wouldn't have been able to capture her," the matron said with a polite smile.

"I understand she was part of your coven at one time, but she has since turned to the necromantic arts, and I feel we can claim her as our own," David said, his smile more saccharine.

The other members of the order filed in behind their leader, including Noah who spared a glance in my direction for a second, and the zombies lined up behind them. If I hadn't known what the magic users were capable of, I would have been worried for their safety.

As for Rose, she looked like one of those wax figures in a museum. Her features and colors were preserved perfectly, but she didn't move, not even to breathe. I didn't know if that would kill her or not, but I figured the magic users knew what they were doing. I also didn't know how long the spell would last so hopefully that wasn't a concern either.

While that confrontation happened, I worked through the rest of the ghosts. I pulled out chains from every chest I could find until all of the summoned ghosts were gone. Wishing I'd counted them for some reason, I kneeled onto the tile and dumped out the contents of Rose's bag. Crystals rolled onto the floor, and I scrambled to catch them before they went too far. There were five in all, and I had no way of knowing if they were empty of ghosts. I was tempted to smash them but didn't know enough to do so in case I would be hurting any of the ghosts that might be left inside.

Other things were inside the bag, including two more strands of my hair, the candle she used to seal the hair onto the crystal, and some other usual things you'd find in a purse, including the tube of ruby red lipstick she wore.

Frustrated, I grabbed the bag and started putting everything back together. I'd have to learn more about the way the spell worked before I could be sure to destroy the crystals. I did take a second, though, to grab the lighter and burn off the rest of my spare hair bundles. There was no way I was going to be a part of her capturing any more ghosts.

"There is no reason for us to fight. We both want the same things—justice and peace, a restoration to the natural balance of things," Cordelia said, spreading her arms out in an inclusive gesture.

David's jaw clenched and the muscles flexed along his lower cheek. His hesitation to respond reasonably made warning bells go off inside my head as I stood and slung Rose's bag over my shoulder.

Justice and peace were what the order wanted, right?

I looked to Noah who was staring down at his leader with a furrow in his brow. He was braver than I was to speak up and risk messing up the tenuous stalemate. "That sounds exactly like what we want, right?"

David didn't turn to look at the young apprentice, instead keeping his eyes focused on the matron. It was almost like they were engaged in a staring contest.

Another necromancer came up behind David and placed his hand on the leader's shoulder. I recognized him as Alberto, one of the others in the order who had helped me back at the vampire seethe. Seeing them stand against the magic users right now was disorienting after they'd been so gracious to help me before.

Alberto's voice was rich with a distinct accent. "Yes, all we want is peace and the natural order of things, but you can see why we would be interested in this situation. Rose was clearly using necromantic powers without the permission of any order. This goes against one of our basic rules, and if this were under normal circumstances, the order would take care of the offending person."

"We can assure you that Rose will not be permitted to use any further necromancer magic. The use of its magic, especially in the way she employs it, goes against the natural flow. We are in complete agreement," Cordelia said with a firm nod.

"What about the ghosts she enslaved?" I asked, finally finding courage enough to approach the fragile situation.

All eyes turned in my direction, and I swallowed thickly. "As a Seer, I feel like I should speak on behalf of the ghosts that she's captured. They need to be set free before anything happens to her, and as I'm not a magic user nor a necromancer, I'm not entirely sure how to undo all she has done. Is there a way to get back the souls she's devoured?"

As I walked closer, I eyed Rose for a second, checking to see if there would be any response. I could only hope she wasn't conscious and able to hear everything. For some reason, having her hear my plans freaked me out, even though she was clearly captured.

Her pet vampire was sprawled out on the tile, thankfully several yards away, stabbed in multiple places with wooden stakes. Zombie corpses spread around the area, and I hoped no one would take that moment to come visit the warehouse of storage units.

"Those are important questions," Cordelia said with a nod in my direction. "Tasks that the coven would be more than willing to assist with. Restoring the ghosts to their natural places is a high priority."

"There is no way to redeem the souls she's taken," David spoke, his voice tense and terse. "While it is admirable that you have found a way to rescue the ghosts from the curse, that is not the biggest concern here. What if Rose were freed to enslave more ghosts? How can we be sure that the magic users are strong enough to do what must be done?"

"How do we know you're not going to just chop her head off the second she's out of our sight? Any ghosts that she's still got trapped will be stuck," I said, glaring down at his spry and wrinkled form.

There still had to be at least one ghost she had trapped that I hadn't seen yet. I refused to think of the alternative. Plus, I still needed to free the three kids that were hopefully behaving themselves back inside the storage unit.

David rolled his eyes. "Such dramatics. Of course we'll interrogate her and get all the pertinent information before we perform a trial of her peers to decide what is best to do here."

"Her peers are magic users. You said so yourself that she was work-ing outside of the order. She belongs with us," Cordelia said, her voice growing in strength as her words turned from suggesting peace to a firm stance.

As tensions rose between the groups, I knew who I was voting to win, even though I still wasn't certain I could trust either of them.

"Please, let us take her so that we might ensure her darkness remains unexposed to the world," David said, surprising me with the please. "We do not want a war with the magic users. We only want what is ours."

"And *we* want what is *ours*," Phoenix said, stepping in for Cordelia. "I'm sorry, but we were the ones who captured her, so we're the ones who get to interrogate her."

"I'm afraid I can't let that happen. We'll let you visit if you're good," David said with a flick of his wrist.

Purple lightning zapped out of the order leader's fingers and pulled a group of zombies from behind, propelling them toward Rose nearly as fast as lightning usually moved. Phoenix had only time to furrow their eyebrows and reach for Rose's arm before the zombies locked onto them and pulled them away before they could connect with Rose.

I didn't know how the teleportation worked exactly but figured if one of the magic users could just touch her, they'd be able to pop right out. They probably hadn't done so yet in an effort to make nice with the necromancers, but David had crossed the line, and it was clearly every group for themselves.

Leah darted around a zombie and got within inches of touching the witch before more zombies held her fast. Cordelia didn't bother to move. Instead, she kept her eyes locked onto David's.

"Your desires are evil. Does your order know the true reason why you want Rose's powers?" the matron asked, her gaze boring deep into David's soul…if he had one.

Alberto's eyes narrowed as he stared at the witch. Noah blinked several times, glancing between the witch and the leader of his order. The other necromancer stood firm behind David, probably not taking any word the magic user said as truth.

If I were them, I probably wouldn't have trusted her either, but something about her words made the skin around David's eyes tighten just enough that I figured she'd struck a chord somewhere.

"I must do what is best for the order," was all David said and nodded, signaling for the necromancers to close in on the magic users, preventing them from getting any closer to Rose.

Phoenix was fiercely fighting to free themself from the zombies, but each time they shook off the slippery clutches of one creature, another reached up and grabbed their arms. Somehow the zombies knew how to restrain the magic user in such a way that they weren't able to cast any spells.

Leah was suffering the same issue, but so far, the zombies had left me and Cordelia alone. The matron had shown no effort to attempt to touch Rose and the frailty of her age, combined with the mass of zombies fighting Phoenix and Leah between her and Rose, there was little chance that she would break away to help.

I shivered thinking about their clammy hands touching my skin. As much as I didn't want to be in contact with a zombie, I didn't want the necromancers to win either.

But I was no magic user. I didn't have the ability to teleport myself out, let alone Rose. David must have known that enough not to worry about me.

Perhaps there was something a person like me *could* do.

Closing my eyes, I pictured each ghost I had freed. I remembered the details of the farmer's hat and the stubble that had lined his chin. I remembered the lace on the Victorian lady's dress and the way her hair had been pulled up into an intricate bun. As each face appeared in my mind, I pulled them to me.

I didn't prefer to summon ghosts without first preparing them for the sudden disorientation of being yanked out of their haunt. In fact, I didn't even know if I could summon a ghost without knowing where their haunt was.

But I figured these ones owed me and may even enjoy enacting some revenge.

Coldness seeped back into the room as I summoned the ghosts, grabbing every single one I could think of, including Frank. Part of me was curious enough to try summoning Brandon, but again, it felt blank on the other end of that connection.

The snarls and grunts of the magic users and zombies wrestling while the necromancers closed in on Rose were drowned out with the bewildered cries and surprised voices of the ghosts. I opened my eyes, pleased to see transparent, blue forms all around, looking at me with various forms of confused expressions.

Telling myself that I wasn't as bad as Rose, I shouted and pointed, "Possess those zombies!"

None were probably as surprised as myself when it actually worked. Ghost after ghost turned to a nearby zombie, stepped into it, and took hold of the creature. Zombies consistently had an emptiness in their eyes, but once a ghost took over, they seemed to wake up and become more aware of themselves.

The zombies let go of the magic users, stepped back, and looked around the room as if they'd never seen it before, despite having been inside it for several minutes now.

The necromancers watched in awe for a second and then struggled to control their zombies with curses and shouts and mighty glares of willpower.

"What's happening?" Phoenix asked as the zombies stepped back.

"We're winning, that's what!" Leah said, pushing past the spacey zombies and at last landing a finger on Rose.

Even though several zombies had started carrying the witch toward the door, probably to the cars the necromancers had taken to get here, wherever "here" was, once Leah touched Rose, they both winked out.

Cordelia gave David one last upturned twitch of her mouth before she also disappeared. It was too bad David missed her classy exit as his eyes were trained on mine.

Chapter 18

A headache had bloomed behind my eyes, and it was increasing exponentially every second as the ghosts used my energy to overcome the zombies. I released my tight control on them and would have slid to the floor in an exhausted puddle if Phoenix hadn't caught me.

"Thank you," I croaked out, both to Phoenix and to the ghosts. "Go back to your haunts. I promise not to do that again."

I wasn't sure how many of the ghosts could hear me, but I pushed the release and promise through our connections.

Frank took at least a second to step in my direction and salute me with an amused smile. I was sure I would hear all about his adventures as a zombie later.

"I've got you," Phoenix said, lowering me gently onto the cool tile.

The fluorescent lights swam and danced above me as I stared at the ceiling, trying to keep from passing out.

"Hanna!" A familiar voice sorted in through my haze before Noah's face was in my field of vision.

Phoenix looked at him warily but let Noah grab my other arm, probably figuring they could teleport us out if anything got weird.

"Noah? Your boss is a real turd," I said, my words slurring. "He probably wants Rose's spells for himself. Have you seen his wrinkles?"

I don't know whether it was my subconscious putting together pieces after Cordelia's words or if I was delirious, but something must have hit home inside Noah because his face changed from worry for me to calculating eyes that moved elsewhere, toward David's position.

I couldn't see the leader's face, and my blinks were getting slower. If my eyes had their way, we'd have already fallen asleep moments ago.

"I should get her out of here before your order decides they want a Seer," Phoenix said, their tone quiet and meant only for Noah.

Noah pressed his lips together tightly as he glanced down at me and took a microsecond to brush a strand of my wavy, messy hair out of my face. "She's done something I'm pretty sure has never been done before. It's smart to get her out of here. Text me, will you?"

I blinked in answer as shouts came from a distance, the necromancers apparently figuring out what was about to happen.

"Stop them!" David hollered, but it was too late.

I woke up sometime later inside a simple, yet elegant room, the style making me immediately assume I was in some part of the coven's safe house. The four-poster bed was finely crafted, the wood carved with flowers and thorns. There were matching side tables, a matching dresser, and the pictures on the walls displayed scenes in nature.

My eyes felt like sand had been rubbed in them, while my muscles felt like they'd been smashed, stretched, and put back together again.

Groaning, I rolled over and hoped I could get back to sleep. Unfortunately, the consciousness had woken my brain up enough to throw memories at me. The magic users had gotten Rose, she was somewhere nearby, probably, and we needed to get the rest of the ghosts out of the crystals, making sure there weren't any others stashed around.

While my family was probably worried sick, there was only one person I was thinking about, determined to find him, unwilling to think of what could have happened to him.

Fighting gravity and the thick confines of the pink quilt I'd been sleeping under, I finally kicked my way out of bed and stood, only to fall back down again when the room spun in ways it shouldn't have been able to.

"Hanna?" someone asked as they opened the door. "Are you okay?"

Phoenix's sturdy hands lifted me off the floor and gently placed me back onto the bed. Their face with sharp cheekbones and steady grey eyes helped ground me as they kneeled onto the plush carpet. Warmth traveled in through their hands as they kept me from toppling back over.

"Just breathe, dear. You've expended a lot of energy, more than I'd ever recommend using if you were a magic user," Phoenix said and then shook their head with a whistle. "Woo, girl, though, you pack a mighty punch! Why didn't you tell me your ghosts could possess things?"

"I didn't know they could. Never tried it before." My words were slurred, but the world was starting to make sense again. "Is Rose here?"

Phoenix nodded but pulled their eyebrows together. "She is, but you're not allowed to go anywhere near her. We've locked her up in a secure place and have since started asking questions that she has so far refused to answer."

"Oh, okay. So...time to pull out some tricks. I'm sure you magic users know exactly how to get people to talk."

"We do. Don't you worry about that. But there is something else…"

I raised my eyebrows for them to continue, not in the mood for playing guessing games.

"You know where you are?"

"Is this one of the rooms in the coven safehouse?"

Phoenix nodded. "Quite so, and your mother and sister are here."

My eyes probably bugged nearly out of my head. "What?"

"You've been asleep for nearly a whole day." Phoenix glanced out the window, but it simply displayed a peaceful field in the middle of a sunny afternoon. And judging from the other windows in this place, I couldn't use that as a measurement of reality. "The matron decided it would be better to bring in your family rather than have them be lost and worried without you. It was an easy decision since they already know about us, have proven trustworthy of our secrets thus far, and have a few secrets of their own that we could…"

"Use if you need to?"

Phoenix's mouth pulled upwards on one side. "Yes, to put it plainly."

"They're trustworthy. You have nothing to worry about. I'm the one who needs to worry," I said with a sigh, imagining all the different ways my mom was going to ground me. "I'll probably be locked up inside my house until I'm forty."

They shrugged. "That's still young in my book."

"Too bad I don't live as long as you."

"There's another thing…but you have to promise to eat a really good breakfast, or early dinner, as the case may be."

My stomach felt hollow and sad, too tired to grumble any more, but there was no way Phoenix could know that. "What other thing?"

"Promise you'll eat well for dinner? You're trembling like a homeless puppy in a snowstorm, and I've seen how little you eat. You're going to waste away."

I frowned, images of ballooning up with so much fat that I'd need a motorized scooter to get around but nodded because I wanted the information.

"Your mom and sister have something to tell you. It appears they've been doing some work while you were gone. I'll let them explain, but Trina and her vampire friend have found some interesting information."

I pulled myself off the bed, noticing for the first time that my feet were bare as they touched down on the soft carpet. I was wearing some kind of nightgown moo-moo thing, and, after wobbling and, getting myself to stand with Phoenix nearby to catch me, I gave them a flat look while gesturing to my person.

They chuckled. "It looked more comfortable than keeping you in those dirty jeans. Your mom brought you clothes from home you'll find in the bathroom. I'll go get them to help you change and shower. They were meeting with Cordelia when you awoke so I was the only one nearby."

I nodded, feeling like a newborn deer as Phoenix helped steer me into the bathroom. They left me hanging onto the counter as they dashed to go get my mom. If I'd had more energy, fear and anxiety would probably have been having a party inside my brain, but as it was, I mostly felt numb.

While I was alone, staring at my sunken cheeks and purple bags under my eyes in the bathroom mirror, threads of doubt threatened to weave themselves into my absolute resolution that Brandon wasn't gone for good. He had to still be trapped somewhere, a place where I could free him. With as strong as a mental wall as I could build, I kept those doubts from coming in.

To distract myself, I wobbled over toward the toilet, hiked up my hideous sleeping gown, and carefully lowered myself to the seat where I could relieve some bodily fluids, even if I couldn't relieve the coil of nerves that had knotted so tightly inside my chest that I was sure I'd never get them loosened.

Mom came by then, knocking softly on the door, and after her assistance to shower and change, I emerged from the bathroom feeling fresh and clean, even if I still didn't feel whole.

"Phoenix told me you had something to tell me," I said as I sat on the bed and pulled on my shoes.

We hadn't talked much in the bathroom because we'd been focused on the immediate tasks, and I was afraid to say much or else risk opening up the waterfall of verbal discipline I was most certainly about to incur.

But I couldn't wait any longer. I was too curious.

After making sure I could handle tying my own shoes, despite the many laces of the worn Converse sneakers, Mom stood, undid her chestnut brown hair from its messy ponytail atop her head, and redid the style, catching all the strands that had fallen out. She looked nearly as worn as I felt. The peeking wrinkles around her eyes made her appear older than I'd ever seen her before.

I felt kind of bad for being the cause of her stress, but I'd had to act. Enjoying a Thanksgiving dinner with my family while Brandon was out by himself had felt wrong.

As she wrapped the hair tie one last time around her bun, she sighed. "Yes. We have a lot to talk about, but we can do that over food. You look like you're about to float away on the next strong breeze."

"Fine," I huffed, and we walked out of the room and down the hallway with linked elbows.

I had no idea where we were in the house or how to get to other places, but my mom appeared to know where she was going as she steered us toward a large, warm kitchen where the chefs were using pots to cook from instead of cauldrons as one might expect from a witches' home.

There were two ovens, a large fridge, and lots of cabinets and counter space. I probably wouldn't have bothered to notice all that if it hadn't been for my mom who was always complaining about the lack of workspace in our own small kitchen. A six-person table set off from the counters and cabinets in its own place inside the kitchen. There was a fireplace nearby that crackled happily with purple and pink flames, perhaps some kind of special witchy fire.

Trina smiled from where she was sitting in one of the chairs as we entered the room. "Wow, Phoenix was right. You look terrible."

"Hello to you too," I said as Mom helped lower me into a chair. Strength and solidarity were returning to my body slowly but eating, as much as I didn't want to admit, would be required for me to recover more.

There were two workers cooking in the kitchen, but they conveniently had something else to do when we arrived and left us to our food and conversation I was sure not to emerge from without some verbal bruising.

I had to admit the spread before us looked pretty good, and even though I wondered in the back of my head if we were actually eating some kind of conjured witch food that would later turn out to be enchanted mounds of mud, I wasn't going to fight too hard to fill up.

And it didn't take much.

After several good bites of fried chicken, a mound of mashed potatoes and gravy, a pile of peas, and two slickly-buttered rolls, I was fuller than I could ever remember feeling. I sat back in my chair to give my stomach room and patted it, hoping it wouldn't look so big for long.

"Alright, let's get this out of the way. Either yell at me and ground me or tell me what this new piece of information is. The suspense is probably going to kill me if I have to wait much longer," I said, sitting up to grab my glass of water and resting back onto my chair.

Mom chewed her roll thoughtfully as she regarded me. "You're right to think you're in trouble. I've thought about how to address this in so many ways, but that was all overshadowed by my fear that you weren't actually going to return home to be yelled at."

I nodded, pressing my lips together tightly. "I get that. I'm sorry. The last thing I wanted was to make you guys more worried. I know how hard you've been working since Dad left, and I really didn't want to add to your stress... It's just... I couldn't..." I tried to fight the emotion that was growing inside, fueled by the food I'd finally eaten.

Mom stopped me with her warm hand on my knee. "I know. I saw how panicked and upset you were. I can't say I agree with your actions, but I do understand that you felt trapped and needed to make some kind of progress. I just wish you could have clued us in on what was happening."

Trina kept bouncing her eyes around the room, probably unsure how much she should be a part of the conversation where her sister was in trouble while still wanting to lend support to her mother or sister, whoever needed it most.

"I knew you wouldn't have let me go. I actually had no idea where I was going at first. I just knew I needed to *go*. It wasn't until Phoenix found me that I got some traction and direction. We both figured the wolves were right on my tail, so they helped me get somewhere the wolves couldn't follow."

"And you turned off your phone," Mom said with an upraised eyebrow.

I nodded. "I'm sorry. I really can't say it enough... Feel free to ground me for life or whatever as soon as..." The lump in my throat was too big for me to get further words out.

Mom and Trina exchanged glances and then Trina nodded as if giving her permission for something. It was then that I noticed Trina's neck was bare. For the first time in my working memory, she wasn't wearing that golden eye necklace.

Chills skittered down my arms as I wondered exactly what she had been up to.

Mom turned to look back at me. "Phoenix filled us in on some of what happened. I still want the full version of the story from you, but we can do that in a minute. First, they said you were able to release and free some ghosts."

I nodded, wishing I felt more relief from it than I did.

"Second, they said that they were able to capture Rose, with some amazing and truly frightening moves on your behalf."

Blushing, I ducked my head. "Yeah... Those necromancers, I'm sure, are mad. It's probably a good thing y'all are here and not at the house. They might try to hurt you or something to get back at us."

Mom's eyebrows rose. "Okay..."

"Should we be worried about Dad?" Trina asked, concern making her eyes wide.

"The magic users will help, and I'm sure the wolves, too. Although I have no idea what Caleb's been up to," I said, trying to backpedal from getting into more trouble.

"Right," Mom glanced at Trina again who had some kind of awkward expression on her face I couldn't place, "Caleb has been helping us, actually."

"What? Helping with what?"

"We'll get to that in a second. The third thing Phoenix said was that they suspected you didn't find a certain ghost that you were looking for." Mom patted my knee again as her eyes regarded me with visible love.

I nodded. "Not yet, I haven't. He's still probably stuck inside one of the crystals. Maybe even one we don't have, hidden somewhere. There was another crystal inside the storage shed where we were trapped inside a picture. Did they tell you about that? It was both cool and super annoying. Anyway, I need to make sure Phoenix grabbed the stuff that was in the shed too. That crystal had at least three ghosts inside of it, and maybe even more. I need to make sure I set them free and yeah, there's still ghosts I need to get to. They're going to be interrogating Rose some more to figure out where all the ghosts are."

Trina and Mom let me ramble on for a while with patient smiles and raised eyebrows. It was kind of funny to see how similar their expressions were. Then I remembered they were both related to me too, and we all shared a strong resemblance.

"Yes, you're probably right," Mom said with a tight smile. "There are more crystals to be found. There's no reason to think that..."

Trina picked up where she left off with a cheerful tone. "I'm sure we'll find him, and any other ghosts Rose has captured, including Brandon's siblings and anyone else."

Mom watched me closely as my sister's words entered my head.

"Wait, his siblings? What do you know about them?" I glanced between their faces. "Did you say that Rose had them captured? How do you know?"

Images popped into my head of the boy's shoes reminding me of Brandon's. It wasn't too far of a stretch to imagine the little brother wanting to wear shoes like his older, cooler big brother.

My heart hammered inside my chest, and there was suddenly a shortage of air in the wide kitchen.

"Did I... Those were Brandon's sisters and brother? Are you freaking serious right now?!" I said, smacking the table and standing up.

"Woah, Hanna. It's okay. Let's go through this carefully, okay?" Mom stood with me and grabbed onto my shoulder, trying to catch my roaming eyes with her own.

I latched onto her strong, steady gaze and nodded slowly. "There's more?"

"A bit, yes," Trina said, her eyes not as steady but just as focused.

Slowly, I sat back into my chair. "Do you know if the magic users got the crystal out of the shed?"

"We'll ask as soon as we're done here, sweetie." Mom sat down again as well, her focus all on me, the afternoon meal forgotten. "Do you think you saw them?"

"Yes. He told me about them. Two twin sisters and a younger brother. He said they died…but he never told me how or what happened. The three ghosts who helped Frank help us escape from the spell were three kids, two twin sisters and a boy. They looked so much like him, now that I'm thinking about it. I can't believe I missed that."

I frowned down at my mostly empty plate and felt my stomach flop with too many carbs and missed opportunities.

"We might be able to fill you in on some stuff then," Trina said, idly tinkering with her fork that rested on her empty plate.

"What? Like what?"

Trina looked to Mom who nodded at her to continue.

"We found his mom, their mom," Trina said, her eyes watching me carefully.

"Alright, you have my attention. Just start from the beginning and ignore any of my outbursts," I said, pushed my plate to the side, clasped my hands together, and set them on the table in a listening and focused stance.

Trina's lips wavered around an amused smile as she spoke. "Do you remember Tracy?"

I nodded, determined to stop interrupting her so I could hear it all.

"Well, after you…left, I decided to pull as many resources together as I could, and that counted ghosts. At first, I took off my necklace in hopes that I would spot Frank or someone who was trying to call for help and knew where you were. Of course, we visited the skatepark, just in case, and—"

"She's forgetting the important part that we were doing this all while we should have been out Black Friday shopping," Mom said, giving me a pointed look.

I winced. "I'm sorry, Mom. I know that's one of your favorite holidays."

She gave me a mockingly angry look which softened. "You're not out of trouble, yet, but I am glad to have you safe and sound."

I gave her a close-mouthed smile in thanks and turned back to Trina so she would continue.

"Right, so during the super way-too-early-hours-to-be-awake-even-for-Black-Friday, we searched for ghosts who might know where you were. The wolves worked on their own search, using smells and clues from where they knew you liked to hang out and stuff, but of course, they didn't find anything. It seems obvious after we found out that Phoenix teleported you."

I winced again. "Sorry."

"Yeah, those poor pups got worn out." Trina's eyebrows lifted as she nodded.

"I'll make sure to apologize to them... Although I did set their alpha's mate's ghost free. I hope that counts for something," I said, the last part mostly to myself.

"So then I... Well, actually, Mom should probably jump in here. Even before you left, she and Caleb had been working on something else that they thought was unrelated at the time," Trina said, turning her gaze toward Mom.

"Right. Do you remember the brunch we had with Mr. Tyler?" Mom pushed her plate aside and rested her elbows onto the table, her chin in her hands.

"Of course. Why?"

"Well, he was going to tell you something else, but after you seemed so upset, he decided against it. Later, he told me about it without you, and we decided it was important enough to investigate, especially after how close you seem to be getting with Brandon."

"Okay…" I said, completely lost as to how all of this added up.

"Mr. Tyler found an article about four kids who were in a car accident, the driver their older brother, the other three kids, his siblings. The three kids died while the older brother walked away, nearly completely unharmed."

Air rushed out of my lungs as understanding for Brandon's pain and inability to talk about the accident soaked in. Of course he hadn't wanted to talk about that. I couldn't even begin to imagine how terrible he felt. The amount of guilt and pain that rested on his shoulders must have really been awful. The darkness I'd glimpsed from inside his soul finally had an explanation.

"Wow…"

"It gets crazier," Mom said, a grimacing flinch echoing through her face and down her shoulders.

"How can it get crazier?"

"Wait until you hear about their mom," Trina said, her eyes widened scandalously.

"Yeah, so the article was about these kids dying, right? Well, Mr. Tyler gave it to me, I took it to Caleb to get his older insight in on the topic, and he worked his vampire magic—"

"Or just used the internet," Trina said, shaking her head with a scoff.

"Vampire magic does sound cooler," I agreed with a nod.

"It took him more than an internet search," Mom said, giving both of us a flat look. "You probably didn't notice, but he was away a lot, looking for answers. If he hadn't assured me that the house was protected with that spell and agreed to allow for a substitute at nights, I wouldn't have felt comfortable without him, but he was able to arrange it."

"Okay, so that explains why I haven't seen him around much lately. What kinds of things did he find out?" I said, purposely not bringing up the night I spent snuggled up with Gryphin.

"He hasn't told me everything, promising to do so once you're safe and sound and ready to hear it, but he did say Brandon's mom's name was Susan, and that after her kids died, she deteriorated until she was an alcoholic homeless woman." Mom shook her head with a frown. "I can't imagine how she must have felt having her kids die."

"Guess where she died," Trina said, puckering her lips expectantly.

"The streets?"

"Yeah, of course. But like...she died under that horrible underpass, and unlike other ghosts who haunt places they didn't die, she kept right on haunting that place."

"Wait, the same underpass where Tracy haunts and where the necromancers want me to find a ghost named Susan?" I asked, starting to piece some things together, remembering my curiosity at the coincidence of the name.

It still did nothing to explain why the necromancers wanted to talk to Susan unless the guy she knew about had something to do with Rose using necromancer powers. Maybe? I was scrambling to get the whole picture, but it was clear we were still missing some important pieces.

"Yes, that very same…" Trina trailed off as she saw all the emotions that waved over my face in quick succession. "Did you just figure something out?"

Slowly, I shook my head, everything swimming around inside my brain like too many fish in a small tank. "No, pretty sure I just confused myself some more."

"It is kind of confusing." Trina nodded. "So I reached out to Tracy after I couldn't think of any other ghosts that both of us had been in contact with, and we worked through some stuff, you know, just trying to brainstorm what we could do next, while hanging out under that terrible underpass, when Susan flitted on by. At first, I didn't think anything about it while the ghosts talked. They were familiar with each other since they'd inhabited the same haunt. After you woke Tracy up from her butter churning, and she had made that first contact with Susan, she'd began to make connections with the other ghosts. Susan came by to investigate another Seer, apparently, and well, long story short, Susan mentioned missing her kids, one of them being named Brandon, and I just knew the connection was too much to pass up. I told Mom all about it later that evening, which was Friday, and we kept working with the angle since we had nothing else to go on. Mr. Tyler had assured us he'd be checking in with the magic users, Phoenix especially, if he could find them, so we found ourselves with supreme anxious energy and nothing to spend it on."

"I'm really sorry to have made y'all so worried." I didn't think it would matter how many times I apologized, I'd still feel bad about it. "Wait, Friday evening. What day is it today? How long have I been gone?"

"Sunday," Trina and Mom said at the same time and in the same annoyed tone of voice.

I flinched. "Wow. How long was I asleep?"

"Not as long as you were trapped in the spell. Phoenix only contacted us this morning," Mom said, grabbing for my hand on the table. "Still, I'm so glad you're safe. I'm sure you were scared."

"Not as scared as you guys were, probably." I shook my head. "I'll try really hard not to ever run away again. I promise."

Mom's lips spread into a thin smile. "That didn't feel like a complete commitment, but I do appreciate the sentiment."

"So what happened next?" I asked, eager to find out everything so we could go ask Phoenix about the three ghosts in the storage shed.

"Well, we figured out how to help with Tracy's unfinished business," Trina said, her head rising from her shoulders with excitement. "I was amazed at how simple it was, but she merely wanted to find out what happened to her family. It took more than a few minutes online, and I signed up for this family history website which could come in handy for other ghostly help too, by the way, and once we read about her sons and their kids, she seemed at peace that life had gone on without her at least okay enough to keep the family line going, and that her sons lived to be the ripe old ages of fifty and fifty-six, which was pretty good back then."

I smiled at the twinkle in Trina's eyes. Despite everything that was going on, it was refreshing to see the change from hating what she could do and hiding it from the world, to helping her first ghost cross over. It hadn't been much different for me just a few months ago, but I had Brandon to help me through it, though I hadn't looked at it that way at first. There was something sweet about her accepting the powers as she accepted a part of herself she'd been hiding from her whole life.

At least one good thing had come out of all this mess.

"It really does feel good to help someone cross over, doesn't it?" I said, sharing my proud smile with her.

"It did. I'm not sure how I feel about the whole being a Seer thing, and I'm not quite ready to reveal it to anyone else, but yeah, it did feel good to help her. I wouldn't mind trying to help others in the future, depending on the situation."

"Yeah, believe me, you want to be careful and don't want to get involved with a crazy poltergeist, take my word for it." I shook my head with wide eyes remembering the little girl who'd tormented the old church-turned-homeless-shelter.

We shared some chuckles.

"So y'all learned where Brandon's mom is haunting and talked with her, helped Tracy cross over, and figured out that Brandon's sadness is caused by his guilt for being the driver in the accident that killed his siblings?" I asked, trying to get a handle on everything.

They nodded.

"And did y'all happen to find out how Brandon died?"

The depressing question put a damper on the room.

"We did not," Mom said, turning her glass around in slow circles with her fingers.

"But Caleb wants to meet with us, with you, and talk more about what he's found out." Trina took a breath. "And that meeting apparently involves Kieran, you know, the vampire queen?"

"Wait, what?" I blinked. "What does she have to do with any of this? I thought she fled town."

"Well, it seems she's been a great source of information about Rose to Caleb, and there's more they want to share with us." Trina shrugged.

"So we have a date with a vampire and his ex-queen?" I raised my eyebrows.

"Looks like it."

After finishing up our meal, Mom showed me how to get to the main room of the coven's house. It was vastly empty compared to the first time I'd been in there. Phoenix and Cordelia were chatting near the bar. Leah had gone home to her coven, and I hoped had been thanked enough for her valiant efforts.

Before Phoenix even had a chance to speak to us, I pounced in on their conversation, uncaring about what I'd interrupted.

"Did you guys get the crystals and stuff out of the shed? I know we left as fast as we could, but please tell me one of you went back before the necromancers ransacked the place?" I asked, walking briskly toward where they sat on the barstools.

Cordelia didn't look surprised at all to see me, so Phoenix had probably told her I'd awakened.

"Hanna, good to see you up. How are you feeling?" Cordelia asked, her manners better than mine, clearly.

"Oh. I'm fine. Thank you. Just need answers. Did you guys go back or not?"

Cordelia and Mom shared an amused look while Phoenix regarded me with a small smile. Trina had wandered off to go look at the large windows displaying different, sometimes impossible, places.

"Leah went back, leaving Phoenix to tend to your ills, and grabbed what she could before the necromancers stormed down the hallway with their anger. We certainly severed several hundred years of tenuous peace between our groups. I'm not sure what we should expect from them." Cordelia sighed.

"Yes, hopefully nothing? What can they really do against your coven anyway? I'm sure this place is well hidden and warded. There aren't as many of them as there are of you guys, and I'm sure the zombies wouldn't be much help against magic users. What's there to worry about? And what did she grab from the storage unit?" I said, finding out I didn't know much at all about the relationship between necromancers and magic users.

Someone seriously needed to give me history lessons on all these different groups. Maybe then I'd stop causing wars or battles or whatever chaos always seemed to follow me around.

Phoenix scoffed while Cordelia shook her head.

"I wish it were that simple," the matron said. "But whatever happens, it was necessary."

We all nodded on that account.

"Leah brought back three crystals, a stack of magazines in case anyone else was stuck inside a picture spell, and a bag of supplies to cast spells with. Obviously, we don't know if we grabbed the right crystals with the ghosts that were helping us, but luckily you're able to check for us," Cordelia said, putting down her glass and standing. "Let's go assess what she found. Follow me, please."

"Finally getting somewhere," I said, unable to help myself from rubbing my hands together.

"Yes," Trina said from beside me as we followed the matron down the hallway, "then we've got a date with a vampire."

"Which I'm sure you're looking forward to," I gave her a side-smile.

She rolled her eyes, but the press of her lips told me I wasn't wrong.

Chapter 19

"Here we go," Cordelia said, showing us into yet another room in the safe house.

It was a storage room with several rows of cluttered shelves, barely big enough for all of us as we shuffled in. A table lined one of the walls with various objects strewn across it, including eight rose quartz crystals that gleamed in the light.

They were all sealed with a piece of braided hair wrapped around them, held in place by white wax. Three of the braids looked like my hair while the rest were a darker hue I didn't recognize.

I picked up the three with my hair and looked at Cordelia who stood across the table. "Do you know how to pull the ghosts out? I know I'm supposed to be the ghost expert, but this spell was done by a witch."

Slowly, she shook her head. "I do not, and even if I did, I suspect the spell can only be used by the one who cast it."

"Alright. You have Rose locked up here somewhere, right? Let's go ask her." I turned toward the door, still holding the bespelled crystals.

Phoenix stopped me with a gentle hand on my shoulder. "I know you're eager to free more ghosts, but you need to let us handle Rose."

I frowned, looking down at the crystals. "Why? Don't you think my help would be good to have? You can't free them without me."

Phoenix nodded and slowly pulled the crystals from out of my hands. I didn't fight them, but for some reason, it felt like they were pulling a lifeline away from me. "Because it's dangerous for you to even be in the same room as her. She's out to get you, honey, and with her track record of harming other Seers, we want to keep you as far from her as possible. Let us work with Rose, and when we're sure we've gotten her where we need her, we'll have you free the ghosts inside. We promise."

I looked into Phoenix's grey eyes and felt calm wash over me from an outside source. I knew for sure it hadn't come from me. My insides were twisting in knots.

Trina put her hand on my shoulder. "Let's go meet up with Caleb and Kieran. It's nearing dark, prime vampire time."

Caleb had darker skin which protected him more from the sunlight, but Kieran was as white as cake flour. She avoided the daylight like all Dracula-inspired legends did.

Slowly, I nodded, knowing that getting more information about Brandon's story and figuring out how everything pieced together would help assuage some of the guilt and anxiety I was feeling.

Hopefully.

An hour later, I found myself on familiar roads. Phoenix had teleported me, Mom, and Trina back home where we refreshed ourselves. Mom and Trina took showers and changed into new clothes while I caught up with social media on my phone.

That video of me talking to myself hadn't gone quite viral, but there were enough comments from students I knew that it was obvious it had gone around the school, at least. I didn't know if I would end up going to school tomorrow, especially since the necromancers might try something, but I wasn't sure I even wanted to go.

Honestly, I shouldn't have cared what the other kids thought. And for the most part, I didn't, but I couldn't help the stinging shame as comment after comment stated how they all knew I was crazy and should be avoided.

I'd gotten text messages from both people who were trying to encourage me and those who were fishing for more gossip. One had even told me to go get an exorcism.

At least Emma and Addy were supportive. They'd started a chat with the three of us, and while I had been silent for the last few days, they'd kept sending me reassuring messages. The thought was sweet and helped me feel a tiny bit better but did nothing to really solve the issue.

I did send them a message, so they at least knew I was alive and working on some ghostly things. The happy texts back made my frown lift a bit, and I felt a twinge of gratitude for having found better friends.

Noah, of course, had left several voice messages and texts trying to get a hold of me. All of them sounded sincere and worried, but knowing who his "family" was made everything suspicious. How did I know they weren't using him to get to me?

Thoughts of Noah reminded me of what he'd said before we'd ran to the zombie versus witch versus vampire-slave battle. Andrea was essentially a zombie.

Sitting alone on the couch, feeling sorry for myself, waiting for my mom and sister to get ready for a vampire meeting we were about to have, it suddenly occurred to me that this was super hilarious.

Andrea, the girl who was so obsessed with her looks that nearly everything she did and said revolved around them, was a zombie. The same girl who was super concerned with who she sat with during lunch or that she had to have the most good-looking boy in our grade on her arm was a zombie.

A stinky, rotting, arm-falling-off-at-some-point zombie.

Sure, whatever spell Noah and the necromancers had to do every day was keeping her in pretty much normal human health, but she was, at her essence, a zombie.

I laughed so hard there on that couch that tears ran down my cheeks. The irony of her being the person to post that video about me wasn't lost on my energy-deprived mind. It was just all so perfect.

Too bad I couldn't get a video of her drooling and groaning for brains. Then maybe we'd be even.

I also thought about what Noah had taught me regarding necromancers. Wouldn't that take a large cost to perform a strong spell like that *every day*? By my reckoning, the kid should have looked older than Mr. Tyler at this point.

What were they doing to combat that cost?

Noah may have looked like a manly-aged high schooler, but he still looked young enough.

The memory of the eagerness in David's eyes floated into my mind, and I wondered if he'd use Rose's harness on ghostly souls for himself. The amazing way it had restored Rose's youth had to have been appealing to the not-quite old guy. If I was a betting type, I would have put odds on the fact that even though David assured us that he knew what Rose was doing was wrong, he wanted to do it for himself.

This line of thought also brought me to the possible retaliation of the necromancer order. We were safe enough coming home for a few moments because Caleb had agreed to watch over us, the witches had given us their number in case they needed to come back here and teleport us out quickly, and the spell was still over our house, hopefully protecting us from any nearby zombies.

"What's so funny?" Trina asked as she came down the hallway brushing her wet hair.

"Uhm," I said around a slightly un-hinged giggle, "long story short, Andrea is actually a zombie."

Trina's eyes widened and she paused with her brush for a second. "That girl you used to hang out with at lunch?"

"That very same one."

"The cheerleader?"

I stifled another giggle at the image of her leg falling off during a voracious kick at a football game. "Yes, that one."

"Oh my gosh."

We both burst into laughter, causing Mom to wander down the hallway to investigate. We filled in her on the details between fits of giggles until all of us had watery eyes.

A few minutes later, Caleb knocked on the door, escorted us to my Mom's car, and we all piled in.

Trina and I sat in back on account of Caleb's long legs. As Mom started the car and pulled out of the driveway, I scooted up so I could give Caleb a meaningful look.

"So I hear you have been busy," I said with a sassy press to my lips.

He chuckled, the now-familiar rumble in his chest warming me to him. I was glad it didn't make me want to kiss him anymore like it had when I'd first met him. "You ladies sure have kept my life exciting in the past few months. I suppose I owe you three a 'thank you'."

"You're welcome," Trina chirped from the back.

Caleb turned around enough to give her a smile that made my eyes widen. "It's been all my pleasure."

Mom and I locked eyes in the rearview mirror, and it was hard to determine which of us was more amused.

"Right," I said, drawing out the word. "So we're going to meet the previous evil vampire queen who has some information she couldn't tell you to tell us?"

The flirty smile faded from his mouth as he turned to look at me. "Well, yes, but first I have to assure you all that we're going to be perfectly safe. Kieran has vowed that she will not harm any of you three, ever."

"Wow. How did you get her to do that?" I asked, remembering how she snarled at me when I was a bit too sassy for her liking.

"And how do we know we can trust a vampire's vow?" Trina frowned in thought.

Caleb took a second to direct Mom's driving so she knew where we were going and then turned back to Trina and I. "Usually, you couldn't, but I do happen to know that while Kieran is a bit of a monster—"

"A bit?" I raised my eyebrows meaningfully.

He laughed. "Fine. A lot of a monster, her vows are usually trustworthy. Plus...she may be wanting something from y'all in return. She didn't tell me what it was, but that's why she's willing to give you more information, that's why she wants to meet with you in person, and that's why I think y'all are safe for the time being. Plus, I'll be there, not thralled by her anymore, and I'm much closer to her as an equal, if not more powerful at this point."

"Wow," Trina said, glancing at me. "We're going to have to help a vampire."

"It better not be as bad as it was last time." I frowned at Caleb.

"I'm sure it won't be anything we can't handle together," he said, his bright smile causing me to blink a few times.

"As long as you're there to help us," Trina said, making me roll my eyes toward the window.

Now I understood why people complained about being the third wheel. This flirting stuff was sickening.

For the rest of the drive, we mused about what Kieran would possibly want in return for information. We knew there were lines we weren't going to cross, murdering any innocents being the top of the list, betrayal to anyone we loved second, but we were going to need to weigh the cost of her info against the cost of what she wanted.

Hopefully, it wouldn't be something too much.

I was unsure how far I'd go to learn more about Brandon if it was going to help me get him back, but judging from the panic attacks and morose attitude that had seemed to seep into my entire personality, I was willing to go pretty far.

When we pulled into the parking lot at the city park, I set my lips into an amused pucker. "Really? She couldn't think of a more clandestine place to meet? I know she has more style than this."

Caleb waited for us to unbuckle our seatbelts as he hadn't used one before popping open his door. "We figured this would be a relatively neutral place to meet where y'all would feel slightly safer. I mean, we could go to an abandoned crypt or something, if that's what you'd like better."

I scoffed and climbed out of the car. "Whatever. Let's get this over with."

A few ghosts flitted around through the trees, wandering aimlessly, while one sat on a swing, moving it slowly and causing the chains to squeak.

Trina spotted the other ghosts and gave me a worried look.

I tried to put on a calming smile. "Ignore them. They'll figure you're like any other human. It's fine."

She nodded, but had we not been in the darkness of the park with only passing streetlights to guide us, I was sure I'd be able to see how pale her face was.

Thankfully, Caleb stopped us by a bench that sat in the halo ring of a streetlight. The vampires had been kind enough to make sure us poor-sighted humans had something to see by, which to be honest, was more thoughtfulness than I expected from Kieran. It was probably all Caleb's doing.

"Still don't know why we have to see her again. I was hoping I'd never have to think about that night again or wonder why we hadn't killed her when we had the chance. It was stupid to let her leave, wasn't it?" I asked as I huddled closer into my jacket. Winter was definitely upon us and while it hadn't snowed yet, the nights were chilly enough that I didn't feel like doing stuff outside.

Caleb's dark eyes searched mine for a moment. "I, for one, think letting her live was a brave thing on your part. I've learned over the years that it's all too easy to kill something or someone that has wronged you. It's much harder to let them live."

"Plus, you'll be grateful once I tell you all I know," a smooth voice announced her presence before our eyes registered.

Queen Kieran...or maybe just Kieran since her seethe had been taken down, stood just outside the circle of light. Despite the shadows, I could make out normal street clothes, which I was honestly surprised to see from her. The only other times we'd met, she'd been sporting fancy, albeit outdated, dresses. Her blonde curls were piled on the top of her head in a messy bun while she wore a cream-colored button-up blouse and a pair of fashionably distressed skinny jeans. The look was finished off with tan, wedge boots that made her dainty frame a tiny bit taller.

Mom and Trina grabbed onto each other as the vampire appeared, but I tried to remain calm and stand my ground. I hadn't let her intimidate me when I'd been her captive, and I wasn't about to start.

"Alright, we're all here together now. Tell us what you know," I said, crossing my arms over my chest.

We formed a half-circle around Kieran with Caleb next to me while Mom and Trina were on his other side. On the outside, Caleb appeared relaxed and unworried, but on the inside, he had to have been as taut as a tightrope. Kieran had easily bested him while she'd been his queen. He was free from her bonds now, but the woman was still a formidable opponent. Caleb had seemed confident that he'd be able to take her during a one-on-one battle, but I wasn't sure his theory had ever been tested.

Kieran held up a slim hand. "Hold on. If it were that easy, I could have written you an email. I've come here to make a deal."

I sighed. "Of course. Everyone wants something from the Seers. We just want to live normal lives, too. Is that too much to ask?"

"Ugh, I have not missed your attitude. Can you cut it out and act like a normal adult for a minute?" Kieran asked, looking at Caleb and Mom for back up.

"She deserves to take a tone with you, if you ask me," Mom said, her defense surprising me and causing warm gratitude. "After you locked her up, she can talk to you however she wants."

Kieran scoffed and turned back to Caleb. "Really? And you're putting up with this?"

Caleb shrugged one shoulder. "They don't talk to me like that...most of the time."

Shaking her head, Kieran put her hands into her fur-lined jacket pockets. "Fine. Whatever. I'm sorry for locking you up. Having a Seer has come in handy over the years. Plus, you can't blame me for wanting to protect you when I know of at least one person who hunts Seers down and not just to capture them."

"Are you talking about Rose? She's safely locked up inside the coven. We don't have to worry about her anymore," I said, making an honest effort to take some of the snark out of my tone but finding it difficult.

"I wouldn't count on that until she's dead. The witches aren't often trustworthy. Just like me, they'll make choices based on what's good for them, not necessarily for everyone else."

I had to admit that Kieran's open honesty was growing on me. She might have been selfish, but at least she was open about it.

"I'm sure it'll be fine. We need to get more information on the rest of the ghosts she has captured, and then they'll deal with her the best way they see fit," I said, trying to push out the unease that was trickling in at the back of my mind.

"Right. Well, that's what I've come here to trade—information for her death. I want to kill her myself."

"You what?" I looked to Caleb for confirmation. He just shrugged again. "Why do you want to do that?"

Kieran's jaw clenched and she pressed her lips together for a moment as if debating something. Finally, she sighed. "Promise me you'll let me kill her, and I'll tell you everything...*without* you having to push a ghost inside to possess me."

I didn't fight the quirk of a smile that perked up my lips as I remembered Gran driving around the queen's body. "That was pretty funny."

Trina giggled quietly.

"Not to me," Kieran said flatly, her dead eyes staring me down.

"Yeah, I don't imagine so, but you deserved it. Anyway, besides all that, I can't say who gets to live and die and who gets to kill who. I'm not tempting God like that. The witches will give a trial, and she'll be held to their law, and I'll go off and live my happy, private life where hopefully the only other occult creatures I will have to deal with will be ghosts with no more of these other dramas."

"Except for your friends, of course," Caleb grumbled good-naturedly.

I nudged him with my elbow. "Of course."

Kieran was shaking her head. "No. I've got to be the one who kills her. The witches may lock her up, at best. Their numbers are so few, their powers are dwindling and aren't what they used to be. They'll keep Rose around, just in case. Not to mention the leverage she gives them over the necromancers. Yes, you can bet she'll live after this. You'll have to watch your back for the rest of your life because I can assure you, if you let the magic users decide, Rose will outlive all three of you and your grandchildren."

Silence sunk in after her words, and I turned to look around Caleb at my mom. She and Trina were still linked at the elbows as we all considered what to do.

Caleb was the first to break the thoughtful pause. "She's right, you know. Rose wants you dead, the magic users will do what's best for them, and they can't be trusted to hold others' needs in high esteem. Until we know Rose is absolutely dead, unable to come back in any way, you won't be safe. And even then..." He scoffed to end his sentence.

"But...it wouldn't be ethical to just agree she has to die and let a vampire take her out," I said with a frown.

Mom finally turned her soft blue eyes on me. "Not even in self-defense?"

My eyes widened. "Are you serious? I figured you'd be wanting to use this as a teaching moment about making the right choices."

"When it comes to my daughters, I will always choose them first," Mom said, letting go of Trina's elbow and coming to stand in front of me. She moved a strand of hair that had come out of my ponytail and tucked it behind my ear. "Sometimes we have to make hard choices, and this is one of these times. It may seem cruel to sentence Rose to a death, taking another's life in our hands, but if there is something more we can do to help our family, we need to do it. Not to mention—protecting a rare Seer. I know you of all people want to feel the relief of safety and no longer having to worry about Rose. Plus, and

I'm not saying this is what happened, but just in case, if Rose really did do something with Brandon's soul and you never see him again, wouldn't you want the assurance that she wasn't able to do it again to someone else?"

The low blow of her statement felt like it had been physical as air rushed out of my lungs. My mom had put words to the unthinkable worries I was furiously trying to keep stuffed in a locked box pushed to the back of my mind.

"Oh, sweetie." Mom pulled me into a tight hug. "I'm sorry. There's still hope, but we need to know all we can before we proceed. Let's agree to Kieran's terms and figure out the rest later, okay?"

"Ugh, humans are so much drama." Kieran sighed and looked up to the stars. "I'm so glad I don't have to deal with this all the time."

Mom whispered into my ear as Kieran talked, talking as quietly as she could while still allowing me to hear her in hopes that the vampire wouldn't pick it up. "Just say yes for now. We can get the info we need and go from there."

She gave me another squeeze and stepped back. "It'll be fine, sweetie. We need to do what's best for our family."

Numbly, I turned to Kieran and gave a small nod. "Sure. Whatever."

Apparently satisfied that my mom had convinced me to do the right thing, Kieran nodded. "Finally."

"First, start with why you want her dead so much," Trina said, the resolution in her voice surprising me.

"Is that really what you want to know first when I know so many things about your ghost friend?" Kieran asked, starting her sentence with looking at Trina but then moving over to me.

Blood rushed to my face, but before I could answer, Caleb spoke. "It's Onyx, isn't it?"

"Wait...the vampire brute that Rose bosses around?" I frowned, remembering his mangled corpse after the zombies had gotten to him. "What's he got to do with this?"

"They were in love," Caleb said, his eyes still on Kieran.

She sighed and shook her head. "I can speak for myself, thank you. He was a part of our seethe about sixty years ago...and yes, I loved him. It's hard being a queen for many reasons, but one is love. It felt like he loved me in return, but I couldn't ever be sure if he did or if he was just getting close to me because he wanted favorable treatment from the queen."

"Oh yes, it must be so hard being a queen," I said, unable to help myself.

She gave me a flat, annoyed look. "Can you please stop talking? You're exhausting."

I frowned while Caleb tried to smother a chuckle.

"So how did he start helping Rose?" Trina asked, giving me a meaningful look, which I took as trying to tell me to mind my manners.

I shrugged but kept my mouth shut. It was probably not good form to make fun of someone who was helping us like Kieran was, but there was something about her that pulled the petulant child out of me.

"I'm not sure how it got started. They must have met somewhere and maybe he agreed to work for her for some money. He always did have a restless spirit, which after centuries of life, appealed to me. There was constantly a scam brewing of some kind, not enough to cause battles between any of the occult groups, but enough to keep things interesting."

"I remember that time you decided to host a contest among the seethe members for how many humans we could enthrall in one night. Kinda unethical, if you think about it." Caleb shook his head with the memory.

"Don't forget to mention how you won that one," Kieran pointed out, her tone dry.

He shrugged. "I have many talents."

"Okay..." Trina gave Caleb a concerned look before turning back to Kieran. "So you think he went to work for her because he was bored and wanted something else to do?"

"Perhaps. Then over time, he became distant, and eventually stopped coming around. I gave him space, but a few years later, I was starting to get annoyed. Using the connecting powers of the seethe's bonds, I tried to pull him back to the house...but there was nothing there. No connection. He'd been taken as someone else's, and there wasn't anything I could do. He was unreachable."

"So you don't know if he went willingly or not into her enslavement?" I asked, curious about how Rose's powers worked.

Kieran shrugged.

"And you want revenge on Rose for taking your lover," Mom said with a nod. "I get that."

Wondering if there was a dig in there regarding her recent spouse's situation, I gave Mom a quick smile and turned back to Kieran. "It's a small world that you two happen to be connected like this."

"The older you get, the smaller the world seems," Caleb said in his broody-vampire way.

I rolled my eyes while Trina swooned.

"Anyway, so that's why you want Rose dead. Now, let's get to the real topic. What can you tell us that will help set all the ghosts free?"

"What? I don't know anything about that. I'm just here to tell you what I've found out about Susan Matthews. Caleb has stressed several times how important she is to you, I'm assuming because she's the mother of your ghost friend, and I figured you might want to know what I know."

I frowned, suddenly feeling like I was on the edge of a rabbit hole. They were right that I wanted to know everything I could about Brandon, especially since the turd refused to talk much about his past at all, but I was beginning to learn that not all knowledge was helpful.

"He already told us that she fell into sadness after all her kids died, became homeless, and we know her haunt is the terrible underpass where lots of homeless people go to for shelter. What else is there to know?" I asked, trying to step back from the details and see the picture as a whole.

"Oh, much more. The reason I know anything about her is because I've been working on plans to destroy Rose for a long time. At first, I just studied. I followed. I—"

"You mean you had henchmen follow her," I interrupted with raised eyebrows and pressed lips. "We all know how you hate going outside. How's that working out for you now?"

She scoffed. "Anyway, I tried to learn as much about her motivations and schemes as I could. People often found reasons to hunt her out, mostly based on her reputation for a powerful magic user, one who was able to bend the rules. This includes a situation where she brought someone back to life, but while most thought it was her magic abilities being stronger than any witch alive, it was actually because she was stealing necromancer magic."

Something pinged inside my brain as she talked, and I remembered the encounter with the wolves. "And that's why Sarah went looking for her. Phoenix must have gotten involved with Rose at some point, and Sarah heard about their reputation and went to find a magic user who was powerful enough to help her have a child. Of course, that all went horribly wrong."

Everyone stared at me as I prattled on about the wolves, not making much sense to the conversation at hand.

"Right. Good for them," Kieran said, going back to her story. "Well, it turns out that Susan also heard about this witch's reputation and had some revenge of her own she wanted to enact. Her husband had left a few years ago, and she found out that he had a second family with three children."

I frowned as a tendril of unease swirled through me.

"So she went to Rose, demanding something, I wasn't there so I don't know exactly how the conversation went down, but she wanted a spell of revenge. Rose told her that magic came with a cost, but Susan insisted she still wanted to go through with it, no matter the cost."

"Uh oh," I said, afraid of where this was going.

Kieran nodded. "Yeah, so her ex's kids died in a mysterious accident involving some carbon monoxide, and then not a month later—"

"Susan's three kids died in a car accident," I filled in, sitting stiffly on the bench behind us.

Mom gasped, Trina looked at me with worried eyes and compressed lips, and Caleb chewed on his lip in thought.

"That's right. Want to know the best part of it all? Maybe once you learn this, you'll agree Rose needs to die," Kieran said with a wicked twinkle in her dark eyes.

No one answered so she continued.

"I know enough about magic users from over the years, having employed at least three witches myself, that casting a spell like the one she used to kill the first three kids would have only required some ingredients, nothing like the cost of taking three other lives. Rose made that whole thing up to Susan so she could take even more ghosts and trap them. Or maybe just to have some fun in an otherwise bland existence, I don't know. What I do know is, those kids didn't need to die, but Rose killed them anyway."

I pulled cold air into my chest, but despite the chill, my face heated up with the influx of emotions. The world seemed even smaller as my brain scrambled to gather the whole picture together. Brandon's siblings had been taken, not because of his poor driving skills, but because his mom had reached her breaking point and an evil, I felt no qualms about calling her evil by this point, witch had taken their souls for no other reason than to enslave them.

Warmth seeped into my shoulder as Mom sat down and wrapped her arm around me. "I'm so sorry, sweetie. Sometimes people just do terrible things. Can we agree it's best to get rid of her now before she does anything worse?"

"Tell her the rest," Caleb's deep voice rumbled from where he stood nearby, "now, before she's too broken down to hear it."

Kieran sighed. "You're no fun, you know? Fine. Have you ever wondered how your ghost friend died? It wasn't covered in his obituary because of course it was too scandalous to report. No one wanted that reflected on a mother already so devastated."

The blood in my veins went from pounding harshly through my body to becoming nearly frozen solid with attention.

"After feeling completely responsible for the death of his siblings while he was at the wheel, your dear boy locked himself in the bathroom, put on his favorite album, climbed into the tub with his clothes still on, and slit his wrists. They didn't find him until long after his body had gone cold."

Chapter 20

Sound and time blurred. I don't know what happened for several minutes as I sat on the bench and stared at my shoes. Each beat of my heart ached for Brandon and what he'd gone through.

No wonder he hadn't told me much of the story. He hurt enough without having to relive it.

I knew instantly that I needed to find Brandon now more than ever. Not just to hug him as tight as I could, but to tell him the truth. It hadn't been his fault that his siblings had died, and, not only that, but they were ghosts that I mostly knew the location of. He could talk to them again. Not to mention, his mom was also wandering around.

Although, after hearing all this, I wasn't sure if he'd want to talk to her. I knew the only thing *I* wanted to tell her at this point was how devastating it was that she'd made those choices. She had probably spiraled for years in her guilt and pain, but even that didn't seem like enough.

A mother like that, more bent on revenge than her own precious children, should have been no mother.

At some point, Caleb's muscled, yet cold, arms picked me up from the bench and carried me back to the car as I was too overcome to do much more than stare. He even gently placed me into the front seat.

Where he went after that, I didn't know or care. Someone got me ready for bed and helped tuck me underneath the blankets.

It wasn't until far after midnight when a heavy and furry presence sunk into my bed that sound and sensation returned.

Gryphin's huge head nuzzled underneath my arm, his wet nose touching my chin for a second, before settling down and letting his warmth soak into my frozen skin.

"Did Caleb send you?" I asked, my voice hoarse and groggy.

He bobbed his head in a nod while my fingers idly played with that stubborn curly lock of fur over his forehead. "Sarah's ghost is free. Did you know? I got her out a few days ago."

After licking my cheek with a tongue as big as a Subway sandwich, he relaxed, and both of our tense bodies slowly released a muscle at a time until I was asleep.

He must have been super worried about me because he was still there when the morning sunlight crept in through the blinds.

At first, I only laid there, watching the dust motes float through the air while stroking Gryphin's soft fur.

I was numb to the several thoughts that demanded my attention and would have usually caused me high levels of anxiety. First, it was Monday morning, and I was already late for school. My mom must have been okay with letting me skip today because she hadn't come in to demand that I wake up.

Even if my life hadn't completely derailed over the weekend, I still wasn't sure how I'd feel about going to school with that dumb video circulating. Although it was tempting to want to get a closer look at Andrea now that I knew the truth of what she was.

Second, of course, was concern for Brandon. Where was he? Had the magic users gotten any closer to finding out about the rest of the ghosts? Were there any ghosts left to free? I was certain I hadn't freed his siblings, but they hadn't been close enough for Rose to eat them during the battle, I hoped.

Gryphin stirred, licked my fingers, and climbed off the bed. The springs and metal groaned as it was relieved from his heavy weight, and I almost rolled off.

"Hanna? Are you up?" Mom's voice came through the other side of the door, muffled.

Gryphin and I froze. He was mid-stretch with his forepaws in front with his back and hindquarters pulled up into the air.

"Uh…" I said, looking wildly at Gryphin.

He finished his stretch, shook out his coat, and nodded his head toward the door as if giving me permission to open it.

"It's okay. I know there's a wolf in there with you. He's still a wolf, right?" Mom asked from behind the door, displaying more self-restraint than I would have.

"Yes, wolf. Come in," I said, still standing next to my bed in pajamas and trying to figure out what to do with my hands.

She opened the door and with her came the fresh scent of shampoo and coffee. Her hair was wrapped up inside a towel and she held a mug. "Caleb suggested that the furry guy come in last night. At first, I was a bit freaked out by letting a boy come into your room, but then I sat with him on the couch for a minute and realized his fur was very soft and his presence quite steadying."

"Yeah, he's a good cuddle," I said, giving Gryphin an amused smile.

His shoulders bounced as if laughing with us. As he passed by my mom, he softly bumped into her leg, making her smile.

"You can change in our bathroom. You probably don't want to go outside in the daylight like that. Mrs. Jenkins would die of a heart attack if she saw you walking on the sidewalk," she said to Gryphin, gesturing down the hallway.

He trotted off, looking even more gigantic in the house.

Mom sat down on the bed and patted the spot next to her with the hand not holding the mug. "How do you feel today?"

"I don't know." I sat down and stared at the carpet. "I guess there are so many emotions that they've all kind of canceled each other out."

She sipped. "I get that. That's why I didn't push school today."

"Did Trina go?"

"Mmm," she said with a nod. "Something about a paper being due. You know how those responsible seniors are."

"Yeah, insane."

We shared a small smile.

"Do you want to talk about anything?" she asked after a few seconds of quiet.

"Thanks for letting Gryphin stay with me. It did help, and I wouldn't worry about him changing into a boy while in my room. First, he loves following rules and respecting authority."

She cracked an eyebrow. "Weird."

"I know, right? Second, the changes are super painful and loud, and you'd totally be able to tell if he was doing it."

A few growling sounds came from down the hallway as if to illustrate the point for me.

"Oh, I suppose it would be hard for the physical body to morph into such a creature. I mean, that kid is *huge*."

I chuckled dryly. "You should see his dad."

"Not sure I want to."

"Yeah. That's probably best... So what now? Have you heard from any of the magic users today?"

"That's what I was going to ask you but wanted to wait until you were ready to face the day. I know you got some intense news yesterday. You were basically a zombie the whole trip back."

"Yeah, I don't remember much of that. Did Kieran say anything else?"

Mom shook her head. "Nothing else important. She's a real piece of work. Are we sure we even believe what she said?"

"Caleb seems to. Have you talked to him yet this morning? It seems like y'all have gotten kind of close in the last week or so," I said, giving her a taunting expression.

"Oh, please. Trina's got heart eyes for him, and we all know it. I wouldn't ever do anything to mess with that, not to mention I'm still technically married, and he's...well, you know."

"Hasn't stopped Trina from liking him...or Gran, either, apparently."

"Yeah...you think you know a person." She was smiling as she took another drink.

I got up and grabbed my phone off the bedside table and nestled back into my bed, but this time up where my pillows were. "The only message I've gotten is from Phoenix. They want me to call when I can, but it's not urgent. I hope they've gotten some information out of Rose."

Mom nodded, pressing her lips together thoughtfully. "I'm worried about the necromancers, too. Caleb assured me he'd keep an eye on Trina while she was at school, and the spell on the house would keep us safe, as well as Gryphin's watchful eyes and nose, but it doesn't change that they're still out there and mad."

I didn't bring up the fact that Noah was a necromancer and had no troubles getting into our house. They could easily use him as leverage if they wanted inside. I also didn't mention that vampires weren't the strongest defense against them since even an apprentice could possess a full-grown vampire. Neither of those things seemed like information I should share with her. If Caleb thought we were relatively safe, then that was good enough for me.

Even though he hadn't been there to see the greedy gleam in David's eyes.

"They want Rose, though, not me. I'm still not sure they would even come after me. What good will that do them?" I asked, having some ideas but trying to help my mom relax and not worry more.

"I don't know. Maybe they figure they can use you against the magic users?"

"And trade a super-powerful necromancer witch for *me*? Hah. Yeah right." I scoffed, keeping my attention on my phone in hopes that she would get the message that I wasn't worried.

At least on the outside.

"You never know..." she said, trailing off and drinking the rest of her coffee.

"I'll call Phoenix and find out what's going on. We've got to find Brandon. We just have to," I said, putting my phone down long enough to convey the conviction through my eyes.

Mom smiled and patted my feet. "Of course, and we will. Let me know what they say. I'll go get ready in case we need to go somewhere."

I nodded and dialed Phoenix.

They picked up after the third ring. "Hey, just the girl I was hoping to talk with. Y'all feel like coming to visit again?"

About an hour later, Mom and I were standing inside the large sitting room of the coven's safehouse. Cordelia was busy attending to some other coven business, so we had the room to ourselves.

"What else have you found out? Has she told you where all the crystals are?" I asked, peppering Phoenix with the same questions I'd gone through over the phone, but hopefully this time they would give me some answers.

Phoenix smiled at me amusedly. "I'm sure it's been hard for you to wait for us to get back to you. It took a few hours to brew up the truth potion, and then several more to get her to take it. She had a lot of protections placed on herself that we had to...work around."

Mom and I shared wide-eyed looks.

"I'm not sure I want to learn more about that," Mom said.

"I'm sure that I do. Being a magic user seriously sounds awesome." Glee bubbled up inside, giving me more energy. Was it possible we were about to find out where Brandon was? I had so much to tell him about his family.

And Rose.

He would probably hate her more than I did...unless she'd already consumed his soul. But she hadn't. I was simply not going to accept that. I'd go into the netherworld myself to find him if it came down to it.

"It is pretty awesome. Yes, she's told us where the last two crystals are. Once we grab those, that will be ten crystals with potential spirits in them that we can free. We only have two problems to solve," Phoenix said, holding up two long fingers with purple, manicured nails.

"Okay, what are they?" I nodded, feeling pumped and ready to take on the world.

"First, the last two are inside another picture spell."

I frowned, waiting for them to continue.

"Second, while we do have a potion to make her tell the truth, we don't have one that can control her actions and force her to cast any spells, and there is no way to get the trapped spirits out without her summoning them. It's just the nature of the spell."

Chewing on my lip in thought, I began to pace between two couches. "Okay, do we know what picture and how to get inside there?"

Phoenix nodded. "It's back in the storage shed...hopefully."

"Well, let's conquer that issue and then figure out the rest. Like Dad always says, 'One day at a time'."

Mom gave me a tight-lipped smile and nodded. "Starting small is good. Helps to combat getting overwhelmed."

Phoenix teleported us to the shed, apparently able to take two guests with them as long as we'd been touching their skin. I wondered how many they could take in total. Maybe it was unlimited as long as everyone could get a good hold on them. Whatever the rules, it was still super cool they could teleport all over the place.

The storage unit was quiet on a Monday morning. There were probably workers and perhaps even customers roaming around in other parts of the building, but the hallway where Rose's shed was looked empty.

Flashbacks from the zombie horde struck me as our feet hit the concrete. Thankfully, someone had cleaned up and had used so much cleaner that the place reeked, making my eyes water. I wondered if the necromancers had at least cleaned up some of their mess. It seemed like it would have been the responsible thing to do, not just for the people who owned this place, but also to cover up their tracks.

I was sure the last thing they would want is a news article about finding a bunch of decomposing bodies inside a building that had clearly been harassed in some way.

The rolling metal door to the unit had been dented and beat up, but it was still functional enough to be closed. If it hadn't been for the damage, I probably wouldn't have known which door it was at all. Luckily, Phoenix seemed to be confident in what we were doing.

They did some circular hand movements over the lock and said some words I didn't understand. Then with a puff of air from their lungs, the lock clicked open, and we were able to roll up the door.

After Mom found the light switch and revealed the insides under the fluorescent drone, it was clear that this place had been picked over at least a few times.

"I wonder why they haven't cleared this place out yet. I doubt they're able to contact the owner," I said, going to a table on the side of the room and starting to look through its contents as Phoenix rolled down the door behind us.

"Not to mention that this was probably the only unit open and clearly searched that night of the break in. I'm betting they want to talk to the owner more than just to find out if they were missing anything,"

Mom added as she went to the other side of the shed and pulled on a shelf to put it upright.

"We'll just make sure to be in and out before anyone notices we're here," Phoenix said, moving over to help my mom.

"What about cameras? They probably have those all throughout the building," I said, picking up a box and accidentally spilling several sticks of incense from out of the other end.

"Oh, we fried those the first time we got here. Not to mention, the necromancers have their own ways of dealing with cameras. I'm pretty confident they wouldn't have gotten them up and running yet." Phoenix bent over and picked up a haphazard pile of papers.

"Well, let's hope, anyway. What kind of picture did Rose say it was? Are we able to access the picture without falling into the trigger point like we had before? Did you guys ever go back for that SUV/RV that we left behind?" I asked, putting the incense back into the mostly broken box.

Phoenix chuckled at all my questions. "Yes, we sent someone to pick up the van. No, we don't need the trigger place that opens the spell to get inside. And she said the picture was a snapshot of her childhood home, supposedly in this unit somewhere."

"Okay...but if we go in the picture, we're not really going to that place in real life, are we?" Mom asked, continuing to sort through the items that had fallen off the shelf, and just like a mom, was putting them back as if actually cleaning the witch's secret lair.

"Right. It's kind of like a mirror world. We won't be traveling to the real place, so we don't have to worry about running into innocent humans or anything like that." Phoenix righted a chair that had toppled over.

"Unless an innocent human has been trapped inside the picture," I added with a mutter as I shuffled through more random items on the table.

"Then we'll just set them free." Phoenix smiled before moving back further into the unit.

We fell into concentrated silence for a moment as we searched through different areas. Finally, perhaps twenty minutes or so after we'd gotten there, Mom called out from behind another shelf.

"Do you think this is it?" she asked, causing Phoenix and I to scramble around the mess to see what she was looking at.

"Let me see," Phoenix said, stretching out their hand.

I peeked around their muscled arm to see the picture. It looked like a cabin in the woods, simple, small, and super old. The picture itself was in that brownish-tan color from old-timey photos.

"This was taken way after she was a child," I said, remembering how old Rose was.

"She must have gone back there when pictures were finally invented." Mom shrugged. "Is there any way to tell if it's been used in a spell?"

Phoenix studied the picture for a few more seconds. "Only one way, really. Just gotta jump in. Perhaps one of you should stay here and keep watch? We won't be going into a trap like the other one, and I'll be able to get us out easily, but it wouldn't hurt to have someone on the outside just in case we run into trouble or someone tries to burn the picture or damage it in some way."

Mom nodded. "That makes sense. You'll probably need Hanna in there to help with the ghosts so I should stay here."

"We'll be back soon." Phoenix nodded at my mom and then turned to me. "Ready?"

"More than you know," I said, feeling excited energy wave up and down my body.

After grabbing my upper arm gently, Phoenix began flapping the picture back and forth while doing more of that magic user chanting. If I ever did learn some spells, I'd have to basically learn a whole new language, it felt like.

The world grew hazy and dark for a moment before coming back into focus in that same brownish-tan as the photo. Everything was the weird discoloration, and I blinked several times trying to get used to it. It didn't work.

Thankfully, Phoenix and I remained our usual colorful selves, they more so than I with their half-shaven bright red hair and colorful, sparkly crop top.

The cabin sat before us while trees ringed all around except for a gravel road that meandered out into the woods. All the trees looked skeletal with darker brown bodies and branches thinning out to fingers reaching for the lighter brown sky.

"Charming. Shall we go inside?" I asked, walking toward the cabin.

"Let's." Phoenix's wedge boots crunched through the leaves behind me.

The porch seemed sturdy enough as I stepped foot onto the stairs. It was made all of wood, just like the cabin, and had two rocking chairs sitting off to the side of the door. Perhaps this would be a nice place to enjoy nature in the real world. Inside the picture, however, it was creepy.

The door squeaked as I opened it into the darkness. It took several moments for my eyes to adjust as I stepped to the side and allowed space for Phoenix to come in as well.

"There!" I said, rushing over to a wooden dining room table that sat in the middle of an area I could guess was the kitchen.

The cabin was a small open space with a stove, a table, a fireplace, and a bed. On top of the table were two crystals, the only things in the room of regular color, pink and white, wrapped with braided strands of hair, and sealed with wax.

Just as my fingers were about to make contact with the quartz, Phoenix yelled a warning too late, and something crashed into me.

Before I could figure out what was happening, I was on my back, body aching from the fall I hadn't had time to brace myself for, and unable to breathe. I recognized the feeling of having the air knocked out of me. I'd felt it before on the playground when I was in elementary school and had run in front of the monkey bars without seeing the kid who was kicking off the platform at the same time.

Trying to get my air back was my first priority but even that seemed not as important as I came face-to-face with some kind of dead, feral cat. My arms had come up to shield my face from the slicing mini-knives of its claws as it yowled and attacked me. It shredded the sleeves of my jacket and sliced into my skin.

I was screaming and hollering but had no idea what kinds of words were coming out of my mouth. The creature's face was half-furred and half-skull. Its legs were just bones, ending in the wicked claws. Parts of its ribs were visible and something black and mushy hung outside of its body. I might have been more grossed out if I wasn't so worried about it tearing off my face.

Then there was a distinct *pop*, and the cat was gone, bursting into a plume of black feathers that harmlessly floated through the air and onto the wooden floor.

"Zombie cat. Nice touch," Phoenix said as they helped me sit up.

"That. was. terrible," I said between breaths, trying to get my lungs to function normally again.

"It didn't smell or look too good, either." Phoenix gently grabbed my arms and extended them for inspection. "We'll have to get you healed up back at the house. I don't have anything on me that could work with these right now. It was smart to keep it away from your face."

"Good job turning...it...into feathers?" I eyed one that sat innocently nearby, worried it would suddenly spring back up to attack me.

They grinned. "No problem. Looks like Rose put an extra precaution over the crystals. She really didn't want anyone to get to them."

We stood, Phoenix helping me until my legs weren't so wobbly, and regarded the crystals. They definitely stood out among the world of brown and white.

"Do we dare try again?" I asked, hesitant to approach.

"Only if you want to retrieve them," they gave me a pointed look.

I sighed, gathered my courage, and extended prodding fingers until I touched the cool, hard surface. Nothing else happened, which encouraged me to gather them into my hands and clutch them to my chest.

"If Brandon isn't in one of these, I'm going to skin that girl alive," I said, turning to walk out of the cabin.

Phoenix followed me with a surprised chuckle. "I'd pay to see that. Skinning a person can be pretty tricky, especially if you're trying to keep the skin intact to use later."

I glanced behind me with wide eyes. "It was just a figure of speech. Good gravy."

The arcanist shrugged. "Us magic users have to do weird things sometimes. Just saying."

I regarded them flatly as they moved their arms around, said more of those magic words, and pulled us back out of the picture.

Mom hopped off the table she'd been sitting on. "How'd it go? Are you bleeding?"

"The torn sleeves make it look worse than it is, but maybe it wouldn't be a bad idea to get a rabies shot or whatever they do to treat that. Zombie cats are no joke, and I hope I never have to see one again," I said, gently placing each crystal into one of my jacket pockets and then keeping my hands inside with them to ensure they didn't fall out or get lost or broken.

"Gross. Looks like you found them. Are they the right ones?"

I shrugged. "I sure hope so. Did Rose say anything else about any more crystals somewhere?"

Phoenix shook their head. "This is it. We could try another truth potion, but again, it takes a little while to brew."

"Right. Well, hopefully this is it. Now we just have to find out how to release the ghosts inside. No biggie," I said, fighting the excitement, trying to remind myself to keep cool.

Chapter 21

After we got back to the safehouse, Phoenix used a poultice on my arms while chanting. I was enthralled by the quick healing of the deep scratches but not surprised. I was seriously starting to think the magic users were capable of anything, given the right ingredients for their spells.

Except, apparently, making someone lose their free will, but I was willing to bet there were spells out there to combat that situation. Someone merely had to be corrupted enough to use them, and this coven appeared to be more on the moral side. Usually, I would have appreciated that, but in my case, it would have been so much easier if we could make Rose do whatever we wanted her to do.

Like summon some ghosts.

"I don't suppose you've asked her nicely if she'll pull all the ghosts out of the crystals so we can free them?" I asked, my tone hopeful as I admired the freshly-mended skin on my arms.

A grin quirked on Phoenix's face. "I suppose we haven't tried that yet, but she's hostile to the point of petulant silence. The only time we've gotten her to talk at all is when we used the truth potion, and she fought it the whole time."

"I know you've said no before, but can I talk to her? It might help mix things up, at least. She could be so angry at me that she'll forget to not be talking?" I put on my prettiest-asking-for-things smile.

Mom frowned from where she sat next to me at the kitchen table, the same one we'd had our meal at yesterday. "I don't think that's such a good idea. She could try to hurt you."

Phoenix nodded. "I agree. There are too many variables from a magic user, even one in captivity. If anything, it makes her more dangerous. Plus, we don't know everything Rose is capable of. She may still be able to hurt you if you're in the same room as her."

My shoulders slumped. "Then what do we do?"

"Can I see the crystals?" Phoenix asked, extending their manicured fingers toward them where I'd placed them onto the table.

"Of course. Maybe you could try to pull the ghosts out yourself? Do you know the spell? Did you get Rose to tell it to you while she was under the potion?" I said, putting on a brave face while my heart clenched in anxiety as they touched them. It wasn't like I thought Phoenix would do anything bad or refuse to give them back to me. It was that they were so precious, I was afraid of any risk.

But all they did was study them closely, roll them around in their fingers, and feel the braided hair. "This is your hair, isn't it?"

"Yes." I sighed and rolled my eyes. "I was so dumb to give it to her. I had no idea what we were actually doing and what she was going to use it for. I've regretted that choice for weeks."

A sly smile pulled up Phoenix's lips. "Maybe it wasn't dumb. Let's go to the other room and grab the crystals Leah salvaged from the unit. I have an idea."

Mom and I shared surprised expressions for a second but scrambled to follow them into the planning room where we had performed the location spell in what felt like weeks ago.

On a side table, Phoenix laid out all the crystals we'd found—the five from inside Rose's bag, and then the extra five, three from the unit, and two from inside the picture spell.

"You know, as I look at them, I can't even say that all the crystals from her bag were emptied. There could even still be some ghosts left over in those," I said, noting that only six used my hair while the other crystals were presumably bound by some other Seer's hair.

Phoenix frowned. "Perhaps. But let's focus on the ones with your hair right now." They pulled the six aside, my lighter hair shining from the overhead light.

"Okay, but why?"

"Do you think the use of Hanna's hair will allow her to mess with the spell somehow?" Mom asked, peering down at the crystals.

"It's worth a try," Phoenix said, sliding the crystals toward me. "Touch them and close your eyes, focus on what you can feel."

With my heart fluttering erratically in my chest, I nodded and followed their instructions. At first, all I felt was smooth hardness combined with the softness of my hair and the rubbery wax, but as I worked to clear my mind, spurts of awareness started zipping inside my consciousness. Chasing after the tugs of thought, I pulled through to them, and for lack of a better description, got out a mental basket and started piling those weird ideas into it, grabbing as many as I could.

I paused with my full basket and empty mind, unsure what to do next.

Then Phoenix's words came from somewhere far away and said, "Gather what you find and simply pull them out. There might be a strand of hair-like rope you can pull that will unravel the trap."

Mentally, I searched around for a rope but saw and felt nothing. Looking back at my basket, I realized it felt softer than the usual reeds or whatever baskets were made of. This one was made of my hair. Unsure I was doing the right thing, I looped the basket through one of my arms while I pulled out loose strands with the other. There were several times where I had to yank really hard to free strands from the braided contraption, but I didn't give up, pulling on everything I could until the basket basically disintegrated into my hands.

Opening my eyes, I pulled my consciousness away from the crystals and was amazed to see all six of the braids had come apart as if pecked at by something sharp. The wax seals were still in place, but the braids were no longer wrapping around the crystals.

"Did it work?" I asked, looking up at Phoenix and then getting lost from what I saw behind them.

Several ghosts were in the room with us that hadn't been there before. I didn't recognize any of them.

Except one.

"Brandon?"

Phoenix had started to talk, probably to answer my question, but I pushed past them in a daze, my eyes stuck on the blue transparent form of a kid from the 90s whose pants were entirely too big and whose hair was naturally spiky.

He looked up as I spoke his name, the confused expression clearing as he saw my face. "Hanna? What's going on?"

Tears welled up in my eyes as my arms shook. Goosebumps skittered and vibrated all up my body, and I had to remind myself to keep breathing.

"Oh, thank God," I said, sinking to my knees and clutching my hands to my chest. "I was so scared you were gone."

Voicing the words unleashed the emotions I'd been trying to smother, and water flowed out of my eyes as I struggled to bring air inside my lungs.

"Hanna!" My mom was next to me, grabbing my shoulders. "What's wrong? Did you see him?"

As for Brandon, alarm and fear washed out that stupidly charming smile that had started to form at the first sight of me. "Hanna! What's wrong?"

His words echoed Mom's, but I was in no shape to form a verbal response. Syllables came out in spurts, none of them connecting enough to make sense. "I—it—wha—."

Dropping to his knees in front of me, Brandon made a grab for the hands I had placed over my mouth. I'd put them there in an attempt to stuff all the overwhelming emotions back into my chest, but it wasn't working.

Frustrated with his incorporeal form, he growled, locked his eyes on mine, and pulled energy from me. He'd used my powers to make himself substantial several times, but I'd never felt the drain of power from it before. Maybe it was because he'd been stuck in the crystal for a while, and he had to drain extra power than was ever needed before. Or maybe I was still weak from my unhealthy eating habits and use of my powers to control the ghosts inside the zombies.

Either way, I welcomed the outside sensation to distract me from the tremors working their way through my body.

As Brandon's hands slowly became visible, the blue flesh turning peach as the colors of life seeped into his form, my mom gasped and pulled back from my shoulders.

The first thing he did was grab for my hands again and pull them away from my lips. "Hanna! What's going on?!"

I fell into his fully-solid arms with a sob and clutched onto the back of his t-shirt with a desperate grip. "I can't—It's just—Please tell me this isn't a dream!"

You wouldn't expect a ghost turned physical to smell good, but he must have brought the essence of who he was along with him, because his scent filled my senses and helped relax my nerves. I'd inhaled it several times during panic attacks at night, and his personal smell like the freshness of an incoming rainstorm calmed me almost as much as his embrace did.

"I suppose it could be a dream," he said, and I closed my eyes to relish the sound of his voice coming from inside his chest where my ear was pressed tightly. "One of the better dreams I've had, I think. Although your mom and Phoenix are looking at me weird. I guess they can see me now, too. Also, I'd like to figure out why you're so upset so I can go kick someone's butt if I need to."

He didn't say "butt", causing me to giggle into his chest as I imagined my mom's eyebrows rising with the scandal. Not a second after the giggle, though, I burst into more tears as I felt warmth from his desire to protect me.

"What is going on?" Brandon asked, holding me tightly to his chest, and, I assumed, looking out at my mom and Phoenix since my eyes were buried into the soft fabric of his band t-shirt.

"It probably doesn't feel very long to you, but you've been trapped inside Rose's crystal for about a week or so," Phoenix answered, their voice gentle.

"Hanna has been so worried about you. In fact, I've never seen her more upset. She tried to be brave but was almost falling to pieces every single day you were gone," Mom said, rubbing my back in between Brandon's arms.

Her words admitted truths I wasn't able to voice, and they served to free more pain and relief, and, unfortunately for the small amount of dignity I was trying to salvage, unleashed more tears and sobs.

Brandon's arms tightened around my shoulders and squeezed, essentially trying to hold me together while I fell apart. "I'm so sorry, Hanna. I didn't mean to make you so upset. I don't even know what to say or what to do to fix it. Tell me how to fix it."

"I have a feeling you're doing exactly what you need to do, though I want to ask how you're manifesting yourself so solidly right now. I have to say I've never seen a ghost like this. It's a pleasure to meet you, by the way. I'm—"

"Phoenix," Brandon supplied. "I know. I've seen you around, although this is probably the first time you've noticed. Nice to meet you, too."

I could tell from his tone that he was wearing that teasing grin.

"It's good to see you again. More than you know," Mom said, referring to the time she'd worn Gran's glasses and had a small conversation with Brandon before. "I would also like to know how you're sitting before us looking like any other kid. Well...except for maybe the outfit choices."

He chuckled, and I closed my eyes to savor the sound. "That's a good point. Maybe I should try and change clothes in this form while I've got it. Then I can look more modern. Got any cool holey jeans and a the Google shirt laying around?"

My hiccoughing sob turned into a choking giggle. "It's Google. Just Google," I managed to say, becoming aware enough to feel bad about the tears, spit, and possibly boogers I was getting onto his shirt.

Mom and Phoenix laughed as well, probably more from relief than from the actual hilarity of his joke.

"Sorry. Fresh out of 'The Google' shirts," Phoenix said. "But we do have some sassy nightgowns laying around. For some reason, witches have a thing with wearing nightgowns. Don't ask me why. I sleep in the nude."

"TMI," Mom said, and I could picture in my head exactly the scandalized look she was giving them.

"Yeah, thanks for that. I feel like I'd better let Hanna explain how I can be here like this. Although, to be honest, I've probably been solid way too long. We don't know what the side effects could be, and I would never want to cause Hanna harm," Brandon said, moving his arms to my shoulders and pulling back gently to see if I'd release the death-grip I had around his chest.

Begrudgingly, I relaxed my stranglehold, let him pull me back, and began wiping the wetness off my face. From somewhere nearby, Phoenix handed me a tissue over my shoulder, and I quickly used it to clean up. "I'm sorry. I—"

Then the world spun woozily and went black.

Chapter 22

When I woke up later, I was in my own bed. Bright midmorning sunlight sparkled in through the blinds, and I stretched, using my body to pull my brain back into reality after the odd dreams I'd had.

"That was quite a nap," Brandon said from next to me where he was laying on his side, his left hand propping up his head.

"Oh, hey." I blinked a few times, washing away the surprise at seeing him. Of course he was there. Where else would he be? I rolled over so I could face him and snuggled back down into my pillow. "What happened? How did I get here?"

"Phoenix teleported you back home and helped to tuck you in. Your mom figured I'd gone back to my haunt when you passed out, so she has no idea that I've watched you sleep for nearly thirteen hours. Funny thing is, I did try going back to my haunt and nothing happened."

"Wow. That *was* a nap. You watched me the whole time? That's only a bit creepy, but I have to say after not seeing you for so long, I can't bring myself to care."

We shared a small smile.

"I'm glad you don't think I'm *too* creepy."

"Nope, just the right amount. Did I pass out? It's kind of fuzzy. Why did I pass out?" I frowned, trying to remember more details. "Oh, and oh yeah, once you get freed from the crystal, your haunt resets. Remind me to tell you about Frank and the movie theater."

"Okay... Phoenix said you passed out because you'd used up too much energy. They assured us we didn't need to go to the hospital or anything. I guess they used their witchy powers to figure that out. Plus, it makes sense after...everything you were going through. How do you feel now? I'm really sorry if I—"

I held up my hand to stop him. "Don't even say it. You needed the energy because I needed you. That was literally the best thing you could do for me right then. I'd choose that a million times over if it came to it, even with the passing out."

A small smile pulled his lips up, but his eyes stayed full of concern. "It was really nice to hold you, but it's probably best if I don't try anything like that for a while. You need to rest up. Seriously, though, how do you feel?"

I rolled over onto my back, closed my eyes, and stretched through nearly every muscle group, pulling and testing to see how my body was doing. "I have to admit, I don't feel great. But it could have been worse. I for sure feel better than I have all week, though. I may even feel like eating something for lunch."

"Your eyes do look a bit sunken. I don't care if you don't want to hear it, I have to say it. I'm so sorry for making you worry like that. I'm so sorry you were in pain and sadness. I promise, if there was anything I could have done to help you feel better, I would have done it. Even if that meant distancing myself from you so you wouldn't have felt the pain of such separation. Although, I also have to admit, the evil side of me is flattered that you cared so much. I'm not sure anyone ever cared that much about me when I was alive."

I turned toward him again and put my hand over his where it rested on the bed. He was in ghostly form, so we didn't make contact, but the thought and intent were there. "You have to stop apologizing. Seriously. I don't know what to say to make you understand, but none of this was your fault. If you had distanced yourself, I would have kept summoning you back until you'd given up. There is no way I'm going to let you go. Not when there is time for us to spend together. We might not have the future, but we have now, and that's more important to me than anything else in the world."

The smile met his eyes that time, and he roamed his ghostly hand over my cheek and hair. "Hanna, I think I love you."

We both froze as the words seeped out of his mouth, seemingly out of his control.

When I didn't immediately respond, he tried to backtrack. "Er, I mean, I love a lot of things about you, and I love—"

I smiled, warmth and excitement erupting inside my chest and interrupted him. "I love you, too."

We were both smiling like big dorks when a knock sounded on my door and my mom's voice called from the other side. "Hanna? Are you awake?"

"Come in," I said, scrambling to sit up in bed and appear not at all like I was confessing my deepest heart's secrets to a ghost.

Brandon stayed where he was, amusement dancing in his eyes.

The door opened and Mom peeked her head in before coming into my room completely. "I thought I heard sounds from in here. How are you?"

I gave her a smile, one probably bolstered by the thrill I was still feeling from Brandon's words. "Great! Well, I mean, I'm sore, and feel kind of weak still, but yeah. I feel better."

Mom smiled as she sat on my bed and patted the blanket where my feet were. "I'm glad to hear it. You look better, at least a little, anyway. I was so scared when you slumped to the floor like that. I never want to have to see that as a parent again."

"I'm sorry. I hope I never have to do that again…" I was referring more to losing Brandon than passing out, but it was still also true that I didn't particularly enjoy passing out either. "But things are on the up and up. Have you heard from Gryphin or Mr. Tyler? Did the alpha feel Sarah's ghost come back? What about Phoenix? Did they say if there were any ghosts left inside the other crystals? I can think of at least three I know we are missing."

"Shouldn't you just be content that I'm here?" Brandon said, returning to his self-aggrandizing comments that Caleb had taught me were probably a cover up for insecurity.

At the same time, Mom laughed and put her palms up toward me. "Woah, sweetie. Let's take a step back. How about we start with a sandwich? Trina ran to the store earlier and grabbed your favorite fixin's. Up for some Doritos?"

"Definitely," I said, grinning as I tossed the blankets off my legs, piling them all onto Brandon, and pulled myself out of bed.

"Hey!" Brandon said with a frown, trying to push the blankets where they had landed through his body. They ignored his efforts.

My legs wobbled some as I stood, and Mom got up to help steady me.

"You're as weak as a newborn baby deer," she said as she put a hand underneath my elbow.

"Nothing a few good sandwiches won't fix." I grinned as she helped me navigate out of the bedroom.

Trina was in the kitchen, pulling stuff out of the fridge when we walked in. "I heard you guys talking and figured y'all would come in here next. I made sure to grab your favorite sandwich stuff. You do like provolone, right? At least that's what you always get when we go to Subway."

Brandon came striding in behind us, his hands in his pockets. "Aw, look at that. She stayed home from school just for you."

"Yes, I did," Trina said with a playful smile, answering Brandon's question and surprising him.

I smiled at his raised eyebrows as Mom merely looked confused for a moment.

We ate sandwiches and potato chips until we couldn't eat anymore. Which, for me, wasn't even a whole sandwich. My stomach was just not having it. Mom said I probably needed to start slow since I hadn't been eating much at all recently.

Trina seemed caught up on all the events, probably from my mom while I was sleeping, but we didn't talk much about it except a few comments on what the witches were going to do with Rose. Otherwise, we mostly kept to the regular things—school, boys, homework, and Mom's photography business.

Brandon, for once in his life, stayed pretty quiet throughout our conversation. He mostly leaned on the table with his head in his hand and watched us, a goofy smile on his face.

After a while, my brain reminded me that there were several unsolved issues I should try to address. I dismissed myself, took a quick shower while Brandon hung out in my room, and plopped onto my bed, finally unhooking my phone from where someone had charged it for me. I took a breath to be brave enough to face all the notifications.

Of course there were texts from Emma and Addy, asking if I were okay and if the monsters had eaten me yet. Those made me smile. The extensive number of texts from Noah made me frown, as I was still totally unsure what to do about him as a person and a member of the necromancer order. Those necroes were not happy with me or the witches, and I wasn't sure what the fallout for that would be.

Gryphin had sent me a few texts saying his dad seemed slightly more stable than he had a few days ago, giving me a good indication that the alpha at least knew Sarah was back in the ghost pack, even if she hadn't crossed over yet. Perhaps the wolves could find some temporary peace until I figured out how to help her more.

The comments on my stupid video had mostly stopped and the number of views seemed to be slowing. Thank goodness it wasn't funny or exciting enough to go viral. It was just enough to make my life at school all the more awkward and isolating. After I filled Brandon in on what had happened and showed him the video, cringing during the whole thing, his response surprised me.

He laughed so hard I almost felt my bed moving from it. We were both lying on our stomachs, feet kicking up in the air, and looking down at my phone.

"What's so funny?" I asked, my lips pulled into a strained pout.

"Oh," he calmed quickly after seeing my expression, "I'm sorry. I thought we were making fun of these comments. I didn't realize we cared about them."

"Of course I care about them. These are kids from school. They think I'm even more crazy than they thought I was before!"

Brandon's mirth shifted into a thoughtful and kind smile. "After all you've gone through, do those kids still matter? I mean, sure they matter as far as human life goes or whatever, but their opinions of you don't matter. You're an amazing Seer. Who cares what some regular teenage humans think of you? As Steph found out, you're much more than they will ever understand during life. Don't let them have any power over you."

I shut my phone off and put it on the bed. "You know what? You're actually right about this. School only matters in that it will help me get a good education and prepare me for college where I can work hard to fulfill my dreams. I can handle some teasing and cold-shoulders if that's what it takes."

Brandon nodded and bumped his shoulder through my own. "See? You got this."

"Listen, there's something I need to tell you, but—"

A light tapping on the window interrupted me. Creasing my eyebrows in confusion, I got up and opened the blinds to find Caleb on the other side. It wasn't like him to come by in the middle of the day like this, but perhaps it was something important.

"What's up?" I said, opening the window and backing up so he could crawl through. Despite his large size and the small window, he always made the entrance look as easy as a stroll in the park.

"Hey there, vampire. Seen any dead people recently?" Brandon said dryly, sitting up on the bed and wearing an annoyed expression.

Heedless of the mocking ghost, Caleb gave me a smile, but it was unlike any of the ones I'd seen from him before. This one seemed sinister and not like the flirty, I'm kinda-dangerous-but-mostly-sexy smile he liked to flash around. It was actually evil. "Hey, Seer. Smart move putting the spell around your house. Too bad you were dumb enough to allow a vampire to bypass it. They do make the most wonderful puppets."

I froze, feeling like ice had spread throughout my whole chest. "Caleb? Are you... Oh no."

Brandon stood, alarmed. "What's going on? That's not how he usually talks to you."

"Yup, that's right. It's me, Rose. Nice trick freeing those ghosts. I didn't know that was possible. I guess it was foolish of me to use your hair with the spell because it allowed you to break it so easily. Ah well, live and learn."

I backed up against the wall, my mind racing as I tried to figure out what to do. If I screamed, my mom and Trina would come running and could get hurt. Obviously, I was no match for Caleb physically and wouldn't want to hurt him if I could, anyway. Rose may have possessed his body, but he was still in there somewhere.

"What do you want?" I asked, hoping I sounded braver than I felt. "Come to return the glasses you stole from us?"

Caleb/Rose shrugged one shoulder. "Oh, I think I'll keep those. After all, it makes having Seers nearly useless, and that suits me just fine. No, I've come for revenge."

My eyes darted around the room for anything I could use as a weapon, knowing it would be useless. "I wouldn't know why you would need revenge against me. All I did was right the wrongs you committed. You never told me what we were really doing with the ghosts. I wish I had never trusted you from the start."

"Yes, quite sad. And now the trust you put in your vampire friend is going to get you killed. Oh, I can't imagine the guilt he'll feel from this, but don't worry, I'll keep him too busy for it to bother him too much. I do need a new pet vampire, after all, since your zombie friends took Onyx. Hopefully Caleb will be more suited to the job."

Brandon was watching Rose carefully, his eyebrows furrowed with his hands pulled tightly into balled fists. "Hanna, what do you want me to do? I don't want to manifest my body because you need to rest, but I can't just stand here and let her win."

Horror flooded my face as my heart beat so quickly, I was afraid it'd vibrate right out of my rib cage. "You can't do that. It's not right."

Caleb flipped a hand into the air where Rose's long hair would have sat on her shoulders. "I do what needs to be done. I'm surprised you, of all people, don't understand that the world isn't so black and white yet. Oh well, guess you're going to have to learn that one in the next life."

Even if Caleb hadn't been working with supernatural strength, I was so weak, I probably wouldn't have been able to stop a regular human. Quicker than I could blink, he'd crossed the room and pinned me against the wall, his large hand easily fitting around my neck.

"You see, I know you're in love with a ghost. The signs were easy to spot, and, sadly enough, you aren't the only Seer to fall into that trap. Don't worry though, because I'm here to help you, just as I helped your grandmother. Honestly, you owe me gratitude for helping unite your souls together for eternity. Let's just hope your haunt is in the same place as your lover's, or I suppose you might be facing a very lonely existence." Caleb's eyes flashed cruelly as he talked.

My fingernails dug into his hand as I fought to free myself, but it was like scratching at marble. I couldn't talk. I couldn't breathe. Stars danced in my vision, but the last thing I saw before Caleb snapped my neck was terror and pain coated all over Brandon's face.

To be Continued...

Don't Hex Witches

Hanna's story concludes in book 5, *Don't Hex Witches*. Available Now!

Trina and her mom, Michelle, go on a ghost-finding mission, visiting all the spirit's favorite places in hopes of finding her haunt. In the meantime, they've made a deal with the necromancers and are trying to complete the tasks the order wants from them, which start with contacting a familiar face.

The threat of Rose returning and finishing what she started has everyone worried. It's made even worse by the use of a certain, once-friendly vampire who can travel around during the daytime.

Hanna is getting used to her new life until a visitor comes by, and she discovers another helpful power that will potentially allow her to reunite with her best friend and get revenge on the magic user who has turned her life upside down and inside out.

About the Author

Jeni Conrad is a wife, mother, teacher, writer, reader, and a human (honest, she can pass those robot tests almost every time!). She usually writes YA fantasy or paranormal stories . Since fifteen years old, she worked in the restaurant business while getting through high school, a BA in English, and then an MA in sociology. Now she works from home while wrangling two small girls, a dog, and two crazy cats.

www.jeniconrad.com

Also By Jeni Conrad

The Lost Guardian Series
Part 1- Game On
Part 2- IRL

The Hanna Sanchez Series
Don't Haunt Ghosts
Don't Bite Vampires
Don't Hunt Werewolves
Don't Summon Necromancers
Don't Hex Witches

The Mirror Islands Series
Peter in Wonderland
Alice in Neverland
Wendy and the Lost Girls